Tomb of Endless Night
Kate Haley

Copyright © 2022 Kate Haley

All rights reserved.

ISBN: 978-0-473-63334-9 (paperback)
978-0-473-63336-3 (kindle)

Cover design by Jared Haley

For Richard
*Thanks for always making sure
I'm going the right way.*

CONTENTS

Chapter 1	1
Chapter 2	29
Chapter 3	55
Chapter 4	67
Chapter 5	77
Chapter 6	87
Chapter 7	99
Chapter 8	115
Chapter 9	133
Chapter 10	151
Chapter 11	171
Chapter 12	197
Chapter 13	209
Chapter 14	229
Chapter 15	243

Chapter 16	251
Chapter 17	263
Chapter 18	277

Visit **www.katehaleyauthor.com** for deals and current news from the author.

1

Darkness doesn't fall. Darkness doesn't descend. It doesn't rise from the depths. It spreads like ink in water. It bleeds out from the center. It escapes from the heart of all things, and from there it consumes all that it has yet to touch.

Vincent meditated in the Darkness. He sat back-to-back with the Prince. The man and the shadow leant against each other, skulls, spines, and shoulders pressed together as they sat in the swirling void. Here, like this, Vincent could see what the Prince saw. His old friend was once again sharing his secrets. Sharing his mind.

In the Prince's mind Vincent could see a butterfly being eaten by a spider. The spider did not trap the food in a web, but rather crushed its thin delicate legs. It mangled the fluttering green and gold insect and began to eat it in squirming pieces. Vincent watched this happen calmly.

The void watched him watch. Above him it spun faster and faster. Soon it was nothing but a whirling insanity.

"Have you found what you seek?" the Prince asked.
"Always," the Hunter replied.

The faceless Prince smiled. He pulled away to stand up. Everywhere they had touched was stuck. As the shadow moved, he pulled from Vincent like sticky tar. His darkness oozed and threaded like web between them, but the Dreamer was still released. He still fell.

The cry of his fall was cut short by the floor of his hut. The old hut creaked in the woods. Vincent lay spasming on the floor for a long time. When he could finally breathe again, he crawled to his hands and knees. Drip. Drip. He could hear the liquid trickling onto the wooden floor from his cheeks. It wasn't natural. When it had first begun, he had been expecting tears. Possibly blood or mucus. Instead he found that a thick, sticky, darkness wept from his eyes when he woke from the Dreamlands. He'd been trying to visit less since it had started three months ago. He knew the trips were slowly killing him. But it was the only way to know.

All across the world people were falling on hard times. Things were getting difficult and more and more people were struggling just to get by. The desperate were searching for alternatives, which meant Vincent's business was booming. Deals with the devil never went well. But random occurrences were hard to keep track of. Untamed black magic springing up all over the place was causing uncontainable damage. Things got out of hand before Vincent even heard they'd happened. That was where the Dreamlands came into it. He could find out about events before they happened. He could get the knowledge he needed to save innocents. He just had to cheat.

***

Cheaters, they say, never prosper. Vincent found himself once again contemplating the vague 'they' concept and who 'them' were as he was smashed into the window of an ornate ballroom. The window frame was strong. It splintered, but held, as the glass in the many panes around it cracked and shattered. Vincent's grunt of pain was lost in the noise. It was possible the injury had just helped click his back though. That was something.

He was being held upside down by the ankle. As he was smacked into the window a second time, he wondered if the 'them' who claimed he wouldn't prosper from his cheating were the same 'them' who said girls couldn't shoot. Those people were very wrong.

The sound of a rifle shot echoed around the room. There was a hideous shriek of pain. Vincent was dropped. He hit the floor with a thud and a grunt.

Above him the monster shuddered and flailed. It was colossal, a gigantic spider-like demon nearly half the size of the room. Its body was a mass of heaving, sticky, dripping hair. Eyestalks protruded from the body to look in every direction. Its hairy legs were as thick as tree trunks. It curled, bent and awkward, in the corner. One leg still thrashed in pain above Vincent, who lay where he'd been dropped on the landing of a sweeping staircase. To his side the stairs descended to the ballroom. At the now broken window they split left and right up to the mezzanine.

The clawed foot hurtled toward him. Vincent grunted as he threw himself down the stairs. It was better than being crushed. The monster gained its feet again. Thick black blood dripped down the injured leg, but that wouldn't stop it. Its many eyes searched for the threat.

Lucy was crouched behind the railings on the mezzanine. Her rifle was pointed carefully between the bars. She fired again. The sound of the shot filled the ballroom. It muffled the sound of a small scream under a table. The holy bullet hit the demon with a small explosion of light. It shrieked in pain again. Black blood splattered across the floor. It was hurt now. It was angry.

The demon charged Lucy. Huge strides threw the bloody, hairy body across the room. The building shook with the force. Lucy ran. She leapt back from the rails and bolted. Her long legs sprinted, and her feet barely touched the ground. The rifle swung from the strap over her shoulder as she flew around the mezzanine. But she was trapped.

The monster was so much bigger. Its strides were so much longer. She raced around the room but, in three massive steps, the creature was bearing down on her. It thrust a leg out to crush her. Lucy yelled and threw herself back. She hit the floor of the walkway as the section beside her was crushed. Rubble rained down in a thunderous clatter.

The monster reared back. It went for her again. Two clawed hairy feet smashed at the walkway. Lucy lunged. She aimed to leap the gap. It was a massive hole, and she didn't have a run up. She threw herself from the mezzanine as it was crushed behind her. She wasn't going to make it. Lucy yelled and strained as she tried to catch the other side of the broken walkway. Her hands lashed out for anything they could grab. She caught part of a splintered beam hanging from the ruins. It didn't hold. Lucy cried out as the beam swung her away and snapped completely. She flew across the end of the room.

The monster saw her move. It snatched for her. One of its eye stalks exploded in a shower of golden light. It screamed and missed. Vincent had rolled onto his side and aimed his pistol. His holy bullet ripped part of its face away.

Lucy crashed down onto a sturdy table on the far side the ballroom. It held her weight, and she skidded off the end of its polished surface. She hit the floor hard. Under the table she glimpsed a middle-aged man clutching his two young children to him tightly. They were well-dressed, yet disheveled with fear. Lucy groaned as she rolled over. She caught their eyes and placed a finger to her lips. The man was too afraid to even nod. Lucy struggled to her feet. She had to get away from the hidden bystanders, before the monster's destruction followed her to them. Her leg hurt where she had fallen on it, but the adrenaline kept her going. She pulled herself up against the table and staggered away.

Behind her, the demon thrashed in pain. Its legs whirled around it like a storm of destruction. More of the mezzanine was smashed away. Debris crashed into the room. The mindless monster screamed and churned. Plaster cracked and shattered as the creature smashed the walls.

Lucy hobbled to Vincent. The old Hunter was using the stair rail to pull himself to his feet. They shared a look. The demon was going to bring the whole building down. It might survive tons of rubble, but none of the humans would. They had to kill it first. Vincent and Lucy took aim and fired. They unloaded their weapons at the demon. The air was alive with bullets and light. Golden bursts showered out of the creature as it shrieked and flailed under the assault. The guns emptied. The Hunters paused. The demon shuddered. It rushed them.

Vincent cursed and bolted up the stairs. Lucy matched his language and went wide. She couldn't reload the rifle at a full sprint. They had to divide the creature's attention. She ran for the side of the room, knowing she was boxing herself in. Vincent was having better luck reloading his pistol. If he could get another shot in...

But the creature was too big. It was massive and furious. It wanted to destroy those who caused it pain. Within a few strides it was on top of them. It lashed out with dripping, wounded legs and snatched. It caught Lucy by the arm. She yelled as its clawed foot yanked her off her feet. It pulled her roughly and tossed her through the air like a ragdoll. She screamed as the force pulled her shoulder from its socket. The pop echoed. The demon threw her across the room. She smashed into the mezzanine debris.

Vincent was racing up the stairs when he was snatched again. Claws dug into his side as he was pinched around the waist. He struggled and writhed, but the monster wasn't taking any chances with him. The leg trapped him tightly, and pulled him in. Vincent could see all the eyestalks pointed at him. Dozens of sickly-green, veiny eyes drew closer. The massive, razor-tipped pincers of its mouth twitched as it dragged Vincent in. Shreds of green fabric hung from its pincers. The remnants of its summoner.

He tried to squirm free. His arms were pinned to his sides and he couldn't shoot. It was no good. Terror gripped him as he realized he was about to be the monster's dinner. There was only one thing for it. This was going to hurt.

The monster drew him in. Vincent kicked and struggled as he neared the demon's face. His foot connected with a pincer and he kicked away, but it was stronger. He thrashed. Still closer. It bit his leg. The sharp points of the pincers sheared into his calf like hot knives. He barely kept back a scream. But now he was where he needed to be. His arm was still pinned down, and the barrel of his pistol was pointed along his leg, straight into the monster's face. Vincent unloaded.

The unrelenting chain of explosions mixed with an unholy shriek. The creature reared. It dropped Vincent. He hit the floor with a wet splat from his bloody leg. The gun was empty. He started to reload again. If he could just…

The monster shuddered and collapsed. In the wake

of the holy bullets, its head was little more than a crater in its twisted and warped body. With a faint and horrible hissing sound, it began to dissolve. Vincent couldn't walk. He dragged himself safely back from the acidic demon corpse on his elbows, leaving a trail of blood along the floor.

Across the room, Lucy staggered from the rubble. There was a cut on her brow that trickled blood down the side of her face, and she clutched her wounded arm. Her view of the room was blocked by the dissolving corpse.

"Vincent...?" she called out weakly.

There was movement across the way. The man and his children were crawling out from under the table. He had taken the lead, and was trying to coax the little one out. They finally followed, only to take one proper look at the mess and begin to scream. It was the kind of scream that had been repressed for too long beneath the table. The kind of scream that had been held back in terror, and now unleashed in wave upon wave of horror. The kind of scream that truly comprehended what had just transpired.

Lucy sagged back into what was left of the doorway by the mezzanine ruins. She remembered what it felt like. It wasn't a sound she had made out loud, but it was one she had felt in her soul before. It had been two years since she had felt it, but she knew the pain of this child looking upon the ruins of the monster and knowing that it had been the fate of their mother. Unlike Lucy's own mother, this poor child's mother had done this to herself.

As she breathed out a sigh, someone appeared out of the shadows near her. A tall thin man with dark skin and very short black hair stepped almost silently at her side. He wore what looked like a butler's uniform, still crisp and clean despite the ruins.

"Can I help you with that, Miss?" he indicated her arm as he spoke. His voice was soft and low, smooth and rich, like black coffee.

Lucy realized what he meant, and she nodded, gritting her teeth. He knew from her expression that she had experience with such injuries. Neither of them said anything, and he offered no unnecessary warnings about pain. She braced herself against the wall, and gave a single pained grunt as he clicked her shoulder back into place. Once it was set again, she breathed sharply and deeply, before looking his way.

"Thank you."

"Surely it is I who should be thanking you?" he cast his eyes over the room, and she followed his gaze. "The world needs more people like you, Miss. All over the globe, the helpless are falling to such dangers, and there are too few like you." He tightened his hand on her uninjured shoulder and leant in to whisper. "You see, it is not enough to have the power to help. You have to have the will and desire. You, Miss, you have the pure soul of someone who helps others because they need it. More of the world needs you now."

"We do what we can," Lucy sighed. "You don't need to thank us, but it's appreciated."

"These people had everything. Now they have nothing," he stated, his words touching a sharp and familiar pain in Lucy. "You are the one who comes to help those who have no one else to turn to. Yet, you always feel you have arrived too late. It is a pity you can't save everyone..."

Lucy watched the child sitting on the floor screaming. Their sibling and father held them and wept openly. She had seen so many sights like this in the last two years. Things were hard for everyone now. People were becoming so desperate. She didn't know how this man knew, but it was easy enough to see. He was right. It was never enough. He squeezed her shoulder once more, and walked away. She was left to sigh alone, and her sigh was deep and troubled.

She edged her way carefully around the melting mess in the center of the room, dreading what she might find. She was relieved, but unsurprised, to find Vincent sitting on the bottom of the stairs. He had a tourniquet around his leg, and was cutting pus from his bloody wound with a knife. He looked up as she drew near, and his face was drawn and pale with pain.

"Do you need help?" Lucy asked.

"I will in a moment," Vincent growled, as he finished cleaning his wound. "Good to see you moving. I feared it may have been worse."

"It was," Lucy admitted. "The butler kindly helped set my shoulder again." Lucy looked back to the doorway where it had happened. Vincent looked with her. There was absolutely no sign of the man.

"I thought the help were long gone," Vincent grimaced.

"They seem to be now," Lucy agreed. For a moment

she half thought she had dreamt the exchange, but the remaining ache in her shoulder was very real. She waited patiently while Vincent bound his injury, then she helped him off the floor. He limped painfully and leant on her offered good shoulder.

The father had quieted his children and ushered them from the room, but they were not moving quickly. Lucy and Vincent caught them up in the hall outside the ballroom. The man looked up and shared a glance with the Hunters. Lucy watched the traumatized children. Vincent met the father's eye.

"The other rooms are safe," Vincent assured him gruffly. "Keep the children upstairs for now, and don't let anyone in the ballroom. There will be officials arriving tomorrow to speak with you."

The man nodded at him blankly. Vincent's words were processed and the orders filed. The meaning not so much. Vincent could see through the shock. The man would do as he was told. He would keep the children safe and away from the damage. He did not yet realize that his house may well be condemned. That he was going to be billed by the Hunters and the government for the extermination and the danger to the public. Vincent couldn't bring himself to clarify it. The man had just gruesomely lost his wife, while fearing for his life and the lives of his children. He had just witnessed a horror beyond that which the normal human mind could cope with. This was not the right time to bring the cruelties of reality down on him as well.

The old Hunter continued to lean on his apprentice as he limped from the building. There had been nothing more to do or say. They exited via the front doors of the mansion. From the front of the house everything appeared to be normal. The darkness that had occurred inside had yet to settle over the land.

Vincent's giant bike was parked out the front. It gleamed like an extravagant junk pile of twisted pipes and secret compartments. Lucy insisted that she drive. He could hang on and keep that leg out of the way. The urge to dispute her rose strong in his chest, but he quashed it. He could accept when she was right. The pain would make it hard to focus. He trusted her to get them home.

***

Arriving back surreptitiously was impossible on such a monstrous vehicle. The bike had a roar louder than most of the creatures it had been designed to hunt. Which meant there was no way Vincent could sneak his injuries inside. Fred was waiting on the doorstep as Lucy pulled up. He swore the women conspired to catch him at his worst. Fred stood with her arms folded and her ever-serious expression framed by jet-black hair. She was not alone.

Her gangly young apprentice was standing away from the steps and crushing out his cigarette as the bike parked. The wide-eyed and gormless boy he'd once been always flickered into life when he saw Lucy return, but there was a permanent shadow behind Tony's eyes now. Over the last two years it had settled from a resounding terror into a comfortable bleakness.

Lucy parked the bike and kicked out the stand. She helped Vincent onto his good leg and climbed off. Fred was already striding down the stairs towards them. Tony looked around nervously and hunched like he didn't know what to do with himself.

"So good to see you home in fine health, Sir," Fred proclaimed. "I remember expressing concern that you were not in a fit state to go, but I can see from the evidence of your resounding success that everything was fine and I was wrong."

Vincent met her sarcasm with a dry glare. Beside him, Lucy shook her head at the cynical mage. The girl didn't have a lot of luck quelling the banter between those two, but now wasn't the time for it. It had been bad, but it would have been so many kinds of worse if Vincent hadn't insisted on going. They were just lucky he knew how to get to these things as they were happening, if not before. That monster could have killed hundreds of people if it had slain the family and escaped.

Fred took in the state of them both, and heeded Lucy's warning. She sighed. Then she whistled sharply.

"Tony! Help get him inside."

"Yes Ma'am," Tony jumped when she whistled at him and scooted straight over. The action instantly jerked him out of his awkward disposition. Having a task gave him focus.

"I'm fine," Vincent protested, more for the sake of protesting in front of Fred than anything else.

"Yeah you are, Doc," Tony agreed, scooping an arm around him so that the old Hunter could lean on him.

"I got you."

Tony was nearly as tall as the old Hunter now, and Vincent grudgingly admitted in the privacy of his own mind that the lad was easier to lean on than his own tiny apprentice. Lucy stayed at their side as he hobbled into the house. Tony's attention was split equally between keeping Vincent supported and flitting constant looks to the young lady at his side.

"Are you alright, Miss Lucy?" he couldn't help but ask as they crossed the threshold.

Lucy shared a fleeting glance with Fred, walking in on the other side of the men. She had told Tony to drop the 'Miss' two years ago, and multiple times since then. Tony was not an easy person to teach. At this point, Lucy was starting to save the reprimanding for special occasions.

"I'm fine, thank you, Tony," she replied.

"You're bleeding..." he pointed out.

"It's just a scratch," she shrugged it away. "How are the lessons going?"

"Oh, um, fine... they're going just fine," Tony nodded.

Vincent chuckled at the look on Fred's face.

"You alright, Doc?" Tony mistook his amusement.

"I'm fine, Tony," Vincent smirked. "We're all fine."

"Really? 'Cause you sure look like you've got a bloody hole in your leg," he commented. "I... um... I could try patch it for you? I know magic isn't supposed to heal, but I felt like the theory is there. I'm getting better–"

"We have perfectly good doctors here, Tony," Fred

shut him down. "Just help me get this dear old doctor down to the bathroom and we'll call one through. Lucy, do you need any medical care, honey?"

"No thanks, Fred," Lucy shook her head.

"Good. Then you can head upstairs and clean up too. Dinner will be ready in an hour. I'll have this grumpy old sack of bones patched up by then."

"Is Tony staying for dinner?" Lucy asked.

Silence fell between them all.

"I think I have to go–" Tony began to make excuses.

"Please stay!" Lucy requested. "Please can he stay?" she implored to Vincent, before turning back to the awkward young man. "I'm not going upstairs until you promise you'll still be here when I return."

Tony was steadily turning a sweet shade of cranberry.

"That's sorted then," Vincent announced. "Segreti, you're welcome, as always. Any complaints, Fred?"

"None that you'll listen to, Sir," she sighed.

"Excellent," Vincent grinned wolfishly. He was going to get in as many digs as he could, before Fred was allowed to poke at his wound. Fair was fair, after all.

* * *

When Lucy descended again she was wearing a dress. She hadn't abandoned the practice completely, but it was more common these days to find her leaping around in boots and trousers with a weapon in hand. The dress was full-length, bias cut, and backless. It draped and clung to her like water, and when she moved, it whispered around her skin like it had secrets. She floated down the stairs in it and caught Tony on the landing. He was flicking through a half-scrunched letter and fidgeting like he needed a cigarette. Fred had banned him from smoking in the house.

"Miss Lucy," he smiled when he saw her, but his face blanched slightly at her dress. "When you asked me to stay for dinner there was no mention of having to dress for it…"

She laughed at him and caught his arm, leading him further down the staircase. "No one dresses for dinner in this house, Tony. Any day we can get Vincent at the table in regular clothes, without getting blood everywhere, counts as a proper dining experience. Most of the time he eats in the kitchen, gobbling and gnawing on leftovers like an animal."

"Well, you're certainly looking all manner of ritzy in your glad rags…" he commented nervously.

"I can assure you I'm not," Lucy smiled.

Tony's expression remained unconvinced. He had that uneasy look in his eye that so often settled there. There were times, and this was one of them, when he was really forced to face the different worlds they came from.

"So, who's writing you?" she pestered, as she dragged him through the house towards the dining room.

"My cousin," Tony replied. "The one who's gone down New Orleans way."

"The one Vincent got a Hunter's apprenticeship

for?" she asked.

Tony nodded. "Giovanni. He's been settling in down there. Mister Ferro wants some Hunters of his own, now that monsters are becoming such a problem."

Lucy glanced sideways at Tony. She knew his cousin Giovanni had been one of the survivors of the massacre in the city center two years ago. Ferro's gang had helped Fred banish the monsters, and the Mafia had decided it would not be a bad idea to get some monster hunters of their own. Vincent had been reluctant for a long time, but apparently, he had seen something in one of Tony's cousins, and had agreed to find him an apprenticeship. He had flat out refused to take on any of the gangsters himself. He had an apprentice already. Also, Lucy was fairly sure that if Vincent had agreed to training for a member of the Mafia, he had only done it on the proviso that said trainee would be sent far away from his boss and forced to build new loyalties.

"Your uncle knows that's not how this works, doesn't he?" she inquired carefully. "He can't just send people away to train into his personal monster-hunting button men."

"So the Doc keeps telling him," Tony muttered wryly. "At length. But Giovanni sounds like he's doing well. He likes the new Professor anyway – says he was pleasantly surprised by him."

"How so?"

"Well, apparently, this Professor Owens is... nothing like Doc Temple," Tony shot her a shifty glance. "He's younger, clean-cut, more academic, more professional, a real wise-head."

"You buying that?" she asked.

"I dunno," Tony shrugged. "Look, Doc Temple knows his onions, for sure. But... you have to admit... he looks a bit like a bindle punk you dragged in off the side of the road..."

Lucy laughed. The sound made Tony grin.

"A very dirty road..." he added gently.

Lucy continued to chuckle as she led him into the dining room. She wasn't going to fight him on that. Vincent was certainly scruffy at the best of times. Occasionally, Fred and Helen managed to get him to shave and doll up, usually if there was something he needed from the university, but mostly he seemed content to live life as a grizzled thunder cloud.

"I do find it endearing though..." Lucy admitted. She turned to face the boy on her arm as he scrunched the letter back into his pocket. There was no one else in the room yet, and Lucy tangled her fingers in his.

"Oh, so the hobo look works for you?" Tony teased. Lucy took one hand back to smack his shoulder playfully, but he was still grinning.

"You know what I mean," she retorted. "He's a good man. Working with him puts things in perspective. He's so busy worrying about the important things that it helps you realize there are much more crucial issues than clothes and credit ratings."

"Says the rich girl..." Tony countered.

"I'm not rich anymore."

"Yes, you are," Tony insisted gently. "Even if you weren't still a Phillips, you're practically a Temple. You have the bees, and dress to prove it."

She frowned slightly as he forced her to confront this. He leant in closer and spoke softly.

"I'm just trying to be square with you, Lucy…"

She grinned wickedly and linked her arms around his neck. Given their respective heights, this involved some stretching on her part. She pressed in against him, smiling mischievously. He hadn't said Miss.

"There's no one else here yet…" she murmured.

"I'm very aware…" he replied. His hands rested gently against her sides and his touch was yearning yet hesitant. "But the others could arrive any second."

"I could take you back out to the stables…" she suggested, turning her lips as close to his as she could.

Tony went scarlet. The memory was over a month old, but it was one of his most vivid ones. He had found her out there on a previous visit, and things had become heated. She had clung to him and kissed him until he was breathless. Collapsed against the back wall, his hands had found their way to the front of her shirt, and she had been encouraging, even guiding, as he felt her up. For a few hot minutes there had been nothing else. He had even wondered how far she would let it go. Then the only witness, whom they had completely forgotten about, let his opinion be known.

Brendan had snorted and stomped in his stall loud enough to get their attention. Lucy had gone to tend to the big grey horse, and Tony had left. He had sat in his car for ten minutes, until his heart stopped racing and the shadows crept back from the edges of his vision. He hadn't told her much about the darkness that still plagued him. Most of the time she was the best cure he had to keep it back. Right now, she looked like she was sharing his memory, and hoping to incite something similar. He leant closer. Footsteps sounded. Tony leapt back from her. His lips had barely brushed hers before he had placed a solid three feet between them.

Helen drifted through the doorway. She had her golden curls pinned up, and her dress was a touch more conservative than Lucy's. One glance over the room caught them, and she grinned. She raised a hand like a gun at Tony and feigned pulling a trigger. The soft gunshot sound she made turned quickly into a bright tinkle of laughter.

"Oh boy," she chuckled. "You look like a startled deer. Did I catch you at something?"

Tony shook his head. "No, Ma'am."

Lucy rolled her eyes. Helen laughed at both of them.

"You must make the worst gangster," she commented sympathetically. "You always look guilty, even when you've done nothing wrong. Well, if you're here, you kids can help me set the table."

"Yes, Ma'am," Tony nodded, moving to help her instantly.

Lucy rolled her eyes again. She drifted up by Helen and gave her a sidelong glance.

"Who says he wasn't doing anything wrong..." she offered suggestively, passing by.

Tony looked mortified. Helen pointed at the stricken young man with his hands full of cutlery.

"Look at him," she answered. "Besides, everyone knows he's a bluenose."

"Wha–" Tony looked like he was about to protest but

didn't know how.

"Who says that?" Lucy demanded, drifting further to corner Tony again.

"Everyone," Helen chuckled. "It's alright though," she looked at Tony. "Means Master Vincent trusts you with her."

"Should he?" Lucy teased, slipping her arms around Tony's waist as she caught up to him.

"Break it up, chippy," Helen warned her. "Fred and Doctor Temple might trust him with you, but no one trusts you with him."

"Excuse me," Lucy feigned mock outrage, but let him go all the same. "I am a lady of modest virtue."

Helen laughed.

"She is!" Tony protested, and had to look between them like he was missing the joke.

"She is," Helen agreed. "But if we left you two alone for too long, she might not be. For all that you're shy, trouble boy, you're a pushover. She'd have her way with you and be out the door like a shot."

Lucy feigned more outrage, but Tony looked unsettled. He'd had time to get used to Helen and Fred, but there was a deep part of his upbringing that left him uncomfortable when either of them spoke candidly, especially when they were together. There was concern in his dark eyes that the women who ran this house might be doing a better job of corrupting Lucy than he was. Lucy wholeheartedly disagreed and had previously spoken to Tony quite firmly on the matter. Several times. It went against everything he believed in, but she was softening him.

She helped him set the table with minimal teasing after that. His discomfort eased as her behavior mellowed, until Vincent and Fred joined them. Fred helped the old Hunter limp into the room, and she sat him at the head of the table. He was clean and dressed, but his permanent scowl was deep with pain, and whatever concoction Fred had given him for the hurt hadn't kicked in yet. His mood didn't improve at the sight of the letters Helen had left by his plate, but at least they distracted him.

Tony liked these people, but two years of working with Fred and trying to court Lucy hadn't made him comfortable around them yet. The witches made him nervous, and Vincent frightened him. It wasn't fair, and he knew it, but the sight of the old Hunter made Tony want to hide under the table. It wasn't just his severe attitude and constant air of judgement. Every time Tony looked at him he felt the touch of the writhing darkness, as he had when Vincent pulled him back from the world beyond.

Two years had done nothing to shift those nightmares. Fred had tried to teach him more, to help him heal. She called them the Dreamlands. Tony called it Hell. He had been there. He had seen it. He had felt it. When night fell, and Vincent looked at him with such knowing eyes, Tony felt the cold creep in again. It hungered for him and, no matter how much he practiced Fred's arts, he felt condemned.

Dinner began as a tense affair, but Lucy was seemingly having none of it, and Helen was of a like mind. Tony couldn't help but smile, even though he tried shyly to hide it, as he watched Lucy ignore Vincent's scowl and inform Fred what had happened during the mission. Fred listened intently and encouragingly as Lucy spilled the beans. Every now and again, she would shoot Vincent a sharp look with a raised eyebrow – the practiced discernment of a detective who is used to conflicting stories. Vincent began reading his letters, and glared at the women over the top of them when he felt Fred looking at him. Tony kept his head down and tried not to chuckle. The fighting in this family was so much gentler than his own.

"Boy," Vincent addressed him out of the blue, ignoring Fred's comment that Lucy's story seemed to contain more honesty than his own had. The old Hunter looked up from the letter he was reading, straight into Tony's eye. "You've heard from your cousin?"

"Yes, Sir," Tony nodded, setting his cutlery down politely. "I just got a letter from him before. He says he's doing well. Uh... your friend is an excellent teacher."

"He is," Vincent affirmed. He lifted the letter in indication. "Owens says the lad shows promise. Says he makes a fine apprentice. It's nice to see them getting on."

Vincent kept his eyes on the paper, and Tony waited awkwardly for a moment. He felt as though he needed to be dismissed from the conversation, but Vincent was drawn back into the letter, and no one seemed to need him. He picked up the cutlery again. Eating was a good enough way to avoid conversation.

"Sir, are you going to eat the food I put on your plate

or do you need me to feed you as well?" Fred asked Vincent pointedly.

"I'll get to it," Vincent answered distractedly as he moved onto the next letter.

"Before it gets cold and starts growing new life?" Fred replied flippantly.

Vincent ignored her and kept reading. Lucy and Tony shared a smile at the cynical attitude that dominated when mom and dad fought. Fred's eyes narrowed as she watched him read. The paper crackled. Helen watched them both fondly, and then also gave Vincent a curious look.

"Forgive my prying, Sir," she addressed him. "But I was wondering what that letter was when I set it down? It had strange runes scrawled on it."

"It's Arabic," Vincent answered her gently. "From Anisa."

"From Anisa?!" Fred piped up sharply.

"Yes," Vincent nodded, keeping his eyes on the letter. His dark gaze scanned it repeatedly, and he seemed genuinely oblivious to the table watching him with bated breath. Tony had no idea what Anisa meant, but he assumed it was important from the way Fred reacted. He'd known his Master long enough to know what that tone meant. Vincent set the letter beside his plate, and then picked up his cutlery and began to eat. Everyone was still staring at him. He no longer ignored them with deliberate scorn; merely inattentiveness. Tony repressed a shiver up his spine. It was unsettling to see Vincent so distracted.

"Sir?" Fred pressed him. He didn't answer.

"Vincent?!"

"Hm?" Vincent looked up from his food. "I'm eating now, woman. What else do you want?"

Fred looked at him helplessly like she was trying not to laugh.

"Yes, Sir, we're very proud, that was not another rebuke."

His response was a confused look at the notion that she might not be scolding him.

"Sir," Fred began patiently, "what was she writing you about?"

Something seemed to dawn in Vincent's eyes. He was distracted; whether it was the pain or the letters or an accumulation of all these things, he hadn't been paying attention to the room. But he was now. The lights had come on in his mind, and they shone behind his dark gaze like headlamps. He hadn't been planning on sharing the contents of the letter with anyone. Although, Tony had now deduced that Anisa was a 'she'. Vincent seemed to consider the situation for a moment, and then decided that there was no reason Fred's curiosity should go unsated.

"They're having trouble in Alexandria," he admitted quietly. "*Alshifaq Alfidiyu* are back, and she's asking for my help. She's worried about Fajr."

"We're going to Egypt?" Lucy piped up excitedly.

"No," Vincent shook his head and turned back to his meal. "We're not going anywhere."

"You have to take me!" Lucy protested.

"I'm not going," Vincent replied, continuing to eat.

A bleak silence settled over the table. Tony didn't

really know what was going on, but he wasn't prepared to ask. He knew it was none of his business. Fred and Helen had a resigned, harsh-but-fair look about them. Lucy looked like she was after another fight before the day was over.

"You can't just abandon them," she insisted.

"There are other Hunters in that part of the world," Vincent explained. "It is their territory and they will take care of it. We cannot just go busting in there, and we cannot leave our territories unprotected against the forces of darkness. You've seen how busy we've been, Lucy. What would have happened to all those people if we hadn't been there to help?"

"But she asked for you..." Lucy pressed. "That means her Hunters aren't helping."

"We're not running off to the other side of the world, Lucy," Vincent sighed.

"You'd really leave her family in their hands?" Lucy demanded.

Silence reigned. A thick black silence of guilt and pain and shame. Tony wanted to hide under the table. He could feel the atmosphere of the room creeping under his skin. It wanted to flay him, rip him raw until his own darkness was naked to the world. Fred was trying to subtly shake her head at Lucy. Vincent was staring her down. Neither of the Hunters were budging. Master and apprentice were both staring at each other like the first to look away would catch fire.

"The first lesson of our Order," Vincent spoke sternly in his powerful and quiet voice, "is that you cannot save everyone. I took you on, safe in the knowledge that I would not have to teach you that lesson." He stood slowly. "Do not force me to make you relearn it."

Lucy looked like he'd slapped her, but he was already turning away and limping from the room. They all watched him go, but not even Fred moved to help him. Tony knew his Master. This was shock, not disapproval, and he didn't blame her. Vincent was the only one of them who wasn't shocked by his ruthless stance, not just with Anisa, but with Lucy. He left them alone with their revelation.

TOMB OF ENDLESS NIGHT

2

Lucy was furious. It wasn't just indignation at the way Vincent had spoken to her at dinner, but his unyielding stance and the casual air with which he condemned others. She knew he was ruthless, but even by his standards that had been cold. He was worn down, injured, and in pain. It wasn't the best state to be making such decisions. Still, Lucy couldn't justify it to herself. He was ignoring someone's call for help. The screams of the child from the mansion still echoed in her ears. The sound haunted her. She could hear the voice of the butler. *The world needs more people like you, Miss. All over the globe, the helpless are falling to such dangers, and there are too few like you... It is a pity you can't save everyone...*

The sound was so deep under her skin she could hear it pounding with her blood. That man had been right. Vincent was right. She hadn't been able to save that child's mother, the same way she had completely failed to save her own parents. They were always too late to save everyone. Not this time. This time they had been given adequate warning, and they had been asked for help directly. The butler had said she was the one who came to help those who had no one else to turn to.

These thoughts were whirling behind her frown as

she walked Tony to his car after dinner. The gangly boy at her side stumbled next to her as shy and nervous as ever. She found his awkwardness endearing. He was more unsettled than usual tonight, but after the experience they'd just had she couldn't blame him. He always looked like he was trying to work out how to wear his skin properly, and his soulful dark eyes begged permission to be a good person. Lucy begrudged the world for making him think he couldn't be.

"I'm sorry he spoke to you that way," Tony muttered to her as they crunched across the gravel drive. "The old Doc seemed in a right foul mood."

"He's just a crotchety old man," Lucy grumbled. "He's lost too many people, and he's losing his will to fight."

"Who's the lady that wrote him?" Tony asked. "You know her? She an old flame?"

"Not likely," Lucy almost chuckled despite herself. "She's Naeem's sister." Lucy paused as they came to a stop beside Tony's car. "Naeem was Vincent's last apprentice... before me. He died a long time ago."

"I'm sorry," Tony muttered, keeping his eyes fixed on the ground.

"I've never met any of them," Lucy shrugged, turning to face him and stepping in close. "But I've heard a bit."

Tony was fidgeting with his grey wool cap, staring down through it to the earth. Lucy took it from him, and reached up on tiptoes to flop it on his head. He grinned wryly at her. She caught her fingers in his, now that they weren't pretending to be busy anymore.

"I got family business over the weekend," he told her. She could hear the reluctance in his voice. "But I got lessons with Miss Winifred next week, so I'll see you again then. Hopefully you and the Doc won't be too busy with him all bunged up like that."

Lucy nodded solemnly, her face a mask of contemplation. She tiptoed up again. Tony took the hint and leant down to kiss her cheek. Lucy placed a firm hand to the side of his face and directed his lips to hers. She kissed him without any hint of bashfulness. He kissed her back, but drew away first and whispered.

"People can see us…"

"So?" she challenged, holding him close and knowing he wouldn't answer.

Sometimes his skittishness was cute. Sometimes it was just annoying. Everyone knew they liked each other, and her reputation had been so thoroughly ruined by the death of her parents and taking up arms with Vincent that nothing else could diminish it further. Tony didn't seem to see it that way. Tony liked her, and he wanted to do right by her. As endearing as that was, Lucy was used to taking risks now. That was her new norm. She wanted Tony to be a part of that. It was about time for a big risk.

"Do you remember, when your cousin first went south, we talked about getting fake papers for that mission with Vincent?" she murmured.

"Yeah," he nodded.

"Did you ever get them?" she checked.

He nodded earnestly.

"Can we still use them?" she asked.

"What for?" he replied in confusion.

Lucy gave him a direct look. He was smarter than he pretended to be, but sometimes it took him a little while to realize that. Comprehension dawned in his eyes.

"Wait…"

"Yes," she replied.

"You can't be serious!"

"I am," she insisted. "Anisa needs our help. There's a ship that leaves before dawn, and I can get us tickets if you can get us papers."

"What, just you and me?" he checked nervously.

"Yes," she confirmed unflinchingly. "I'm a Hunter. You're a mage. We can help them. If Vincent won't, it's our duty to protect those in need."

"Doc Temple said there were Hunters in that part of the world though," Tony reminded her.

Lucy stared him down. "The Hunters in Egypt were the people who murdered Naeem. I wouldn't ask that lady to go to them for help, and I wouldn't expect her to. Vincent should know better. Now, are you with me or not?"

Tony stared at her for a long time. Lucy had watched him freeze like a deer in headlights fairly frequently. She could almost see him trying to weigh everything up in his mind. With a sigh, she leant close again and whispered.

"Go home. Get those papers and pack a bag. Drive back here after midnight, I'll meet you by the front gate and we can leave for the ship."

Tony seemed to think about this for a long time. She

wondered if she could up his processing speed. From memory, he could react very quickly in a fight. It was just when they tried to involve his brain that the system encountered problems. Then, very slowly, he nodded. Lucy grinned at him. Tony looked slightly dazed, as though he was deeply concerned about what he had just agreed to. He kissed her once, fleetingly, but of his own instigation, and then quickly climbed into his car. Lucy watched him drive away. The slight frown she had worn out to the car had been replaced with a small smile. Once he was out of sight, she went back to the house to see how surreptitiously she could pack.

* * *

The night was dark and still. A faint fog was settling over the city, but it cleared the closer they got to the harbor. Tony had met her exactly as she had asked. He had picked her up from the corner of the drive and brought the papers she had asked for. To her eye they looked good, but it didn't stop her nerves as they tried to board. A tall man with a short beard and a grim expression looked over their passports and tickets.

Lucy stood with one hand clutching her bag, and the other interlocked with Tony's. She didn't know how nervous she looked, and she was impressed that Tony didn't look nervous at all – especially given that he had looked like he was going to have a heart attack when she had lent him one of the two rings she had 'borrowed' from the house. Apparently trying to fake your way onto a ship with false papers scared him a lot less than pretending to be married to her with a ring that had been borrowed without permission from his Master. When she thought about it, she could understand why that might be.

The man finished looking over their papers and tickets and handed everything back with a gruff nod and short sharp directions to their cabin. Lucy felt a wave of relief sweep through her as she and Tony took their bags up the gangplank. The fog hadn't lingered over the harbor, but the air was damp enough that the lights were extra bright. Tony kept a tight hold of her hand and led her across the deck to the internal door.

They descended into the bowels of the ship to the guest cabins. The steel walls were worn and gritty, and the grated stairs clanged beneath their feet. Lucy smiled to herself as they traipsed down and clunked along the corridor. Three years ago she would have been horrified to board such a pedestrian ship. This was starting to feel like an adventure.

Tony opened the door to their cabin. It squeaked surprisingly little. The room was austere, with four stacked bunks bolted to the floor and a small window looking out at the darkness. The electric light in the ceiling was harsh, but the carpet was nice. It was a thick midnight blue, and didn't even seem too badly scuffed. Lucy dropped her bag and looked around. There wasn't much to see. It was just a cramped ship's cabin. She couldn't stop grinning at it.

Tony shut the door behind them and neatly stashed his suitcase under the bunk against the far wall. He shrugged out of his jacket and hung it on the back of the door. Instinctively, he took off his cap and began to fidget with it, pushing his mop of dark hair back out of his eyes. He rolled up his sleeves, passing the cap between his hands, and smoothed his waistcoat before sitting down on the bed, hunched so as not to knock his head on the bunk above. His big dark eyes scanned the room apprehensively. Trepidation rolled off him in waves that matched the gentle rocking of the boat.

Lucy unfastened her thick overcoat and hung it beside his. Her thin white button-down shirt was cold in the cabin, but that was just the chill of night seeping through. She kicked her bag in beside his, under the same bunk, and perched down beside him. She was still smiling. She couldn't help it. He looked as nervous as ever. She took his cap from his hands and tossed it onto the bunk above them.

"You calling dibs?" he finally smiled.

"No," she shook her head. "I just want you to be able to relax. The ship will set sail soon. I booked the whole cabin. We're safe here. You don't have to be so jittery."

Tony looked away. His expression was apologetic and reluctant with all the things he didn't know how to put into words. Lucy leant in against him and rested her head on his shoulder.

"Um..." Tony started to stammer, fidgeting with his fingers after having his other option confiscated. "You... um... do you know how we're finding this sister? Y'know, when we get there, I mean."

"There was a return address on the back of the letter," Lucy replied. "I copied it down. We'll start there. As soon as we find her I can explain who we are."

"You think that'll work?"

"I'm sure it will." She smiled and reached out to take his hand. Her fingers laced themselves between his, with her hand resting over his palm, and her fake wedding ring gleaming in the harsh light. He was so cute when he was nervous, sitting in their private bubble of light, surrounded by the silent dark world of early morning. They were all alone. No one else. They were on an adventure, and she didn't want to play it safe. She didn't want to play anything safe. She leant in to kiss him, but he shied away.

"Miss Lucy..." he hesitated.

"Drop the 'miss', Tony," she warned him. "I'm not 'miss' anything anymore."

"Yes, you are," he insisted, closing his hand over hers and holding it between them. "Those papers are fake. I can't use the lie to take advantage of you."

Lucy tried not to laugh, but a small chuckle escaped her. She took her hands from his to touch his face, leaning in to kiss him again.

"It's not stopping me from trying to take advantage of you..."

"You couldn't," he whispered, kissing her back.

Tony didn't so much have walls as terraces. Lucy found they were easy enough to climb, if she tried. She pressed her lips to his, and tangled her fingers in his slick hair. A flush raced up her chest. Her skin felt hot. Her pulse quickened. She clutched herself to him, careful not to knock the top bunk as she climbed onto his lap and straddled him. She heard his breath catch, and felt him pause. His lips drew back from hers.

"What's wrong?" she whispered. Her fingers brushed his cheeks as her eyes sought his, but he wouldn't look up at her. "Tony? What are you scared of?"

He kept his eyes down. She kissed his hair. His arms still held her on him, but his grip wasn't sure. She pressed herself against him harder and felt him shiver.

"Why does nothing scare you?" he muttered nervously.

"Lots of things scare me," she answered honestly. She kept her face as close to his as he would let her. Her nose gently poked against the side of his face, and she kissed his cheek. "But not this. Not you. Never you, Tony. You're where I go to feel safe."

He finally met her eye. She could have elaborated, but she didn't need to. She saw that he understood. His gaze was always so tortured, but the hope she longed for in his eyes had sparked at her words. She smiled at him, wondering if it was too much to hope that he would smile back. He didn't, but he kissed her. He kissed her like he meant it. His arms wrapped around her tightly and pulled her into him. The force of his grip made her blood surge. She opened her mouth against his, gasping at the intensity with which they kissed. Heat flared up the back of her neck as his fingers traced her spine through her shirt.

Lucy pushed him back, guiding him onto the mattress beneath them. The bunk creaked as she crawled over him. Her lips searched across his skin as she unbuttoned his waistcoat. Hot sweat beaded his neck as she kissed down his throat.

"Lucy…" he whispered.

She returned her lips to his, silencing him. She didn't know what he was going to say, and she didn't care. She didn't want to hear him tell her they shouldn't be doing this. They shouldn't be doing any of the things they had done tonight. That was half the fun. They were in the right disobeying Vincent and leaving to help a stranger. Why couldn't they be in the right about this too? She didn't want to know why, she just wanted to taste him. She pushed her tongue into his mouth as she reached between them and fumbled with his belt buckle.

Tony's hands shot down and caught her fingers instantly, pulling them away from him. She was still sitting on top of him and could feel his desire for her, but she could hear his fear in his breath. His mouth panted against hers, torn between terror and hunger. He just needed a little encouragement.

Lucy sat back, still straddled against him, and unbuttoned and removed her own shirt. She wore nothing beneath it. Tony lay under her, his chest rising and falling like he was struggling to breathe.

"You can touch," she told him, guiding his hands to her bare breasts.

He groped her hesitantly at first, then eagerly as she lowered her body back to his. Her lips sought his kiss again as his hands squeezed her chest. He gasped as she kissed him.

The door banged open. It moved so fast the creak was lost, but it knocked against the bottom of the other set of bunks. Lucy yelped and leapt back. She snatched her shirt up and clutched it to her front. Her legs were still tangled over Tony's, but her back was pressed to the wall. He looked just as startled, half risen on his elbows.

Vincent stood in the doorway. He had the top of a cane tightly clasped in one hand, and a battered suitcase in the other. His eyes looked over the room, but barely seemed to take them in. Fred stood just behind his shoulder. He turned to her.

"What do you know, Fred, you were right. They are getting themselves in trouble without us." He said nothing else, but limped into the room with the aid of the cane. He stashed his suitcase under the other sent of bunks. Then, without removing any of his heavy outer clothing, he lay himself down on the bottom bed. His great, tattered overcoat clinked when he moved but it covered both man and bunk like a thick, dirty blanket. He tipped his hat to cover his eyes and lay still and peaceful.

That left Lucy and Tony to out-stare Fred, which was somehow worse. Fred stood in all her severe glory in the open doorway. Lucy hugged her shirt tighter to her body, now painfully aware of how exposed she was and how hideous this moment could have been if their mentors had been five minutes later. Fred stepped into the room and shut the door. No one else moved or spoke. She was also carrying a bag, which she moved to stash beside Vincent's, but paused first. Her black eyes pierced Tony mercilessly.

"Top bunk, Segreti," she ordered him. "Where I can see you."

Lucy resented the instruction, and the swiftness with

which Tony scrambled to follow it. She wanted to protest that they hadn't been doing anything wrong, but she knew it wasn't true, and trying to claim it would only make things worse. Instead, she settled for arguing her mission.

"Anisa needs our help," she stated. She tried to keep her eyes on Fred, but she kept glancing up to the top bunk where she knew Tony was now huddled, probably fidgeting with his cap.

"Does it look like anyone is dragging you off this boat?" Fred replied as she stashed her bag.

"What happened to 'we cannot leave our territories unprotected against the forces of darkness'?" Lucy pestered.

"I have made other arrangements," Vincent told the room firmly. He didn't move, and his eyes stayed closed under his hat. Lucy knew he wouldn't elaborate. He so seldom did. She glowered.

"How did you find us?" she inquired petulantly.

Vincent spoke gruffly again from under his hat. "You called ahead to book tickets with my name and my money. Did you really think we wouldn't notice?"

Lucy glowered at both of them. Vincent didn't see or care or move. Fred didn't care either, but she stared Lucy down so hard the girl actually began to feel ashamed. Fred was the only one looking at her now, so she carefully pulled her shirt back on and wrapped it around herself. Lucy huddled down on the bunk under Fred's watchful gaze. The mage stood at the end of Vincent's bunk, with a full view of both apprentices.

Lucy wished she could still see Tony. She wished he

was still with her, that she could hold his hand, even if Fred was supervising. But she couldn't. Her great plan for sneaking away with her fake husband had been shattered. Resentfully, Lucy slid the ring off her finger and held it out to Fred. Fred's lips twitched in a small smile and she shook her head.

"Oh no, little one," she declined. "You're going to have to keep that safe for me, at least until we get home. Your papers say you're married. So, when we're in public, you two will be living that lie."

Lucy slipped the ring back on and contemplated this. Then she saw a ring on Fred's hand. Confusion gripped her for a moment, until realization dawned with stunning light.

"Wait–"

"Yes," Fred confirmed. "If anyone asks, we're your parents."

"You're my what?!" Lucy exclaimed.

"Mom and dad," Vincent muttered under his hat. "Your papers might say 'Moretti' but that is formally 'Temple' now."

"And you're Missus Temple now?" Lucy taunted Fred.

"What do you mean 'now'?" Fred replied.

"We never told the kids, Fred," Vincent reminded her.

"Never told us what?" Lucy demanded.

"Legally, Fred and I are married," Vincent admitted, slightly muffled. "She's a Temple, and the beneficiary of my will."

Lucy heard Tony move on the bunk above her. She

wondered if he was staring as hard as she was. Vincent lay completely still on the bed, with no care for the bombshell he had dropped.

"You… you two are… married…?" Tony stammered at the room.

"For some years now," Fred nodded.

"But…" Tony protested.

"But what, Tony?" Fred challenged.

"But…" he protested meekly.

"It was a legal decision, Tony," Vincent told him from under the hat. "We don't advertise it, but it made sense. I love Fred. I trust her. I've had too many near-death experiences not to prepare for eventualities. The decision wasn't going to impact our lifestyles, but it would help keep the estate and the collection safe. You should understand better than most how important that is."

Everyone fell silent. Tony would have sunk back down at that reference, and Lucy didn't want to further disturb the waters now that they were rippling. He still wouldn't speak about what had happened to him. Not properly. Lucy knew a little, pieces she had gleaned from the other three. It had been horrible. It still haunted him. It might haunt him for the rest of his life. As if to prove her point, a small mutter came from the bunk above her.

"We're all going to burn in Hell…"

"So pessimistic, Mister Segreti," Vincent replied. "That may prove true, but it will have less to do with our behaviors than you think. Not to mention, it's probably preferable to other places you've ended up."

Lucy glowered at her mentor for continuing to push the memory, not that he could tell she was doing it. She'd been giving him dark looks since he arrived, and he was yet to know about a single one. Or, perhaps, he knew very well that she wouldn't stop glaring at him, and couldn't give a damn. Fred could see, but she didn't care. The darkness hung over all of them now, and the ship began to move. Lucy felt the gentle lurch. The vibrations of the engine grew louder as the ship pushed away from the docks. They were stuck together now. Lucy was getting her mission. She was getting her wish to help Anisa. Provided the four of them could survive two weeks living together in the same cabin. This was not the trip she had signed up for.

* * *

Vincent napped away the morning. It helped him ignore the pain in his leg, and made up for the sleep he had missed getting to the ship in the middle of the night. The lull of the engine was a comforting white noise, and the rocking of the boat was soothing. All of these things paled in comparison to the knowledge that he had nothing to do. There was no pressing monster to fight, no research weighing on him, no dire need for training. Well, there was a bit of a dire need for training, but nowhere they could get away with it. So he could sleep peacefully.

Daylight from the small window filled the room when he woke. He lay peacefully for moment, before all the aches and pains of his age and condition drifted into his consciousness. He still lay on his back in his coat and fumbled in his pockets for all the different bottles. He pulled himself onto his elbow and removed the cap of a little brown bottle of tonic. Unlike his homemade brew, this one was designed to alleviate pain. It worked rather well too. He took a sip and replaced it in his pocket.

Above him, he could hear the gentle sound of Fred snoring. The kids were nowhere to be seen. That was his problem now. With a weak groan, Vincent slowly hauled himself off the bed. He perched himself on the edge of the bunk and unhooked his cane from the end. The hat he was prepared to leave on the pillow. He pushed himself to his feet and limped out to find his ward.

It didn't take him long, and he was surprised to find them keeping out of trouble. Although, as he thought about that, he wondered if it was perhaps unfair of him. With the exception of the last twenty-four hours she was usually very well behaved.

Lucy and Tony were on deck, beneath a bright cloudy sky. The breeze was gentle, and the ocean calm. They leant against the railing, arm in arm, and looking for all the world like young newlyweds. Vincent almost didn't want to interrupt, but now that he was rested there were things that needed to be addressed. He limped over to join them. They heard him approach and Tony untangled himself from Lucy. She didn't fight him about it, but she stayed close and rested a concerned hand against his back. Tony didn't look good. He looked tired and haggard. There were dark bags under his eyes and the ever-present grimace on his face. He fumbled a cigarette out of a silver case from his pocket and lit it as Vincent approached.

The old Hunter watched as the boy's fingers trembled, before steadying again when the familiar action and nicotine comforted him. Tony waved out the match and inhaled deeply. This was as close to relaxed as the kid ever seemed to get these days. Vincent remembered the nervous errand boy from two years ago and wondered if Tony regretted saving Fred's life in that dark corridor. It had cost him dearly, but Lucy wouldn't love him the way she did if he hadn't done it. In fact, if he hadn't, it was possible none of them would still be here.

"How's it going, Doc?" Tony asked once he was in earshot.

"I've been worse," Vincent answered. "And you?"

"Same," he answered, nervously exhaling a stream of smoke. Tony looked to Lucy, as though passing on the question and including her in the conversation.

"Are you here to scold me?" Lucy asked, folding her arms.

Vincent smiled. He looked out across the endless blue ocean as the breeze rippled his grey hair.

"What you did was rather brave," he commented. "You defied me, boldly and fearlessly, in the name of helping someone you've never met, just because they took the time to ask."

"You can't really have meant to leave her to her troubles..." Lucy insisted.

Vincent continued to smile at the waves. "I really did. Egypt is not my place. It is not my land, nor my protectorate. I once hoped to train Naeem to care for it as it should have been cared for, but Britain does not like to relinquish its colonial hold over even the smallest things. My disapproval of the Order's habit of coming into foreign lands and upsetting ancient traditional magics to introduce their own has led them to exclude me in many areas. I have not been excommunicated like some of my brethren, I still hold a seat on the Council, but my advice is unwelcome under the Chancellor, and I am uninterested in theirs. The Brotherhood of Hunters is an archaic order. They cling to so many traditions because they are traditions, regardless of whether they help or hinder." Vincent's smile had faded to a grimace as he spoke.

Lucy and Tony shared a look, but they didn't interrupt him.

"The Order have representatives in Egypt that will not be pleased to see me back," Vincent continued. "It was a fight I did not want to start. I trusted the Brotherhood to keep the Darkness at bay, even if that meant people like Anisa and her family were neglected in the process. So many suffer... who am I to gift special protection to some and not others?"

"But that is what you do," Lucy reasoned. "That's why you let everyone live at the mansion. That's why the estate has so many staff. You do protect some of us over others. That's what it is to be human, to care for the people you love."

Vincent gave the horizon a considered nod. "Perhaps. Perhaps you were right, and that is why I am here now, sailing to a place I never thought I would return to." He gave the children a grim look. "We have a long way to go, but be careful when we get there. If Anisa is right, and things are stirring, it won't just be the Order that doesn't want us in Egypt. No one can know why we are there or what we are doing. If anyone asks, we are visiting old friends. I have sent a telegram back to Anisa and will pick up her reply went we stop in Spain. I imagine we shall be staying with her and her family. She has a husband, Anwar, and a daughter, a little girl called Fajr. This is a pleasure trip. A social call."

"And what do we say when we start shooting stuff?" Lucy asked pointedly.

"Say we're American," Vincent shrugged.

Tony snorted. Vincent flashed him a grin.

"By the time we're shooting, most people won't be watching," he replied honestly. "Either they need the help, or they're too far gone. I'm hoping we can wrap this up quickly and be on our way."

"You really like our odds on that?" Tony muttered around his cigarette.

Vincent gave him a long look, but the boy's tired eyes didn't budge. The old Hunter cast his gaze back out to the sea. He wasn't interested in tempting fate with an answer.

"She told you about Naeem?" He changed the subject and indicated Lucy. "You know what we're walking into?"

"He was your first apprentice," Tony recalled. "Killed by your own people, and they covered up the friendly fire."

"Before the Great War," Vincent nodded bleakly. "I didn't have you two dragged off this ship when we caught you, although I had half a mind to, but if I am going to let you be a part of this, I need to know you will look after each other."

"You really worried about that?" Lucy asked drily. She almost sounded like her fake husband when she said it.

Vincent bit back his smile, but his eyes conveyed his understanding. He was not worried about these two protecting each other, or even himself and Fred. That was inevitable. They were still young and idealistic. They were doing this to protect others. He was mostly worried about what they would need protection from. Dark clouds were looming on his horizon, and the threat of the future grew ever nearer.

* * *

The distrust and resentment didn't linger for long. By the first night Tony was back to his reserved and obedient self, and Lucy had outgrown her frustration at being caught. Fred was still keeping an eye on them, but they seemed happy enough to retire to their respective bunks. Vincent didn't want any of it to be his business, but he knew it should be. She was his ward. He was just grateful they all seemed content to keep to themselves and not mingle with the other passengers. Lucy was becoming evermore of a wild child, and while that had aided her instruction with him, and her abilities as his apprentice, he did wonder what it would mean for her life outside monster killing.

The ship rocked gently on the waves as night stained the landscape. There was nothing but darkness as far as the eye could see. Vincent sat on his bunk and watched the endless void of black out the window as he listened to the others sleep. Every now and again, a light from the ship would reflect off the water, and he would glimpse a sliver of ocean. The peril of what lay before them was still chasing old memories around his head. He couldn't shake it.

Everyone else was fast asleep. He'd been waiting for it, and now that it was here, he hesitated. Perhaps the reluctance was fear of terror or pain, perhaps it was the knowledge that if Fred busted him, she'd hang him over the side of the ship by his ankles. Eventually, he pushed aside the fears. Their room had a private water closet. Vincent snuck inside and shut the door. He sat on the floor with his back against the door and crossed his legs. From his pocket he pulled a small vial that didn't have painkillers in it. Not the good kind anyway.

He didn't have candles or a circle, but with the rhythm of the ship and the endless ocean he wouldn't need it. The act of travelling was its own shift between realms. He would be able to find his way. With trembling fingers, he removed the cork. The shaking in his hands reminded him of Tony trying to light his cigarette. He wondered if he looked as bad as the boy did. Maybe, but he had a good number of years on the lad. He should look worse. But maybe not. Maybe that was just what that place did to people. He downed the contents of the vial.

Darkness engulfed him, like a warm, deep bath. He didn't even have time to feel dizzy. He sank through the steel floor like he was going home. The pain in his leg and the aches of his old bones faded to nothing. He was comfortable here. So much more comfortable than sitting on the cold bathroom floor. He stared up into the sky. Galaxies swirled through forever in faint hues of color. He watched a star explode. It wasn't happening in his lifetime. Either a long time ago, long before this earth, or a long time from now, perhaps when life had been reclaimed. A star shivered and wobbled. It heaved and boiled. It exploded. Too far away for anything else to know about it yet, but they would. Other debris would feel this birth.

Where the explosion began the light was too bright to look at. In the center of it was darkness. A darkness so pure no light could wash it. From there, tentacles thrust out of the fire. They writhed, pushing and squirming from the center. Millions of them, reaching into forever.

Vincent felt hands on his shoulders. A firm and amorous grip. He relaxed back into the hands of a friend, safe and secure beneath the end of all things.

"It's beautiful, isn't it?" a smooth, rich voice whispered in his ear.

"Very…" Vincent whispered back, meaning it at the time.

"And what brings you to me this time?" the Prince asked. His hands tightened reassuringly.

Vincent leant back further, like he was sinking into a deep soft bed. He'd never been this comfortable, and he wasn't sure he knew the answer.

"Fear?" the Prince whispered hungrily. "You are afraid?"

"Of so many things..." Vincent answered dazedly. "I need to know what's coming... I need to know..."

The tentacles were reaching for him. They twisted closer and closer. Slime dripped from them like acid rain across the world. They shared the Prince's hunger. A hunger so deep a million galaxies could not sate it. He could hear breathing as they neared, a million groping fingers reaching for his body. The breathing came ragged and rough, like someone struggling for air. Tense moaning interspersed it. Though whether the sounds were made in pleasure or pain Vincent couldn't tell.

"Reality is calling you," the Prince whispered. "You have to wake up."

His breath was hot by Vincent's ear... but that didn't make any sense. There shouldn't be breath. The Prince had no face. Or did he?

"Wake up," his deep voice ordered.

* * *

Vincent jerked awake on the floor. Everything hurt. His leg was twitching in pain from the way his wound had twisted when he slumped. His whole body throbbed and heaved. He gasped desperately, trying not to puke. Even his eyeballs burned. He could taste blood. It was stronger than the aftertaste of the tonic. There was crying coming from the other room.

He pulled himself up, shivering and retching. The basin made a good enough crutch until his uninjured leg could hold him. He propped himself up against the walls, wiping his face and checking the mirror. No ooze. No darkness. Thank goodness. He spat and rinsed away the blood as quickly as he could. Then he used the walls to keep himself standing as he limped back into the bunk room.

Tony was on the floor. Fred and Lucy were bent over him as he writhed and moaned. His hands clutched at his head and he cried weakly, struggling on the carpet. Vincent staggered over and crashed down at his side with the others.

"Sir!" Fred caught sight of him.

"Seasick," he answered gruffly, using the back of his wrist to wipe away a trace of blood and sticky saliva from the corner of his mouth. He pushed through the women and grabbed Tony by the shoulders. The boy struggled in his shaking hands. "Come back to me, Tony," he encouraged. "Follow the sound of my voice, boy. Come back. This way. Wake up."

Tony shivered and cried, squirming in Vincent's hands. The old Hunter tightened his grip. He dug his fingers deep into Tony's shoulders, firm enough to hurt. Tony writhed and snapped. He jerked awake with a yelp of terror. His huge dark eyes looked massive in his skinny face. He blinked at the ceiling in confusion and distress. His eyes scoured everywhere at once, trying to get his bearings.

"Tony?" Lucy touched his face gently. She leant over him, taking up most of his vision.

He stopped panicking, but he didn't look any happier. He lay back against the floor, closing his eyes and letting his head relax. Vincent let him go, but Tony clutched himself. His arms wrapped around and hugged his body tightly as he shivered uncontrollably.

"Tony... what happened?" Lucy pressed him.

"Let him be," Vincent growled, placing a hand on her shoulder.

"No, what happened?!" Lucy insisted. "Is he alright?"

"He's okay," Fred sighed, sitting back. She looked weary, and she ran her fingers through her black hair. "You get this happening a lot, Segreti?"

Tony rolled over, burying his face in his hands and hiding his expression against the floor. Fred reached out a hand and rubbed his back comfortingly. That was enough of an answer for her.

"The boys say I got ghosts..." Tony muttered tearfully; his voice muffled by his hands.

"I'd say you do at that..." Vincent sighed. "Nothing wrong with ghosts. Lots of us have them."

Tony didn't respond. He just lay on the floor and cried. His shoulders shook, and Fred kept a hand there, rubbing him soothingly like a caring mother.

TOMB OF ENDLESS NIGHT

3

Time did not improve the situation. They sailed on in close quarters for two weeks. Tony had nightmares almost every night. After the first night, Lucy swapped bunks with him so that he wasn't in danger of falling in his sleep. Two nights later, she took her blanket and crawled into his bed with him. Fred withheld comment. There was nothing untoward for her to worry about, and Tony whimpered less with Lucy curled up beside him.

Vincent knew Fred had been worried. They had talked many times over the past couple of years about the damage Tony had done picking up that book. Fred was happy to train him, but his power was strange. It was unique and dangerous, and it had come at a great cost. Vincent honestly didn't know if his friend watched the children everyday like a hawk because she wanted to keep them from doing something inappropriate, or if she was worried about the foreboding peril of her apprentice. It might have been six of one...

He wasn't faring so well himself. His leg was healed now, or close enough, but his own nightmares were causing problems. The Dreamlands weren't helping. He was trying to keep his visits infrequent, but it lingered.

He had waited a week after the first incident with Tony before trying again. The second attempt hadn't been particularly more insightful than the first, but it had left him bedridden for the entire stop over in Spain. Fred had found him vomiting blood, and was using her magic to help heal him, on top of acquiring the services of the ship's doctor.

Vincent was taking a tiny sip of tonic each night to try and get himself back into the Darkness. There were things he needed to see. He needed to know what the future held. He also needed it not to kill him. He was walking the knife's edge, and it wasn't paying off. The dreams were as tantalizing as they were taunting. He never quite saw what he needed. Even now, they spun him through infinity.

He stumbled. His feet tripped on the sandy ground as he staggered along. Dunes of dust rose and fell around him. The powdered remnants of the bones of those that came before. Every now and again a lingering fragment, worn smooth and shiny, glinted in the moonlight. He knew the crescent hung above him like a beacon, but he dared not look up. That way lay madness. Without the Prince to guide him, the stars were pure insanity. That was why he sought the Prince. Somewhere… somewhere in the bone dust…

Vincent stumbled and fell. He hit the sand. His hands lashed out to catch him as he went down, sinking into the dust. He kept falling. The dunes sucked him in. Their soft, dry touch was cloying… suffocating. He could feel the dust of the dead, millions of desiccated lives gone, sifting through his clothes and hair, coating his skin. He tried not to breathe. It was so hard. He needed air.

The dust released him. He fell further, and hit a cold, hard ground. He could breathe here. The air was toxic and acidic, like all air in this world. It was stale and bitter down here, but at least the sky was gone. It left the darkness absolute. He crawled weakly across the ground. The floor felt like ancient, pockmarked leather. His hands were still dusty, and the dirt was rough and scratchy.

The Darkness shifted. It moved in a graduation of greys. Vincent couldn't call it light, because there was no light, but there were different levels of darkness to perceive. A cave so huge and deep it could hold the heart of the world. Vincent felt that he could hear it beating. The floor rose and dropped in broken terraces, with sharp spikes of rock piercing up through the ground. Stalactites dripped from the uneven ceiling like the clotted blood of an ancient deity.

In the cave, another deity was rising. More ancient than anything that had bled here before. Far in the distance, Vincent could see a pillar rising up in the center of the cavern. It stood taller than a dozen men, and atop the natural stone a throne had been carved. Upon it sat the Prince. From his royal peak he surveyed his domain, Master of all Worlds, and he watched the barren, lifeless stone with glee plastered across his absent face.

Vincent crawled towards him, hauling himself across the broken ground. The world lurched, and he fell from the cracked ledge.

And jerked awake in his bunk. Beneath him, the ship swayed on the waves and rocked him gently. He leant over the side of the bed, covering his mouth as blood and slime dripped from his lips. He didn't want to cough. He didn't want to wake the others. Moonlight sifted in faint patches through the clouds. He could hear quiet snoring above him.

Pained and trembling, he dragged himself from the bed and crawled to the door. It was so hot. He needed air. He staggered into the corridor. The wall kept him propped up as he leant against it with his shoulder, and dragged his body up the staircase. He broke out on deck like a wounded soldier fleeing ambush. The air was warm still, but much cooler than it had been inside. The Mediterranean Sea was black beneath the night sky. It lapped gently at the sides of the ship. Vincent staggered to the railing and gulped in the salty midnight air. He hadn't realized he was panicked until it took him a moment to calm down.

The Dreamlands had that effect on him. They were toxic and painful to travel to when the trip was forced. There were those who could make it there alone. Strangers who slipped through when they slept and stumbled through the terrors and the wonders, waking with only the gnawing horror of memory. Vincent needed more. Dreams weren't enough. He had to go there, he had to interact with the realm on his own terms. That meant the tonic. That meant a slow and steady path to madness and death.

He breathed deeply and let the air burn his aching lungs and stinging throat. It was a good feeling. A rejuvenating sensation. It meant he was still alive. However, he was having to admit the trips were dulling his senses. He had missed most of the trip across the Atlantic, and now he was missing most of the trip through the Mediterranean too. A Hunter was nothing without their carefully honed wits to keep them aware of danger. He had never been served a harsher reminder than this one.

He heard the rasp and saw the flame. It was sharp in the darkness, much closer than any of the ship's lamps. Vincent watched the end of a cigarette come alight. The flame went out. Tony blew a thick trail of smoke over the railing, and snapped his cigarette case shut. He pocketed the silver case. Vincent watched the glint as it disappeared. It was a nice box – nicer than anything else the boy owned. A gift from the family, no doubt. Perhaps for his sixteenth birthday. He was probably the only man in his family who hadn't been given a gun for the milestone. Vincent didn't know if that was because they didn't think he needed it, or if they were scared of what he'd do with it.

It was also possible that Tony hadn't needed a new gun. His first one carried holy bullets and he took good care of it. Vincent knew the boy could make his own bullets, but he didn't know exactly who had taught him. It was possible Lucy had done it. It was also possible his uncle Elia Ferro had taught him, given that Vincent had taught Ferro. The recipe was supposed to be a trade secret of the Hunters, but Vincent needed help and the Council could kiss his ass. In the past two years the Mafia had helped him kill more monsters than the

Brotherhood to which he was sworn.

"You don't look so good, Doc," Tony commented. He kept a respectful distance down the railing, and tapped ash over the edge. His black eyes reflected the darkness of the night, but his face was pale and tight.

Vincent spat the dregs of bitter blood from the back of his throat over the edge of the ship. He was grateful Tony stood downwind. The last thing his lungs needed right now was tobacco smoke. It would probably make him vomit.

"The ladies have been awful worried about you," Tony continued. "Been listening to them talk, chatting to the doctor and whatnot. They're worried you got poisoned by that thing that bit you. Some kind of slow acting poison Miss Winifred didn't catch at first…"

Vincent didn't reply. He knew what was coming and he didn't want it to get here any faster than it had to. But he didn't look away. He kept his eyes on the boy and watched him seriously. Tony met the look.

"You gotta stop, Doc," he muttered. "I know where you're going, and you gotta stop."

"I can't," Vincent shook his head.

"You promised Fred you'd stopped years ago," Tony protested. "You told her you stopped after you got Toby back. She believes you."

"More fool her…" Vincent murmured.

Tony gave him a look. "You wanna tell the lady she's a fool, Doc, you go right ahead." He took a long drag on his cigarette and let it out. "Miss Lucy can say nice things at your funeral. Uncle Elia probably would too."

"And what about you?" Vincent grumbled.

"I can say something if you'd like," Tony offered reluctantly.

"I mean your dreams, Tony," Vincent pulled him back on track. "You're here to criticize mine, but what about you?"

Tony smoked nervously and stared into the darkness. Vincent waited. The kid could be a little slow sometimes, but he wasn't as dim as he seemed. It just took him a while to process things. He had probably learnt as a child that it was better to say nothing and appear to listen respectfully, than blurt a thought and get smacked for it. Vincent knew that Tony had been beaten when he was younger. No one had hit him in the last two years though. Not since he'd blown up half a town square full of demons.

"I... I got no choice," Tony answered finally, once he'd had a think. "I got ghosts. I don't get to go there like you do. I get dragged into Hell, kicking and screaming. You choose it. You bring the Darkness home. You carry it over the threshold, and you give it a doorway to look back through."

"That's a rather dramatic way to look at it," Vincent commented.

"It's true, even if you don't see it," Tony insisted.

"The Dreamlands aren't Hell," Vincent told him. "They might be unpleasant sometimes, but they're not Hell."

"Just 'cause you like visiting don't make it not Hell," Tony muttered. "That is the home of evil, even if it's not an inferno. Going there willingly... it might be your business, Doc, but you're making it ours. You put everyone at risk doing what you do."

"I protect everyone," Vincent growled. "I go there to keep the world safe. How many Hunters my age do you know?"

"I don't really know any other Hunters, Doc Temple..." Tony reminded.

"Hmph," Vincent grunted. "Hunters my age are a rare breed. Most die or retire. Anyone still fighting the good fight after living half a century is getting by because they cheat. Somehow. There are different kinds of cheating, but it's necessary. The best Hunters have to cheat because we're so dangerously outmatched." He gave Tony a long look in the half light. "It's not a job like any other, boy. If you screw up, you die. If you really screw up, the world could die, cities could be razed, countless lives could be lost, all life could fall to madness and chaos. Going to the Dreamlands... there is a price, yes. There is a price to everything. But it lets me see the future – to an extent. It shows me things this realm won't let me see."

"It's killing you," Tony warned softly.

Vincent grinned at him. "Without those trips I'd be long dead. I'd rather hurt myself learning to dodge, than take the full blow in perfect health. The blows struck by the Darkness are so often lethal, and once you're out of the fight, there's no coming back."

Tony leant on the railing, deep in thought, and smoked contemplatively. Vincent watched him. He could tell the boy was struggling with this. His fear of the land that had once swallowed him was a haunting nightmare he could never escape. It was all consuming, and he couldn't understand anything beyond it.

"Perhaps," Vincent suggested, "if you try it, it won't be so awful. Perhaps going there on your own terms would give you some control."

Tony shook his head violently. Vincent watched as the boy struggled not to recoil.

"Control ain't what worries me," Tony muttered sickly.

"Then what does?" Vincent pressed. "Because I know what worries me..."

Tony balked. A hot blush rose in his cheeks. "I... I di... w-when you got here– Doc, it's not– what you saw–"

"That isn't what worries me, Tony," Vincent sighed. "Although, Lucy's discretion and self-preservation are a touch concerning, I'll grant you."

"But that's what you're worried about, right? Her? That... that I'll... that she..."

"I'm not worried that you'd do anything to hurt her, boy," Vincent assured.

"But you're worried that she'll get hurt," Tony muttered. "Because I got ghosts... I'm... I'm broken. I got the Darkness in me now. It's under my skin. When it comes for me... I put her in danger, just being close to her..."

"Yeah," Vincent agreed gruffly. "That's a concern." He glanced again at the stricken boy and spoke with a soft sincerity. "She loves you."

The look Tony gave him was heartbroken. It only served to reinforce Vincent's impression that the boy felt as intensely about Lucy as she did about him, if not more so.

"She loves you," Vincent repeated, "and she regularly throws herself into the path of more danger than you pose. Being my apprentice should be more dangerous than being with you... and it concerns me that you're even competing."

"I know she deserves better than me, Doc," Tony mumbled. "I know you want better for her... but I love her. I do. More than anything. I'd marry her if she'd have me."

Vincent sighed deeply. "I know that, Tony."

"If I could get the Darkness out I would... but... but Fred says it don't come out. She says I got it now... and... I just..."

"You have to live with it," Vincent agreed. "Some of us do."

"Miss Lucy didn't know though," Tony continued miserably, blowing smoke through his nose. "She didn't know how bad I was. Now she's been nothing but kind about it. That's all she ever is. I want better for her too, but... but I'm not strong enough to let her go..."

"I want better for both of you," Vincent sighed. "But the world is what it is, and there's no point hiding from it." Vincent stood away from the railing, stretching his back. "You've always been harsh on yourself, boy. We all wish we could be better than we are. I wish I could roll back the Darkness and leave a better world than the one I found. I wish I could do it without visiting the Dreamlands, but I can't. Just like you can't exorcise your darkness. Just like you wish you could strip it out and be a normal man in love with a normal woman. Lucy isn't normal though. She gave that up. I do worry about her, about you both, but for what it's worth, I wish nothing better for her than someone who loves her as much as you do. I've lived long enough to know that is worth more than money or titles."

"You… you think so…?"

"I know so," Vincent assured. "You're loyal, respectful, and attentive. I've never seen anyone do better than those qualities, and she seems to recognize that. If she's chosen you, it's not my place to tell her no. My place is to keep the demons at bay."

"It's not your place alone, Doc."

"No," Vincent smiled. "That's why the four of us have each other. Every Hunter does better with a mage, Tony. That's why I have Fred. Lucy seems to have her sights set on you, and I have no objections." He paused. "She will keep trying to take advantage of you though…"

"I'll be good," Tony promised instantly.

Vincent laughed. He couldn't help himself. He was trying to advise and console the kid, and didn't want to belittle his intentions, but it was funny. At least one of the children was responsible.

"Just be safe," he counselled.

Tony had already recoiled, and he didn't appear to be listening. He flicked his cigarette over the railing and it vanished into the dark waves. Vincent didn't have to ask. Tony's expression wasn't directed at him. The fear and anger were completely different. Vincent met his eye.

"There's something here…" Tony whispered.

"You're sure?" Vincent checked.

Tony nodded, his face pale and pinched. "I can feel it…"

Vincent put a hand out and guided Tony away from the edge of the ship. They stalked back towards the door. If the kid was right, Vincent was going to need a gun.

The silence was suddenly eerie. The waves lapping at the ship were booming echoes. The rattle and hum of the engine was a deafening roar. Vincent's ears strained to pick up any sound that shouldn't be there. He steered Tony back inside. Their footsteps on the steel stairs were dull, echoing nightmares. The boy moved cautiously. Vincent didn't blame him, except nothing seemed to be wrong. He couldn't sense anything, and he couldn't hear anything out of the ordinary, which was almost strange in itself, like a thick blanket of silence was smothering the noise of the ship.

A strangled scream pierced the stillness. The ship lurched. Vincent and Tony crashed into the wall. The scream had come from outside. Something was here.

"Miss Lucy!" Tony called, rushing for the room.

Vincent staggered to his feet and raced after the boy.

4

Vincent burst into the room right behind Tony. Lucy was already up. She had a big coat thrown on over her nightdress, and thick boots on her feet. Her rifle was slung over her shoulder and her hands were loading a heavy .45. Vincent felt surge of pride.

"Sir," Fred called to him. She tossed his sword and a loaded pistol. He caught them and strapped them on.

"Thanks, Fred."

She gave him a nod and adjusted her pajama legs over her ankle boots. Tony was grabbing his gun from the bag beneath the bunk.

"What's out there?" Lucy asked.

"Let's go find out," Vincent volunteered, taking the lead. He didn't wait to see if anyone was following him. He took his weapons and made for the deck.

The ship was sailing right again, and there had been no other screams. Everything was back to normal, but even Vincent could sense it now. Something was here. Something silent. He stalked out the door, moving as quietly as his body would allow. In the stillness of night came the faintest of sounds. It was nearly drowned out by the noises of the ship and the sea. Wingbeats. Massive flapping rhythms, like sails caught in the wind.

But the air was still. Or was it?

Vincent felt the softest breath against his skin. It was the only warning. He lunged aside and drew his sword. Something swooped above him, and he whirled to slice at it. His blade grazed flesh. In the faint light of the deck he glimpsed a shadow. It was little more than that. It gave no cry when he cut it, and no noticeable blood spilt. Vincent stalked up the deck in the shadows.

The moonlight was feeble, and the ghostly air of midnight teased his dreams. He blinked back the darkness. He wasn't in the Dreamlands. He needed to remember that. It was impossible though. His other world tugged at him. It pulled yearningly. Everywhere he looked, reminders danced before his vision. It was like he could see the worlds overlapping.

Lucy was the next one to sneak out on deck. Vincent saw it coming before she did.

"Behind you!" he ordered, raising his pistol and firing.

He saw the shadowy hand sneaking out of the darkness above the doorway towards the girl. He took aim. The holy bullet flashed as it struck the creature. A shower of sparks lit up the night. The only sounds were the gunfire and the splatter of the bullet tearing flesh. The creature collapsed dead from the roof. Its corpse slapped onto the deck. Lucy and Vincent stared down at the body between them. He didn't know what the girl made of the creature, but he was shaken.

It had the shape of a man, with horns, black leathery wings, and a barbed tail. Its skin was dark and rough like frozen lava. It was faceless. There was nothing there but emptiness, smooth and blank. There were no eyes to see. No mouth to scream. Vincent recognized the Prince's Children, but they shouldn't be here. They couldn't be in this world. They belonged to the other.

Wingbeats sounded above them. Lots of wingbeats.

"Get down!" Vincent bellowed, leaping out of the way.

Fingers grazed the back of his coat as he dove. Their grasping touch tickled at his skin. He hit the deck hard.

Behind him, gunfire sounded. Lucy ducked down in the doorway, and unloaded her pistol into the night. There were no screams of pain, but showers of sparks lit the night and marked her success. The silence was eerie. It fell between every echo.

Vincent grunted as something tugged at his leg. Sharp spikes scratched his skin. A tail wrapped around his ankle. He slashed his sword towards it. Another tail caught his hand. He yelled as the barbs tore across his fingers, snatching the blade. He grasped for it. The silver whooshed into the air, and then fell. It clanged against the deck at his side as red light filled the air. Vincent snatched it up and staggered to his feet. Red lightning crackled between a dozen of the Prince's Children, lighting the sky and the hordes about them.

Fred stepped beside him, hands aglow with the same red light.

"Got your back, Sir," she told him.

He gave a nod of thanks, and shot into the sky where he could see the creatures swarming. The ship creaked and groaned. Then it shook. Something exploded below them. The lightning vanished as Fred staggered.

Vincent steadied her. He cursed. He knew the sound of an engine going.

"They're tearing in!" Tony yelled. The boy had shot his way to the railing, and was staring over the edge. "They're swarming the ship!" Tony fired his pistol over the side. It was impossible to know if he was doing any good. The demons were tearing their way into the hull. That meant the ship was taking on water. Tony raised a hand and Vincent saw the red light. It flickered around the boy's fingers, and the glow from his magic on the side of the boat reflected off the waves. The ship grated painfully, but it was still moving forward. Fred lent her power to Tony's and the ship became a storm of red lightning. It flared, but she couldn't sustain it.

Above them came the sound of breaking glass. Followed by a scream. The demons were attacking the bridge. They had smashed through a window. One of them caught a man by the shoulder and dragged him out the hole.

Lucy had unhooked her rifle. She took careful aim as the creature swooped and sagged under the weight of its prey. She fired. The demon's head exploded. The man cried as he fell, and shrieked as he hit the deck covered in black goop. From that height his leg had broken. Vincent could see the injury. He gave the man's uniform a nod.

"Captain," he greeted him.

A tail lashed out towards the injured man, and Vincent cut it clean off in the middle of the air. It flopped weakly onto the deck. The demon flapped desperately away. Another one jerked out and snatched

Fred. She yelled in fury as it caught her under the arms. Vincent lunged. He dropped his empty pistol and caught it by the tail. The barbs bit into his skin. He hissed in pain, but tightened his grip. Blood began to drip from his fingers. Fred struggled. Her hands began to glow. The creature dropped her. It started to writhe as she burnt it. Fred landed catlike on the deck, her hands positioned like claws as fire erupted across the demon's skin. Vincent let it go. It swooped up like a torch into the darkness. One more leapt from behind. Vincent roared as it crashed into his shoulders and pinned him down.

Another scream came from the bridge. A struggling sailor was pulled shrieking into the night. Lucy couldn't shoot him down. She was staving off nearly a dozen of the creatures. Bodies were piling up in melting lumps around her. She yelled as a demon snatched for her. Her guns were empty. There was no time to reload. It caught her around the waist and pulled her into the night.

"Lucy!" Tony yelled. The faint red flecks of his magic flickered out. He thrust his hands forward. Magic erupted. Golden light burst off him like an explosion. Vincent buried his face in his arms against the intensity. He felt the weight on his back fade as though disintegrated. Even with his eyes covered and turned away, it was brighter than the sun. It took seconds. In the time it took Vincent to draw breath, the light had faded. The wingbeats were gone. The ship groaned and chugged along. Her remaining engines were working overtime. The ocean lapped against her.

"Tony!" Fred called.

Vincent raised his head just in time to see the boy's eyes roll back as he fainted. Fred ran straight to him and began to check him over. Vincent struggled to his knees. There was no sign of the demons. None, except for the ash, which drifted in tiny black flakes through the air.

Struggling and clinking alerted him to the side of the ship. Lucy had fallen when the creature carrying her had disintegrated. She had caught her rifle in the rails, and was using it to pull herself back up the side of the boat. Vincent staggered to his feet and rushed to help her. He reached over, grabbing the back of her coat as she pulled herself up the railings, and helped haul her over.

"You okay, kid?" he asked.

"What happened to Tony?!" Lucy cried, ignoring Vincent and rushing to the fallen boy.

Vincent stretched his back out painfully. That answered his question. If the girl was running and talking, she was probably fine. He was scratched up, but it wasn't so bad, and the adrenaline of the fight made him feel better than he had before. He approached the others.

"That boy has been touched by God..." the Captain muttered in an awed daze, no longer aware of his pain. "I saw the light..."

"Yeah," Vincent replied gruffly, "but we don't like to advertise it." He carried on to where Lucy and Fred were fussing over Tony. There was always something. At least this time the pressing question hadn't been 'what are those things?' or 'is the end of days here?' Instead, the pressing issue was Tony. Again. Vincent loomed over the others. "How is he?"

"I think he'll be okay..." Fred mused. "He's still with us, just out cold."

"Let's get him back inside," Vincent advised.

The three of them gathered the boy up and carried him carefully downstairs. Vincent stopped and stood aside to let some of the sailors run by in search of their Captain. He'd have to deal with that later too. For now, it was enough to get Tony back into their room and tip him into his bunk. Lucy took her coat off and draped it over the boy, staying perched at his side. Vincent watched the way she looked at him, and knew that everything he had said earlier was true. He tore his eyes from the children to share a look with Fred. He jerked his head at her.

They left the room and ducked down the hallway. There was a dining room reserved for guests, separate from the crew's galley. It was unoccupied in the middle of the night. He held the door open and let her through, before following inside and shutting it behind them. Fred sighed and pulled up a chair, sinking wearily into it. Her adrenaline was long gone. Vincent's was still going.

"You weren't kidding..." he said.

"Nope," Fred shook her head. "I've been telling you about it. What he did when he banished that formless one... the town square massacre... what he did tonight. All of it. I don't know if he's blessed or cursed... but I've never seen anything like it."

"He's powerful..." Vincent agreed. "Too powerful..."

"I wouldn't call it too powerful, Sir," Fred disagreed. "He just helped us win a fight we were losing – a fight where I don't even understand what instigated it."

"What do you mean?"

"What were those creatures, Vincent?" Fred asked. "Why were they here?"

He didn't answer. He wasn't sure he could. Fred pressed on.

"Does someone know what boat we're on? Someone who doesn't want us to make it to Egypt? Is there anything you're not telling us?"

"Not off the top of my head," he lied. "It doesn't smell like a coincidence, I agree. Possibly the cult know Anisa asked for help, and they're trying to dissuade such assistance."

"How would they know to find us here?"

"They wouldn't have to know," Vincent shrugged. "Tony could sense them long before we saw them. I don't doubt they could sense him the same way. Monsters can smell their own."

"What are you saying?" Fred demanded.

"I'm just worried," Vincent shrugged. "I've never seen magic like that, Fred. Neither had you. I don't know how he got it, and that concerns me."

"He's a good kid, Vincent," Fred warned. "I know I give him a hard time, but he's good. Miraculously so, given his family."

"I know," Vincent nodded. "But there is something inside him that neither of us understand, and it is more powerful than we are."

"I, for one, quite like forces of good that are more

powerful than I am," Fred retorted. "It takes the pressure off."

Vincent smiled. "But are we sure it's a force of good?" he asked patiently. "Just because the boy is, doesn't mean that what he's carrying isn't evil. It reeks of darkness, and it haunts him."

Fred fell silent. Vincent knew how she felt. They wanted this to be good. They wanted Tony to be alright, but they didn't know enough, and there was nothing more they could do. They just had to keep an eye on him, look after him where they could, and hope like hell for the rest.

Their cautious conversations about the children and their concern for Tony took them to the dawn. Vincent could see the first kiss of light touch the horizon. Dawn brought a sandy coast and marshy landscape with it. Massive clumps of reeds rose up from the water, and marked the end of their voyage. Ship horns sounded. They had arrived.

TOMB OF ENDLESS NIGHT

5

It had been years since Vincent had been here. The hot sun, strong smells, and bustling noise and life of the port was a stark contrast to the Egypt that haunted him. He had spoken at length with the Captain as they had come into the harbor. Given the number of crew and passengers, there was no point trying to spin a tale about what had happened to the ship. Rumors would spread and they would just have to let them. Besides, what were they going to try and convince them of? Giant bats?

Tony was awake again, but the boy remembered nothing. He was dazed and exhausted. Lucy hung about him like a curious butterfly. To the best of Vincent's knowledge, the girl wouldn't have seen anything like Tony's magic before either. Still, she seemed far more concerned with the health of the boy than enamored with his talents. Vincent watched her fuss over him delicately as they stood in line to disembark. If he didn't know them, he could almost believe they were a young married couple. But he did know them, and they were too young. They were just kids. He couldn't even remember being that young. Of course, if he asked Fred, she would tell him that he had been born a grumpy old man. She might not be wrong.

Down on the docks, a crowd had gathered to gape and gossip at the damaged ship. Vincent could spot runners in the crowd and hoped they would hurry up getting the passengers off before anything else went wrong. He didn't have to wait long, but it was longer than he would have liked. It was long enough to bring trouble knocking.

He came down the gangplank with Fred and the kids, each of them managing their luggage despite their weariness. Vincent saw the suit before he saw the pin. Then he saw the face. An older man in a white suit with a matching moustache caught Vincent's eye with a sharp look. A golden pin glinted on his lapel. Vincent knew the symbol well. He knew the man better.

"Vincent Temple," the man glowered at him as he approached, his strong English accent haughty. "I should have known. What are you doing here? What happened to this ship?"

"You'll have to ask the Captain, Chancellor," Vincent replied coldly. "He'll have an official report he's handing in."

"Don't give me that bullshit," the man sneered. "Why are you in Egypt?"

"That's my business," Vincent answered. He was trying to keep the others behind him, but their curiosity was getting the better of them. The Chancellor noticed.

"Who are these people?" he demanded.

"It's the family, Nigel," Fred told him darkly, stepping up beside Vincent. "We're here to visit friends."

"You really expect anyone to believe that, Winifred?" he scoffed, looking over Vincent's group.

Vincent held the man's gaze silently. He held the look so long he started to believe the lie himself, and he could see the old man's confidence waver. He let Fred stay by his side, but kept vigilant. Fred despised the Chancellor, and Vincent knew she was prone to exposing her feelings on such matters. The last thing he needed was his rogue wife hexing the leader of his organization.

A little hand clutched at his arm.

"What's going on?" Lucy asked, grasping his sleeve and looking over. "Who's this?"

"This is Nigel Whitehall," Vincent answered, without taking his gaze from the man. "He's the Leader of the Hunters. The Head of the Council of our Brotherhood." He paused. "Chancellor, this is my daughter Lucy, and her husband."

Nigel's moustache bristled. He looked wary, but he couldn't prove they weren't telling the truth. Besides, seeing the children had clearly surprised him. It was only getting more surprising.

"Pleased to meet you," Lucy told him politely, holding out her hand.

Guardedly, the old man took her tiny hand in his and shook it gently.

"And you, young lady," he nodded, but it was mere seconds before his eyes found Vincent again. "You never mentioned a daughter."

"I don't tell you everything about my life, Chancellor," Vincent replied dismissively.

"You don't tell me anything," Nigel growled. "You've barely spoken to me in twenty years, and even then it was only out of necessity."

"Well, my family and my visit are my business," Vincent replied. "I won't keep you, Chancellor. You have a ship to investigate."

"And you?" Nigel growled. "What are you investigating? Don't try and pull one over on me, Temple. I know you. You could never let anything lie. We have the situation here under control. Egypt doesn't need you anymore."

Vincent eyeballed the old man. The worst part was knowing that Whitehall really believed that. He was running around this country like he owned it, governed by his British entitlement, with his enlisted followers from the home country doing his dirty work. He didn't trust anyone else, and he stormed through the world convinced he could crush old magic with colonialism. Vincent wanted to shoot him. He wanted to gun down the man in the white suit the same way Nigel's people had gunned down Naeem twenty years go.

"We don't want trouble, Chancellor," Vincent warned. "I just brought the family to visit some friends."

"Tell it to someone who'll believe it, Temple," Nigel sneered. "We have the situation in hand. Don't get involved."

"Wouldn't dream of it," Vincent lied.

Nigel gave him a disparaging look, and then turned and left. He rounded up his cronies, all loitering in the crowd, and had everyone converge on the ship. Vincent directed his party as far away as they could get, as quickly as possible.

"Who was that?" Lucy asked as they wandered down the bustling street away from the docks. "I mean really, who was he? He can't actually be your boss if he looks at you like that."

"You've met Vincent, right?" Fred teased her. "If I was his boss, I'd smack him upside the head every time I saw him."

"You're good at your job," Lucy pressed him. "You're one of the best."

"That doesn't mean I'm well-liked," Vincent replied gruffly. "Or that I like them in return."

"Is this about Naeem...?" she asked in a small voice.

Vincent felt his feet slow almost unwillingly. A deep concern ground him to a halt, and he turned on his young apprentice warningly.

"Do not let him know," he muttered.

Lucy looked between him and Fred in confusion. Fred looked as dark in the eyes as Vincent felt. She knew what his concern was. She knew all too well. Lucy clearly didn't understand. She stood in the street, puzzlement furrowing her brow, as Tony stood guardedly at her shoulder.

"I do not think we will have seen the last of Nigel," Vincent continued under his breath. "Do not let him know that you are my apprentice. All he can ever know is that you are my daughter, and that I have taught you to defend yourself."

"This is about Naeem," Lucy growled.

"Nigel's people shot him," Vincent admitted, proud

that he managed not to choke on the words. "And then they blamed me for it. I raised it with the Council – the Council that run the Brotherhood. But Nigel runs the Council... so nothing happened. He told me I had shown a profound lapse in judgement when choosing my apprentice, and that any fallout from such a mishap was mine to bear."

Lucy's face was pale and pinched as Vincent told her this. Her lips were set in a hard line, and he knew he had only managed to confirm what she had already been fearing.

"Can we go back and shoot him?" she asked.

Fred laughed. She put an arm around Lucy and kissed the top of her head.

"No," Vincent answered.

"Why not?" she pressed.

"You don't want to kill someone, Miss Lucy..." Tony muttered.

"Don't act like you're protecting me, mafia-boy." She blew a loose strand of hair out of her face and eyeballed all of them. "I've shot and killed people to protect the world before. Just because this guy doesn't wear black robes and chant in ancient languages doesn't mean he's safe. If he is responsible for the deaths of others, and we can save people by getting rid of him, don't we owe it to his potential victims to do exactly that?"

"We can't kill a man for crimes he hasn't committed," Vincent disagreed.

"How many deaths does he need to be accountable for before we decide his isn't worth more than theirs?" she pressed.

"That is very dangerous thinking," Vincent growled. "And I don't want to hear it again."

"You already want to shoot him for Naeem. I know you do."

"What I want," Vincent warned, "is for Nigel to own that what happened was wrong, and make sure that justice is served against the person who killed my friend. That is never going to happen if I put a bullet in his head. Even if I want to, it makes me no better than them."

Lucy fell silent. Vincent was grateful she saw reason and backed down, but he was unsettled by her uncanny ability to see straight into people's souls. She wasn't wrong. Nigel had become the face of Naeem's injustice in Vincent's mind. That was where his anger was directed, and where he wanted to dispense his own justice. Lucy saw that pain. That meant he wasn't hiding it. He could still hear Nigel's voice ringing in his ears, telling him that if he was going to apprentice natives then how were the real Hunters supposed to tell the difference between Vincent's associates and the cultists. He wanted to shoot out the old man's kneecaps and drop him in the harbor. Instead, he turned and continued on. Naeem may be dead, but his sister had asked for Vincent's help, and if Nigel was back in town, she probably needed it. As they continued down the street, Vincent heard Fred speaking to the children.

"He was Vincent's mentor," the witch told them softly.

"What?" Lucy replied.

"Nigel Whitehall," Fred muttered. "He was

Vincent's mentor. Taught him like Vincent's teaching you. If you're wondering why he's grumpier than usual."

Vincent steadfastly ignored them and led the way to the carriage stand. The faster they could get away from this mess the better.

* * *

If Vincent was honest, he didn't know Anisa well. She was Naeem's younger sister, and at the time had not shared her brother's interests. In the twenty years since Naeem's death, Vincent was aware that she had married and had a child of her own. He had told her that if she ever needed anything, she had only to ask. He'd never expected her to take him up on it though. Not after he'd gotten her brother killed.

When they pulled up at the address, Vincent was not at all surprised to find a large house on the hill overlooking the harbor. The building was pale stone Mediterranean-style architecture. Her family had always had money, and she would have married within her station.

He led the others to the door and knocked. They were admitted by a servant as though expected, their luggage left inside the door for someone else to collect, and Vincent followed the attendant through the house. The others stayed close behind him.

They were led to a veranda overlooking the city down to the ocean. Seated at a table was a woman Vincent barely recognized. She looked up at him with tired, dark eyes and a curious smile. Her posture was relaxed as she reclined in her chair, but Vincent felt it looked like her ease was more from exhaustion than any peace of mind.

"Doctor Temple..." she mused when she saw him. "You actually came..."

"You sound surprised, Anisa," he replied.

She shrugged and indicated for them to sit. Vincent noted the curiosity in her eyes as she looked at the others. He introduced them all by name as they joined her at the table.

"Your family?" she smiled.

"In a word," he agreed, not wanting to complicate things. "And yours?"

"Anwar will be through in a moment," she said of her husband. Her attention was diverted as servants brought in a pitcher of hibiscus juice and a platter of dried fruits.

"And Fajr?" Vincent asked. "You said you were worried about your daughter in your letter."

"Yes," Anisa sighed. "For all your effort, Doctor, I'm afraid you're too late. Fajr is gone."

TOMB OF ENDLESS NIGHT

6

"How gone?" Vincent asked.

"She's been missing for a week," Anisa replied. "We haven't seen or heard from her or anyone who might know where she is. Vanished without a trace."

"We'll find her," Vincent promised. "Tell me everything."

"I don't know when the cult started coming back," she sighed. "I don't know how far or deep it runs, but their attacks started springing up over a month ago. Whitehall wasn't far behind them. Fajr didn't have anymore luck with the man than her uncle did."

"What would she be doing near Whitehall?" Vincent demanded.

"Trying to intervene with the cult herself," a man's voice answered.

Everyone turned to the doorway. A broad man in loose linen clothes, with hints of grey touching his dark hair, strode into the room. He had a neat, thin moustache and tired eyes. Vincent stood and shook the man's hand.

"Anwar," the man introduced himself. "Thank you for coming, Doctor Temple. We weren't sure my wife's letter had reached you."

"What was your daughter doing trying to intervene with the cult?" Vincent asked. "Doesn't she know how dangerous they are?"

"We told her to stay out of it." Anwar spread his hands helplessly and flopped into a basket chair beside his wife. "I don't know how many times I told her to stay away, but she has a temper. Then Whitehall showed up and everything became worse. She wouldn't listen. The Limey bastard came here just before she vanished and accused her of attacking his men. She might be indiscreet, but she wouldn't attack men who were trying to drive back those monstrosities."

"Unless they shot at her first..." Anisa muttered fiercely.

Anwar reached over and took her hand reassuringly. Vincent glowered. He didn't direct the look at them, but at the world in general. A cold and dark dread was settling over him.

"You are talking about a man who wouldn't give his approval for me to train your brother," Vincent growled. "In his eyes, a woman would be even worse. Nigel and I have grown very far apart in our ideals and methods over the years, but I still know him well. He would have a fit if he found a colored girl among his ranks, but I do not believe he would shoot a child, no matter how much he might disapprove of them."

"She's barely a child anymore, Vincent," Anisa countered. "She's older than your girl."

Vincent looked between Anisa and Lucy as he tried to process this. It couldn't possibly have been that long.

There was no way Fajr was older than Lucy. He did the math in his head. It was possible, but it was extremely unsettling.

"And she's trained...?" he pressed, already knowing the answer.

"To defend herself," Anwar retorted. "It's not like we live without threats, and I wasn't going to leave my daughter vulnerable to the evils of other worlds."

"Or this one," Anisa added.

Vincent nodded. He wasn't about to fight them on that. As far as they were concerned, he had done the same thing. In many ways, he had. He looked over at Lucy who was watching everything unfold with big eyes. She was the real reason any of them were here. He turned back to Anisa.

"Do you have any clues to her whereabouts? Anything at all?"

"She was armed when she left," Anwar admitted. "She has taken to stealing off with the *shafarat muzdawija*, uh, the twin blades our family safeguards, but she has never failed to come home before... we don't know if she was injured, or kidnapped, or... or worse..."

"The blades are magic?" Vincent queried.

"A little," Anisa confirmed. "Mostly they are holy."

Vincent stood. "May I see her room?"

Anisa nodded. When she stood, everyone followed suit. No one was getting left out of the action, and there was work to be done. Vincent led his team through the halls of the large house, following behind Fajr's parents. The girl's room was a mess. Anwar gave them an apologetic look then they opened the door.

"We raided it for clues ourselves when we realized she was missing, and we haven't set everything back yet," he explained.

"Only half of it was us," Anisa defended. "She left the place in a state."

The bed was unmade. The wardrobe was open and clothes were strewn across the floor. Vincent beelined cautiously for the desk and the mess of papers and books on it. Most of the books were occult titles he recognized. Some of them were ones he owned, although almost all of them were in Arabic. There was a stack of journals on the desk. Old journals. They were hauntingly familiar. He leafed through a few pages and looked back at Anisa.

"You gave her these?" he asked.

"I did," she replied coolly. "They were her uncle's, and I saw no reason not to. She never met Naeem, but she has always been curious about him. If your people hadn't killed him, they would have been close."

"These journals contain almost everything I ever taught him, and then some," Vincent countered. "She could get herself into a lot of trouble with the knowledge they contain."

"Or she could get herself out of it," Anwar disputed.

Vincent didn't argue the point. It was concerning, but so was everything about the situation. It was only looking back at the girl's parents, still hovering near the doorway with their guests, that Vincent finally spotted something wrong. He had continued searching through the work on the desk, and, even only glancing at it, was impressed with Fajr's research on the cult – but his secret weapon was ticking.

"Did she own any prohibited magic?" he asked.

"No," Anwar shook his head. "We are not mages. Protective items I will collect, but dangerous tomes or artefacts I have always sent to the museum. I forbid their use under my roof."

"Are you sure?" Vincent pressed.

"Yes," Anisa argued. "Why?"

Vincent shifted his gaze ever so slightly. "How're you doing, Tony?" he asked.

"I'm okay, Doc," the boy shivered. He was white as a sheet, and his whole body trembled. He looked deeply unwell.

"Tony!" Lucy cried. "What's wrong?"

"I think I'm just a little warm in this heat..." he mumbled. Fred stuck her hand on his forehead.

"He's freezing," she told Vincent.

"Hot or cold, Tony," Vincent called to him, moving slowly down the desk. "Where is it?"

"What's wrong with him?" Anisa asked. "Is he sick?"

"Worse," Vincent answered. "He's cursed." Vincent watched Tony shiver and moved his hand down the drawers. He stopped. His fingers closed over the handle. Tony moaned as Vincent pulled the drawer open. There it was. He reached in and pulled out the small, slim volume. It looked like another one of the journals, bound in black. Tony started spasming as soon as Vincent removed it from the drawer.

"Fred!" Vincent barked.

Lucy was already on it. She tackled Tony as he lurched for the book. She was deceptively strong for her size, and she brought the lanky boy crashing to the floor. His eyes had rolled back and he was speaking in tongues. His arms reached out longingly towards the book. Lucy kept him pinned to the floor. Vincent kicked away the rug and mess at his feet, exposing the stone floor. Fred was already striding to him. He dropped the book on the pale stone. Fred raised her hands. Red light tingled around her fingertips. The book began to smolder.

Tony screamed. He lurched up. Anisa grabbed his shoulder and helped Lucy pin him back down. Fred focused her magic. The book caught fire. Hot orange flames burst through it. Tony whimpered, but his struggling became feeble. In less than a minute, there was nothing left of the book but a pile of ash, and Tony lay limp and groaning on the floor.

"What was that?" Anwar demanded.

"You know what that was," Fred replied.

"It was only a chapter of it," Vincent growled. "They did that sometimes, when the monks transcribing the book went insane, or if they couldn't have the same person working on it for too long, they would only copy down and publish a chapter at a time. Sometimes they did it because it was easier to smuggle pieces of the text between countries than the entire tome." The old Hunter turned his dark eyes on their hosts. "Your daughter has been keeping things from you."

"How do we find her?" Anisa begged.

"I have an idea," Vincent admitted. "Before we

begin, is there anything else you can think of?"

"Her journal is missing," Anwar added. "She was always scrawling in it. Some of the pages on the desk have been torn from it. She often kept it with Naeem's collection, but it's not there."

"She will have packed it," Vincent sighed.

"You think she packed a bag?" Anisa shot Vincent a look.

"You don't?" he replied. "You went through her things first, you don't think she took more than just the swords?"

"I know she's been running into trouble with Whitehall," Anisa glowered. "That is my primary concern."

"She was hunting the cult long before Whitehall got here," Anwar admitted. "You think perhaps she found something he didn't?"

"I'd say it's more than likely," Vincent nodded. "If she's been following the code of the journals, she knows a good Hunter always keeps their eye on the target. She won't have let the Chancellor distract her from the cult. Eliminating them is still the goal, no matter who gets there first."

"You just burnt the best clue we had!" Anwar cried, pointing at the pile of ash. "That was probably where she found the information Whitehall doesn't have!"

"Unlikely," Vincent disagreed. "And the best clue you have is me. I'm not on fire… yet." He turned to Fred. "You and Lucy look after Tony, maybe see if you can get him in a bed or something. I'll be downstairs in the main room, where the swords were kept."

"Very good, Sir," she nodded. "What are you about to do?"

"Investigate," he replied. He swept from the room without further explanation. It would only risk outing his tactics if he tried. He barely limped anymore, and he couldn't help but wonder if the remaining touch of limp was more from habit than injury. It was hard to know. At his age, with his lifestyle, everything always hurt.

He had glimpsed the naked bracket over the mantle on the way through the house earlier. Now he was heading back there, because if he couldn't trace the girl, he might be able to trace the weapons. He was aware of Anwar following him; the patriarch of the house made no move to hide it. He was curious about Vincent's methods, and had every right to be.

Vincent stopped by the mantle and looked up at the bracket, where the twin blades would have hung in an X. Fajr had taken them both. That meant she was adept at duel-wielding. Vincent scratched his cheek. Someone should get that girl a gun. Maybe once they found her, he could make eternal enemies of her parents by teaching her how to shoot. The world was moving forward. Hunters had to adapt to the times, and holy bullets were worth the effort. Not that he could call her a Hunter. Still... if the girl had what it took...

He quickly pushed the thought from his mind. That was what had gotten her uncle killed twenty years ago. He was here to rescue her and put a stop to the cult. That was it.

Anwar was watching him patiently when he turned around. Vincent eyed up the furniture.

"I need to clear a space and set up a circle," he stated.

"I have some chalk," Anwar offered. "I keep some chips of it in the office. Will that do?"

Vincent nodded. "The circle is just a precaution. We should be fine with something simple and flimsy. Hopefully I'll only need it for a few minutes."

"I didn't realize you were a mage as well," Anwar commented.

"I'm not," Vincent admitted. He pulled a small vial of tonic from his pocket. "I do this the hard way."

* * *

Anisa had helped Fred and Lucy get Tony up and into a room. He wasn't shivering anymore, but he still twitched, and he was unsteady on his feet. Fred dumped him on the bed. Lucy didn't take her hands off him as he slumped onto the end of the mattress.

"No…" Tony slurred, trying to stand again and falling back down. "We got… we got to go stop him…"

"We don't have to stop anyone, Tony," Lucy soothed him. "You're safe here."

"Stop… Vincent…" Tony mumbled, trying to pull himself up again. "He's… drinking…"

"That's not illegal," Lucy reminded him, pushing Tony's hair back from his eyes.

Fred met the boy's unfocused gaze. That wasn't what he was worried about. It was something else. She knew Vincent and Tony drank back home. Neither of them would have cared if Vincent was downstairs having a whiskey. That meant the old bastard was using again.

Fred vanished from the room. She moved so fast it was almost impossible she wasn't running, but somehow she wasn't. Her long strides carried her through the halls and down the stairs. She could hear the others stumbling along behind her. They followed too slowly, but she was too slow as well. When she burst into the main room, Vincent was already sitting in the middle of the floor and there was an empty vial beside him. The furniture had all been pushed to the sides of the room to make space for the rough chalk drawing on the floor. Anwar was sitting in one of the chairs at the edges, watching patiently.

"What the hell is this?" Fred asked of the floor.

"It's the arcane circle he drew," Anwar replied.

"Is it now?" Fred responded, all of her disapproval and anger apparent in her tone. "And if you need to explain that to me, what the fuck does he think it's actually going to do?"

"Miss Winifred!" Lucy scolded from the doorway. She still had Tony's arm hauled around her shoulders, and his cap in her hand. She dropped him sideways across a padded armchair, and he collapsed back with his head on one arm and his knees over the other.

Fred was not in the mood to be scolded by anyone. She was in the mood for Vincent to wake up so that she could beat the ever-living shit out of him.

"What I'm trying to say," Fred grated, "is that when my three-year-old son shows me a page he's drawn with a blob that has four lines coming down from it, and tells me it's a horse, I need that clarification, because the world is never going to recognize the blob as a horse. That blob is to a real horse what that scrawl is to an arcane circle. It looks like Toby drew it. So what—" Fred took a deep calming breath, "—does that drugged up idiot think he's doing?"

"He doesn't think the circles matter," Tony muttered from where he lay. "He wasn't using them on the boat, so he's not worried about it so much anymore."

"What do you mean he wasn't using them on the boat?" Lucy asked.

"He told me he quit," Fred hissed. "He told me he quit after he found Toby. I didn't even know he had any on him."

"I don't think he ever quit..." Tony mumbled. "He... he said he cheats... I don't think he ever stopped. He was using it on the boat. That's why you thought he was poisoned. I only realized before the attack. I... I didn't know what I was feeling. I thought it was just ghosts, like normal, but... but I can feel him go..."

Lucy rested against the side of the chair and stroked Tony's hair back from his pale face. He looked pained, and Fred wasn't interested in yelling at the boy. She knew better than to put any of her anger at Vincent on someone who was trying his best. She couldn't expect him to know better.

Anisa followed the others in and delicately surveyed the scene. Everyone knew she had heard Fred yelling through the corridors.

"If Vincent thinks this is the best way to find Fajr, we have to try it," she insisted.

"Maybe," Fred shrugged, reluctant to deny someone

else the help she had been given. "But it's killing him." She scuffed her shoe against a rumpled rug that had been pushed away. "Maybe get a bowl or something for when he wakes up. Lord knows what will come out of him when he gets back."

Tony's eyes shot open and he jerked hard enough that Lucy leapt away. Everyone stared at him. He stared at the ceiling.

"Something's here," he announced.

7

Vincent walked alone through the grey landscape. The ruins of a city surrounded him, and the Prince's Children flapped between the crumbling buildings. He walked alone, but he was not alone. The Prince lounged contentedly over a pile of rubble. His faceless head turned to regard Vincent fondly. Vincent met his absent gaze, and the Prince smiled.

"I'm looking for someone," Vincent stated.

"You always are," the Prince replied, his deep voice reverberating softly, like a shiver from Vincent's toes to his skull. "Another child. You should be more careful with your children, Doctor Temple. For creatures so irreplaceable, you misplace them a great deal."

"They're not my children," Vincent clarified.

"Are you sure?" the Prince taunted. "Are not all the people of the world your children, hero?"

"I'm not here to debate philosophy with you. I'm here for the girl. Tell me where she is."

The Prince shifted. His naked, shadowy form seemed to ooze upwards until he had risen from his comfortable recline into a standing position. No particular limb moved or bent. One minute he was simply standing, when the moment before he had not been. He didn't rise like a man, but he stood like one. He stood close, and his faceless head drifted near to Vincent's, as though he could smell him, as though he could see him.

"You came here unwarded," the Prince warned. He spoke so closely that Vincent could feel it. Not breath, for there was no mouth, but words. The Prince's vocabulary traced itself lovingly, soft and cold against his skin. "You are not safe here. You are not protected. Not here. Not there. Danger plagues you. Why are you in my land, Doctor Temple? Why have you come to my home?"

Vincent didn't know how to answer.

"You are looking, Hunter," the Prince whispered. "Always searching. A Hunter knows how to stalk their prey. Why, then, are you always at my door?"

"Because you know the answers I seek," Vincent answered, knowing it wasn't quite correct, but unsure what the truth was. At least his answer had been a truth. He realized his head was cloudy with tonic, and he was no longer as sure as he had been. The Prince knew things, that was why Vincent came back to him again... and again... and again... and again... and again... and again... and again... and again... and again...

Vincent shook his head to clear it, and his face nearly collided with the Prince's blank expression. The smooth blank mirror where his face would have been rested ever so close to Vincent's cheek, and he wondered what would happen if they touched. Sometimes when they connected it seemed as though the Prince melted over him, or through him. Sometimes he was as solid as a person, and sometimes he was the pervasive darkness, sticky like tar and impossible to truly clean away.

Vincent stepped back. He wasn't really sure how he did it, but he found the will. The Prince smiled, and Vincent wondered how he always knew what his expression was when there was no face to convey it.

"You've come a long way, Doctor Temple..." the Prince whispered. "What are you searching for? Be sure."

Vincent knew there were multiple answers. He knew the Prince was searching for a specific one. However, he only had one answer he knew how to give. It was all he could think.

"Fajr," he answered. "I'm looking for the girl Fajr. Take me where she is."

"The journey is yours then." The Prince bowed floridly, stepping aside and extending an arm in invitation. His hand hovered towards a doorway in the rubble. An ornate, arched doorway set in the stone, and filled with darkness. It was cold. Right now everything was cold, but just looking at it Vincent knew the path would chill him. He didn't falter. Without a glance back, or any show of thanks, he set off through the doorway into the depths of truth.

* * *

Lucy was armed as soon as Tony gave voice to his warning. These days there was nothing she could do faster than get a loaded gun in her hands and point it where it needed to go. Fred and Tony had their pistols at the ready, and Anisa and Anwar took up swords that Lucy assumed could deal real damage to monsters. Vincent had taught her that swords were easier to enchant against the Darkness than bullets, but a bullet could keep you safer.

Now, he sat still and pale as death in the middle of the floor. Fred had warned them that his circle was useless, which meant that he couldn't defend himself from whatever threat Tony had sensed. They needed to keep him safe. Lucy was worried about Tony too. He had leapt up, but he stood against the armchair, and she knew he was using it to keep himself upright. He was still weak from whatever burning the book had done to him. His ghosts.

Those ghosts hadn't told them anything new about his perceived threat. Everyone was poised for attack, but nothing came. Lucy strained her ears. She couldn't hear anything... well, anything unusual.

"Maybe it's a dud?" she suggested to the room, straightening up and turning her attention back to Vincent.

Something wet splattered down the hall. Everyone turned to the noise. It was followed with a series of pops like firecrackers. Then the doorway exploded.

Lucy yelled as Tony tackled her to the ground. Bits of stone and plaster rained over the room. She pushed him off. Tony covered his mouth with his sleeve and coughed. His clothes and hair were white with dust. He'd used his body as a shield and protected her from most of it. There was no time to berate him. A massive shadow loomed behind the clouds. Lucy pushed Tony behind her and aimed her rifle at the shadow. She fired.

An unholy screech filled the air. Lucy cried out, dropping her gun in her lap to cover her ears.

Fred stood behind them all. She had leapt to Vincent when the doorway went. She stood with her hands outstretched. A barrier of red light separated her and the Hunter from the danger, but it wasn't big enough. It definitely wasn't strong enough.

Something lashed out of the dust cloud. Anwar was helping Anisa up when it grabbed him. He yelled. Anisa slashed at the limb snatching her husband. Her blade sliced through thick rubbery skin, but the injury was slight.

Something monstrous slithered into the room in a mass of tentacles. Its gelatinous body quivered in the center. A giant maw opened as it screeched again, exposing endless rows of fangs spiraling down like a whirlpool of death. Suckers slapped and popped over the floor, ceiling, and walls as it hauled its grotesque form into the room. Grey ooze dripped from a small hole in its heaving body where Lucy had shot it.

Anwar hung from one of the tentacles, stunned from the horror and barely struggling. His eyes bulged in his face as he beheld the monster. Anisa was not so shaken. She yelled in fury and fear as she rushed to attack. Her blade was fast and her aim true. She slashed and stabbed at the tentacle grappling her husband. Like a tornado of robes, she whirled and twisted. Grey ooze spurted where her sword struck. The monster shrieked. Anisa slashed and twirled, but it wasn't enough. The creature lashed out. It used Anwar to strike her full in the chest, throwing them both. They crashed into a wall and Anisa fell limp.

Lucy was on her feet. She and Tony were directly between the monster and Fred, who was still crouched over Vincent. She went in, guns blazing. Each shot from the rifle resulted in a shriek and spray of grey goo. The thing was massive, bulging through the doorway and oozing into the space. It wasn't hard to hit. But that meant the .308 caliber holes weren't very impressive either. She leapt like a panther, every movement fluid and sequential, coming up shooting.

Tony crouched behind the armchair, using it as cover as he unloaded his pistol into the nest of tentacles. One writhing appendage smacked the chair out of the way. Tony's eyes widened. He backed up. The tentacle smashed down to crush him. He dropped the empty gun and threw his hands up. Red light encased them. A small red barrier appeared above him. He winced as the limb beat against it.

The creature was hitting its stride. Nothing seemed to slow it, and it had more arms than they did. Anwar was on his feet. He was dazed, but he stood over Anisa, blade drawn, and slashed at the writhing tentacles that came their way. Lucy had abandoned the rifle for her pistols, and was backing towards them, ducking and weaving.

Fred's shell had become a small dome of red light surrounding her and Vincent. Tentacles rained down on it, pounding relentlessly as it tried to break through. It beat at all of them, flailing wildly. Tony winced as the suckers smacked down on his thin magic. His small shield cracked. The power flickered and failed.

"Oh no," he managed.

The tentacle smacked him. He crashed across the floor and struggled up.

"Tony!" Lucy yelled.

He was on the other side of the room, and there was half the creature between them. Tony tried to crawl away, but the tentacle caught him around the waist. It snatched him up and smashed him into the ceiling. He yelled as it threw him around like a ragdoll.

"Use your golden light on it, Tony!" Fred bellowed. Her dome was beginning to crack as tentacle after tentacle beat against it. Sweat dripped from her brow with the force of holding the magic in place.

Tony gave a garbled cry in response. Words were hard to discern, but it sounded like he couldn't just do it on command. That wasn't new information. Lucy knew he would have done something already if he could. She leapt under a tentacle. It lashed over her head. She felt the wet suckers brush across her hair. One boot collided with a fleshy limb. She launched herself up. Another tentacle snatched for her. She kicked off it, firing across the room. Both pistols were aimed at the tentacle beating Tony. She unleashed. Bullets tore through the thick hide. Grey ooze sprayed across the room. The tentacle ripped half off, dropping Tony. He hit the ground hard. Thick monster blood squirted up to the ceiling. The creature shrieked and flailed.

Anwar used the distraction. He dove for an opening, rolling beneath a thrashing tentacle. He came up swinging, his sword in one hand and Anisa's in his other. The blades sheared through tentacles, cutting halfway through the bases of the two either side of him. He leapt back as the grey blood spurted from the wounds. The damaged limbs still tried to thrash, gushing ooze. Anwar moved to dodge. But another tentacle came over the top. It caught him as he leapt. He yelled as it snatched him from the air.

Lucy swung around. She jumped and fired. The monster smacked her out of the air. Her bullet caught the tentacle, but barely enough to draw blood. The creature smashed Anwar against the ceiling like it had done with Tony. He wasn't going out so easily. He roared and swung his swords at the limb twisted around his legs. The slithery tail of it severed completely. Anwar cried out as he fell. He tossed one sword back towards the monster, stabbing it near the center. The other he barely avoided landing on. He twisted awkwardly, hitting the ground with one knee. There was a sharp crack. His face went white.

Tony struggled up. Lucy was caught amidst the writhing mass. She struggled and fought to get free. Her yells were lost in the noise of the creature. Another crack sounded as Fred's shield struggled.

"Tony!" she bellowed.

He braced himself against the wall and focused. Red lightning burst from his fingers. It shot out wild and uncontrolled. The monster took the brunt of it, faltering and wailing as the light exploded and scorched its flesh. Lucy took the opening and leapt out of the way. The lightning faltered and sparked out. Tony cursed and slumped against the wall. With renewed fury, the monster screeched and slashed out. It smashed through Fred's shield. Fred roared in pain and fury. The red light shattered around her, but she drew it in and fired. Lightning far stronger than Tony's blasted from her hands. At the same time the monster whacked her into Vincent. She crashed into him and they sprawled across the floor.

A giant smoldering gash appeared through the monster's body. It looked like it had nearly been blasted in half. It shuddered and squirmed weakly. Lucy ran up, sliding new bullets into her rifle. She clicked it shut, aimed, and pulled the trigger.

* * *

The darkness pressed in thick and cloying. It was practically comforting. This was how it was supposed to be. Vincent stalked through it. Nothing was visible. There was nothing to see. Nothing to smell. The only sounds were footsteps and breath, and the hope that they were his alone. Echoes of his journey. He wasn't even sure he was breathing air.

Eventually, the faintest shades of grey permeated the darkness. Vincent found himself walking between the ghosts of shelves. They rose up around him like a maze, and he stalked down the aisles, hunting his quarry. There was no sign of the girl, but that didn't mean he was alone. He heard the sound, more than just his echo. He stopped. So did the other footsteps. Vincent turned towards the sound as slowly as he could.

A man stood behind him, only a few feet away.

Vincent's emblem embroidered on his long coat.

"You're looking for me," he stated.

"No, my friend," Vincent sighed. "Not for a long time. I'm looking for your niece, Fajr."

"Only the dead walk here," Naeem replied. "Are you dead, Master Temple?"

Vincent looked down at his hands. Was he dead? Not yet, he hoped. A hideous scream came out of the darkness. The shriek echoed like the roar of a beast, and turned into a thousand human screams, all echoing off each other. Vincent looked up. Naeem stood right in front of him, his dark eyes clouding over with death.

"Only the dead walk here," he repeated. The ghost reached up, grabbing his own face and ripping it in half the way Vincent had done in a nightmare visit before. Vincent leapt back as the ghost's head tore in half. Blood sprayed and gushed from the wound. Vincent fled the stench of it. The body collapsed, blood pouring from the hole. So much blood. More than any real body could hold. It surged out like a fire hydrant; the aisles began to flood with it.

Vincent clambered up the shelves. He didn't know what was happening, or what would happen, but he knew he didn't want the blood to touch him. The shelves went high, but the tide of blood kept rising. He scrambled up. The ledges became smaller, harder to grip. The shelves were filling up. Vincent reached up. Books. Books were filling the shelves and making it harder to climb. He grabbed a handful and threw them beneath him. One more ledge. He did it again, making small handholds to climb. Just a little more.

He struggled to the top of the bookshelf, the blood rising beneath him. Before him, the path across the shelves spiraled like a maze. Vincent ran and leapt atop the bookcases. He didn't know where he was headed, until he saw the light. The tiniest flicker, like a candle dancing between the shelves in the distance. He raced towards it. The screaming was back, but whether beast or man Vincent could no longer tell. He could sense the blood rising behind him. That threat wasn't eluded yet.

Vincent stumbled and staggered across his dizzying path. He reached the edge, the source of the light. He looked down. Nestled between the bookcases was a small table with a lamp. A robed figure sat amidst piles of books, reading from ancient tomes. The blood had come this far. It swirled around the ankles of the student, although they seemed oblivious to it. The hideous shriek came again, and they looked up, startled. They could hear it too.

"Fajr," Vincent whispered, recognizing the reader as the soul he searched for.

The girl turned to him, but he never caught her eye. He never saw her face. A loud rushing came from behind him and he turned. A wave of blood crashed over the shelves, smashing Vincent full in the chest and knocking him from the bookcase. He fell, engulfed. He couldn't breathe, and he dare not try. He was drowning. Drowning in the blood of his friend. The blood of those he had lost. He fought against the wave. Had it caught Fajr too? Did she need saving?

The harder he fought, the deeper the ocean. He couldn't win. Only the dead walk here. It felt like a warning. A warning from the Prince. Vincent had gone searching for the wrong thing. He would have to be wiser next time. If there even was a next time. Only the dead walk here... the sentence echoed around and around in his dying brain. Only the dead... but he wasn't walking. Not anymore.

* * *

Vincent woke in such pain he wished he had died. He could feel himself still drowning. Still choking. He rolled onto his side and opened his mouth. Liquid poured out, hot and bitter and salty. He really hoped it was just blood, but he couldn't bring himself to open his eyes. A great weight was pressing down on him. His bones felt brittle, as though they had just been burnt and all he had left was the pain and the ash. The weight shifted away. Breathing became easier.

"Vincent!" Fred's voice exclaimed right beside him.

A touch he recognized as hers came warm and heavy. He felt like he was being crushed again, but he knew Fred was just pulling him onto her knees. He groaned and opened his eyes. It was blood dripping from his mouth. A lot more than was healthy. That would be why she was yelling.

He heard gunfire, but he was too weak to move, even when he realized what it must mean. It stopped abruptly. There was a gross gelatinous sound. Squelchy. He couldn't lift his head, but was comforted by the noise of small footfalls on the stone ground, and the appearance of Lucy wandering into his vision. She looked fierce.

"Sir," Fred's voice came firmly just above him. "If you don't want me to slap you back to last Tuesday, you're going to explain yourself right now."

"Only the dead walk here..." he whispered through the blood. Then he fainted.

* * *

When he woke, he felt better than the last time. Someone had cleaned him up for a start. Three guesses who. She must have resisted beating him with a stick, because he didn't feel like he was home to new bruises. Maybe if he stayed asleep that would continue, but he couldn't. He had to find Fajr. He was the only one who knew where she was. He opened his eyes and pulled himself up slowly. He had been lying on a divan, propped up, with a pot on the floor beside him. Whatever he'd been bringing up seemed to be over now, but he knew they were wise to prepare.

Voices sounded from the other room. He stood and slowly shuffled towards the door.

"I think they can feel it, like I feel them," Tony was saying.

"You think the monsters are drawn to him dreaming?" Lucy pressed. "That they sense it?"

"They would still have to be summoned," Fred warned sharply. "Whether or not they can feel the Darkness inside him and are drawn to him, they still have to be summoned into this realm by someone here. That means someone is onto us. Someone knows we're here. Given the flock of demons on the boat, and now this gruesome monstrosity, I think it's safe to say that someone doesn't want us to find this girl."

"But we will," Lucy insisted. "Vincent will know what to do. He always does."

"He does," Fred agreed cautiously. "But I would hesitate to rely on that alone, kid. He promised us that he gave up that awful tonic. That toxic piss is killing him, and he won't always be there to hold up the fort if he doesn't quit it." The disappointment and frustration were plain in her voice. "I can't believe he was lying to us all that time…"

"I can," Lucy muttered. "I thought it was fishy that he always knew about these shenanigans before things even went south."

"Things still always went south." Tony sounded like he was mumbling around a cigarette. "Let's face it, ladies, we've always been behind the eight ball in everything we do. I know it's a hazard of the profession for me… but sometimes it feels like Hunters chase the big sleep faster than us mugs."

"Mafia gangsters aren't exactly our desired comparison," Fred agreed. "But the Darkness is a more dangerous dance partner than crime." She gave a dark and derisive snort and spoke through gritted teeth. "I cannot *believe* he was still taking that poison this whole time."

"And I thought Uncle Nilo had a drinking problem…" Tony sighed.

Vincent shuffled into the room. The others were all bathed and changed. Tony was lying on his back over on a couch, smoking at the ceiling. Lucy was perched on the end beside him, sharing a grim look with Fred. Fred saw him enter the room. She was lounging in a chair across from the children, and turned a severe glare towards him as he entered.

"Where are our hosts?" Vincent inquired. The children started in surprise, but Fred didn't flinch.

"Recovering," Fred replied. "Anisa has a concussion, and Anwar broke his leg. They put up an admirable fight though."

"A fight?" Vincent echoed.

Tony had sat bolt upright at the sound of Vincent's voice. His big eyes considered the old Hunter apprehensively. Lucy rested a hand on his shoulder to calm him.

"A monster attacked while you were dreaming," she told him. "We had to fight it off. Fred protected you because your circle wasn't drawn properly, and Tony thinks that bridging yourself to the Darkness is attracting the monsters."

"But I'm not certain," Tony defended. "It was an awful thing, Doc, and it wanted to get to you. I could feel it. Without the ladies here, it might have chowed you into bean paste without you even realizing. Miss Lucy killed it good though. She shot it dead after Fred blasted it."

"You didn't just turn your lighthouse beam on it, Segreti?" Vincent queried.

"No, Sir," Tony shook his head in embarrassment. "I can't just turn it on and off when I want to. Sometimes it happens, and sometimes it doesn't…" He shot Fred a look, but said nothing else.

"I don't know how he does it," Fred sighed. "So I can't train him in it."

"Maybe it requires heightened emotion," Vincent mused. "Perhaps the panic of the fight helps–"

"I assure you, Doc, I was panicking just fine," Tony muttered, puffing away anxiously.

Lucy rubbed a hand soothingly against his back. He didn't look like he was panicking now.

"Well, perhaps–"

"We're not talking about Tony, Sir," Fred interrupted.

"We're not?"

"No." She stood, staring him down. "We're not."

The kids moved to leave, sharing a nervous glance and quickly scrambling up. Vincent stopped them. He raised a hand and they froze like rabbits in headlights. Neither knew who to obey or what to do. Vincent put them out of their misery. He gave Fred a firm look.

"Spanking me is going to have to wait, Fred," he ordered. "As furious as I'm sure you are, the lecture won't be a new one, and we have more pressing matters. Everyone ready yourselves for our first daytrip. I know where to look for Fajr."

8

The day was hot and dusty. A faint sea breeze teased the air, but did little more than nudge the stench of beast and man. Lucy knew her life was privileged, apprenticeship considered. She had seen all manner of horrors, but the terrors of beyond couldn't frighten her like they used to. It was the conditions of civilization that surprised her now.

Vincent had spoken to Anwar and Anisa. Both had wanted to come to search for their daughter, and both were in no state to do so. The old Hunter had talked them down. They had called him here to help; now they needed to let him. The understanding hadn't been too bitter, and they had organized a coach to take Vincent's team into the city.

Lucy sat in the back with Tony, who let her hold his hand. Vincent and Fred sat across from them in indignant dispute. She was letting him have it. He bit back sharp retorts like an old dog determined never to change. Lucy tangled her fingers in Tony's, feeling her little hand stretch to fit his larger one. She personally thought Fred was in the right, but she wasn't going to get involved. Fred was perfectly capable of eviscerating her mentor without any help, and Vincent knew he was in the wrong. He was just fighting because that was what he did best.

The coach pulled up outside the bazaar, and Lucy peeked out the window at the fascinating warren of stalls. It was close enough to their destination, and she was almost grateful they weren't being dropped at the door. Not just because it gave her an opportunity to see more of this enchanting new land, but because she had concerns about where they were going and what it might entail. She had packed very carefully for this adventure. Mostly bullets, to be fair, but she had a horrible sinking feeling in her gut that had encouraged her to prepare for more.

They climbed out and Vincent paid the man, haggling briefly over the price. Lucy didn't speak the language, so she couldn't tell which way it went. Possibly Vincent was done fighting for the day, or possibly he was taking out his frustration on their driver. Lucy patted the horse and waited patiently, adjusting the tall canvas bag over her shoulder.

Vincent led the way with the rest of them trailing behind. Fred followed close on his heel, but she seemed done with her scolding for now. Lucy strolled after her, with Tony bringing up the rear. Lucy kept hold of his hand and dragged him along like a puppy. He wasn't resisting, but he wasn't enthusiastic either. She wondered if he was worried about the same thing she was.

It didn't take long for her to discover her fears were well-founded. They traced the road between the market and the tall iron fence of their destination, before coming to the gates of the library. Lucy felt her heart flutter. Of course, it wasn't the Great Library of Alexandria, but it was technically the Alexandria Library, which was as close as anyone was ever going to get.

Tony's hand was clammy in hers, and she felt his fingers tense. There was a reluctant tug. It wasn't intentional, but he couldn't help it. She looked back at him. He was pale and unsteady. His eyes were already starting to glaze, and he looked dizzy.

"Vincent!" Lucy called, coming to a stop just inside the gates.

Vincent and Fred both turned to her. They took in Tony's condition instantly and descended on them.

"I'm okay," Tony protested before anyone could say anything. He swayed slightly and dabbed at the sweat beading his forehead. "Just... just the heat, I think..."

Fred put her hands to his temples and closed her eyes. They waited. Lucy slipped a hand into her bag. She'd been waiting for this. The odds of a library like this one containing dangerous texts were just too high. Maybe they were in a back room, or a vault, or somewhere under lock and key, but they were in there, and Tony would be drawn to them. Fred lowered her hands and opened her eyes. She shook her head.

"I won't be a burden, Doc," Tony insisted.

"If she says it's not safe for you, boy, then we listen to her," Vincent sighed.

"We can't just leave him unsupervised," Fred muttered. "Even out here, if something calls to him and we're not here to stop it, we might lose him for good."

"Don't need to be ranked!" Tony protested. "I can resist it! I–!"

In one fluid movement, Lucy handcuffed him to the iron railing of the fence. Everyone stared at her. She ignored everyone but Tony, who she looked up at with sympathetic adoration.

"I was worried this might happen," she told him, sealing her concern with a kiss. "Don't do anything stupid until we get back. This shouldn't take long."

Tony stood completely dumbfounded, whether from the kiss or the cuffs or both it was unclear. Lucy was already turning to go. She didn't want to give him a chance to get indignant when they all knew this was for the best. Vincent cast her a sly glance. He patted Tony's shoulder while the young man stood in complete bewilderment, and turned to follow Lucy. She led on with Vincent and Fred following on behind her.

"That was very much a Hunter's attempt at problem solving," Fred commented drily as they started up the raised steps to the front door.

"Yes, it was," Vincent smiled.

Lucy took the praise stoically. They pushed the doors open and strode into the building. Her heart was thudding, and she wasn't sure if she was excited or worried. She hoped Tony would be okay out there.

The library was dry and dusty and dark. Darker than it should be. Darker than it had any right to be. It was like walking into night. High windows let in thin beams of sunshine, illuminating the dust in the air. These were few and far between, and the light seemed muted by the darkness present. Electric bulbs had been strung up around the ceiling. The glass glinted in the faint light, but none of them were on. Vincent found a switch by the entrance and pressed it. Nothing happened. It clicked repeatedly at his insistent attempts. Nothing. Lucy watched him.

"Keep your eye on the room, kid," he warned.

She turned back to the high-vaulted space with its small windows and rows upon rows of shelves. The area immediately before the door was vast and spacious, with a service desk in the middle. It was empty. Trolleys of books sat by it, untouched and collecting dust.

"This isn't creepy at all," Fred commented under her breath.

"Shouldn't there be staff here?" Lucy asked.

"My thoughts exactly," Fred muttered, pulling a handgun out from under her light jacket.

"Maybe they're just out in the shelves," Vincent suggested, striding forward and running a finger along the books stacked in a trolley. He rubbed a thin veneer of dust between his thumb and forefinger.

Lucy strode up to his side, unpacking her rifle from the bag over her shoulder.

"Maybe they're not out there alone," she added.

"Maybe," Vincent agreed, drawing his pistol. "Even if libraries are supposed to be quiet and dusty. Stay close. I'd rather take longer and play it safe than spread out and lose everyone in the dark."

"Yes, Sir," Fred agreed.

Vincent took point and Lucy fell in obediently behind him. He stalked his way towards the shelves, weapon in hand. It was his dream they were following anyway. He knew what to look for. Lucy just prayed they would catch up to Fajr in time, before anything awful happened. She couldn't bear the thought of going back to Anisa and Anwar with tragic news.

The shelves stretched high and long, disappearing into the darkness. Vincent took out a torch and stepped softly. Lucy followed in his footsteps with practiced care. She noted that he was walking better. Fred followed along behind them. Vincent's handheld beam of light projected through the dusty air, lighting it up and exposing increasingly suspicious normality. The shelves sat unused and unruffled. Books lined every one patiently, content in their neglect.

"What are we looking for?" Lucy asked, trying to distract her imagination from the atmosphere and stay on task. If she had a better idea of what they sought, beyond a girl her own age, she might feel more useful.

"Any sign of Fajr," Vincent replied softly. "Any sign of the cult or dark magic." He paused for a moment, not in movement, but in speech. Words hovered about him, and he added cautiously, "Any sign of death."

Lucy nodded. Those were things she was familiar with. So was the darkness, and the silence, and the waiting; the hideous expectation of dread settling over the area like a blanket; the creeping fear. The deeper they walked, the more intense the atmosphere became. Lucy could feel it like a chill in the air. It should have been comforting after the heat of the city, but it wasn't. It was a diseased cold. A fatal one. They continued on, minutes disappearing between stacked bookcases.

Weak sunshine tumbled down into a gap between bookshelves. There was a reading desk set up in the space with four chairs set either side of it in pairs. Two of the chairs had been knocked over and the desk sat askew, as though it had been bumped. Vincent approached it cautiously. Lucy had a horrible feeling in the depths of her gut. She thought about Tony again. At least he was safe enough outside. Certainly safer out there than in here.

Vincent hovered around the table, inspecting it. Lucy and Fred stayed close. Lucy glimpsed something down an aisle in the faint light.

"Vincent," she whispered, indicating.

He turned and shone his torch over her discovery. A shelf had been knocked over. Books were strewn across the floor. They approached the mess cautiously. There was no sign of whatever had knocked them. Silence still reigned. Vincent kept his torch locked on the fallen books as they stalked down the aisle towards them. As he came out into the clutter, Vincent started and moved quickly away. Lucy sped after him. Fred gave chase. He hadn't gone far. There was another desk with fallen chairs. Books were spread over one side of the table. Some still lay open. Vincent moved to them instantly. He set down his torch and began to leaf through them. Lucy watched him nervously. She nudged some of the fallen books with her toe, but no great evil rose to smite her.

Fred joined Vincent at the table. Lucy could see the books they were perusing. There was no place for her there, everything was written in a foreign script.

"What are you thinking, Sir?" Fred whispered.

"She was here," he replied. "This is her research."

"There's pencil shavings on the desk, but no sign of any notes," Fred commented. "No notepaper, nothing circled in the texts…"

"The notes are gone," Vincent agreed. "And so is the girl."

Movement sounded nearby. Lucy jumped. Instantly, Vincent had his eyes up and his gun ready. They all looked to the bookcase blocking the direction of the noise. Vincent switched off his torch. He kept it in hand, aligned with his gun, as he stalked the shadows. The soles of his boots moved silently across the floor. He braced himself against the bookcase, using it as cover. Lucy and Fred hunkered down, waiting, ready. The sound came again. Vincent whirled around the bookcase, gun raised. He blasted the torch.

A startled human cry met his light. More than one. Vincent lowered his torch and weapon instantly. Lucy couldn't see what he could, but his expression said it all.

"Temple!" a familiar and indignant British accent reprimanded.

"Fancy seeing you here, Chancellor," Vincent replied. He kept his weapon lowered and stepped back into the faint light near the desk. As he backed up, other footsteps followed him loudly, all pretense of stealth forgotten.

"We could have shot you, you fool!" Whitehall cursed.

"And I you," Vincent retorted. "But we didn't, because we're all better trained than that, aren't we?"

There was a dangerous edge to his voice, as though daring Whitehall to admit his people weren't trained well enough to avoid shooting innocents.

"I told you to stay out of it, Vincent," he growled. "What are you doing here?"

"Sightseeing," Vincent replied without missing a beat. "I can't take the family to see the library of Alexandria?"

"You're awfully well armed for a trip to the library," Whitehall retorted, eyeing Fred and Lucy distrustfully.

"We got rights, Nigel," Fred replied in her best American drawl. "With monsters and your amateurs running around we have to be able to defend ourselves."

"I'm not going to fight with you, Missus Temple," Whitehall said. "I won't be baited, but we both know that the best thing for everyone is for your lot to stand down and get back on a ship home. You shouldn't be bringing your daughter into such danger. This building became a place of interest this morning. If it weren't for your ship radioing in, we would have been here first. No one has been seen leaving in the last 24 hours. You best run along and be the first."

Lucy wanted to slap him for his condescending tone, but she was still reeling from the concept of Fred as 'Missus Temple'. If it was only a disguise it would be funny, but there was a ring of legal truth to it that unsettled her. Although, she had to admit they did argue like an old married couple.

Whitehall's men were slowly spreading out around them. They were trying to be subtle about it, but there were nearly a dozen of them. They snuck out from behind the bookshelves, like grunts trying to pass off casual snooping. They were investigating a scene, it just so happened that they were also surrounding Lucy and her faux-parents. One of them, a man with a sliver more intelligence in his eyes, noted the books on the table.

"Some light reading, Temple?" he accused.

"Those books been here longer than we have," Vincent replied. "Dust has already settled on them. We're just having a look around."

"Given the quantity of dust and deterioration in so short a timeframe, I would guess there's a curse settling here," Fred offered. "I don't know what kind of magic was used, but the atmosphere isn't normal. Something is corroding the space."

Eyebrows were raised at her, and she smirked in return.

"Get yourself a mage, Nigel," she advised. "I'm sure there's enough stuffy old coots on our council that you can easily make friends."

"Your kind have their value," Whitehall conceded. "But any given witch is only a few bad dreams away from being a cultist. Magic isn't meant for humanity. It corrupts the soul."

"Only dark magic," Lucy protested. She felt a burning need to defend Fred and Tony, even if he wasn't actually there.

"All magic is dark magic, girl," Whitehall countered, and no one disputed him. As he spoke he drew closer to them, his steps bringing him softly across the floor.

Lucy knew Fred and Vincent had no respect for

Whitehall's acolytes. They were still in training, and it was far less intensive than Lucy's was. For all that the old Englishman might have lost his teaching edge, Lucy could see in the way he moved that he himself was still a good Hunter. He was older than Vincent by some years, but he carried fewer injuries and walked with a spry agility. His white suit was a spotless beacon in the faint light, as though his ability to kill without muck was a point of extreme pride. His steps brought him to the table, and he used the barrel of his pistol to turn the page of a book.

"You're following that native girl," he commented.

"Her name is Fajr," Vincent replied. "Her parents are worried about her, and they want her home. You haven't seen her anywhere, have you?"

"Not for a few days," Whitehall admitted. "It's been a blessed relief to have that wild child out from underfoot, but it doesn't bode well for her health."

Lucy kept her eyes on Vincent, but he didn't react. If anything, he looked like he had been expecting that response. The two old men were watching each other, and everyone else was watching them, so Lucy saw it first. The darkness moved. It was so big it was hard to see. Deep in the depths of the library, where no light could reach, where the curse was at its thickest, half the room seemed to shift. As though a mountain rolled and heaved through the hall.

"Vincent!" Lucy hissed. It was coming towards them.

Vincent turned at her warning, and everyone else followed his lead. To the eyes of even a half-trained

Hunter it was obvious. The darkness was growing and surging forward. Something was blocking the light as it rushed them. It was growing louder. Whatever it was moved fast across the shelves.

"Want to take bets on what it is this time?" she asked her mentor.

Vincent didn't reply, but his expression was grim. He lifted his pistol and torch. The light wasn't bright enough to reach over the rows of bookshelves. Everyone raised their weapons and took aim. As soon as it was in range there was a chorus of gunfire. The hail of bullets was met with the sound of a thousand screams. Then it hit them. A twisted human hand, the size of four men, crashed onto the bookcase above them. Grey fingernails the size of skulls bit into the wood. Something shuddered and uncurled above it, coming into the light.

It looked like a hundred of Frankenstein's worst nightmares. A hideous mix of limbs and faces and ribs jutted obscenely from distorted angles, all enlarged ten times their human size. The flesh was blotchy, torn, and decaying. Entrails strung it all together, as though a dozen giant corpses had gone through a tumbler. But it moved. Blood dripped from the bullet holes riddled through the mess. The faces lifted to the ceiling and screamed in unison.

"What is that?" Lucy gasped.

"That's what happens when magic goes wrong," Whitehall growled. He aimed for an eyeball and fired. The holy bullet hit true and exploded the eye socket. It was hard to know what would constitute a mortal wound on such a monstrosity, but limiting its visibility was a good idea.

It screeched and lashed out. One massive hand swung down. Everyone leapt away. The desk was crushed. The hand reared back, splinters protruding bloody and vicious from its fingers. It barely seemed to notice.

The group scattered, collectively reloading their weapons. Lucy ducked behind a bookcase and hunkered down. She shoved bullets into her rifle. Two pistols hung from her hips. They were still full, but they didn't hit as hard. She waited for the sound of movement. Her own panicked breathing pounded in her ears. There was something truly awful about that creature. Something worse than a monster. Something previously human. Magic gone wrong. It lit a brand-new terror in her. A terror that made her fear for Tony.

The abomination roared and shifted. Lucy leapt out and fired. She wasn't the only one. Another hail of bullets tore through muscle and sinew. Organs exploded. They were superfluous anyway. The thing didn't slow down. It moved forward, away from Lucy. Some of the limbs went over, flipping the body around. There didn't seem to be a top or bottom, or front or back. It moved like a mutant crab, shuffling this way and that as though directed by many brains, or none.

Lucy kept in cover and fired again, aiming for an eye. She missed, but half a cheek ripped clean off. Vincent and Fred were nowhere to be seen, but any of the other bullets firing out of cover could be them. The creature stepped forward, one giant hand reaching out and crushing everything under it. Screaming began. Human screaming. Lucy couldn't see what was happening. The thing was the size of a house, and the danger was on the other side, for now. It moved so fast, with such a reach, she wasn't sure if she could avoid it if it turned her way.

Multiple hands smashed down on the bookcases away from her. She peered through the carnage as the screaming filled the library. Giant hands picked up one of the acolytes. Blood stained his leg like it had been crushed. Multiple hands snatched for him, ripping him into pieces as he shrieked. Another man was snatched by a different hand. It brought him straight to one of the mouths. Blood spurted like a fountain as he was bitten in two. The creature snapped and screeched as different hands and mouths all fought each other for a share of the spoils, shredding everyone it could grab.

Lucy leapt down. She hid back behind her bookcase, fighting the bile in her throat. Her body heaved. She pushed it down. It heaved again. Every inch of her wanted to throw up, but she kept it back. Tears stained the corner of her eyes. Just when she thought the creatures from beyond couldn't scare her anymore. She'd never seen anything so awful.

Then it turned.

The whole body shifted and warped. Different pieces moved in and out between each other as more of the heads turned in her direction. It was looking for fresh food. She didn't even think. She ran. The bookshelves divided the room into aisles, but a straight line here meant death. Lucy ducked and wove. She shoved bookcases, letting them fall, then bolting the other way. There was no time to see if the distractions were working. Her heart pounded. Her lungs ached. Her mind was clear of everything but terror. More screams started behind her. She kicked over a bookcase and stopped. The air was alive with sound. Everywhere bookcases crashed like dominos. Most of them were knocked over by the creature. It had given chase, but another victim had distracted it.

Lucy raised her rifle. Killing it was more effective than running. She shot it again. She fired until the rifle was empty. The creature continued to rip through the fallen shelves like nothing was happening. Paper and blood sprayed around it as it dug for its prize. Lucy reloaded. She was running out of bullets for the .308. She looked up. One of the heads was looking straight at her. Massive glassy eyes, foggy and wet, blinked in her direction. It moved forward. She broke and leapt.

The bookcase behind her was smashed down. To pause for thought was fatal. It had to be instinct. She ran faster. It wasn't fast enough. It couldn't be. She felt a shadow pass over her. She screamed and threw herself as far as she could. The cold, clammy touch of death brushed over her. Then exploded like fire.

Lucy hit the floor hard. She heard a screech behind her. The hand that had grasped for her was mangled and shredded. The smell of burning flesh filled the air. Red lightning still crackled in the holes ripped through the limb. Some distance back, the tell-tale crimson glow of magic marked Fred, hands ablaze with power. Lucy stared up at the abomination in wonder. It was well distracted from her.

A lithe figure had run up one of the arms, sword in one hand and pistol in the other. Lucy stared as Vincent ran across the twisting creature, shooting and slashing. It cried out and swatted at him. Vincent ducked through a mutated joint, slipping through the gross organs. The creature smacked itself and staggered. The face that had been struck snarled and bit at the hand that had struck it.

Another face lunged for Vincent. Gigantic teeth, dripping with grey saliva, gnashed at him. He leapt back. His foot caught in a ribbon of entrail. He tumbled. Lucy cried out, but he caught himself. Vincent stabbed his sword into the side of the creature. His blade caught him, tearing a deep gash between two arms. He began to pull himself up. A giant hand swiped for him. Lucy couldn't get a good angle. She didn't have to. A bullet destroyed half a finger and the hand reared back. Whitehall stood two shelves down from Lucy, gun aimed. He readied his next shot.

"Move, Temple!" he roared.

Vincent ripped his sword free and dropped to the floor. The creature twisted horrifically in and out of itself as various parts of it tried to reach him. Whitehall emptied his weapon into it, removing eyes and jaws in an attempt to take out the heads. He cursed as the gun ran empty. Quickly, he moved to reload. The monster took the opening.

"Chancellor!" Lucy yelled. She sprinted and dove, tackling him out of the way. A giant hand smashed down, destroying shelves and sending books flying.

"Get off me, girl!" Whitehall roared. He pushed her

away. The hand swung towards them. Lucy rolled onto her back and fired. Her bullet ripped through a tendon in the wrist, but the hand kept coming. It snatched them both. Lucy cried out as it caught her by the legs. Whitehall was completely pinned in its grasp. Lucy swung wildly, unable to aim. The hand pulled them in towards a broken face. One empty eye socket seeped dark ooze over a bony, rotting cheek. The dripping mouth opened wide, cracked teeth glistening. Lucy wriggled fiercely. She grabbed her canteen, ripped the cap off, and poured it all over the face.

The monster shrieked. It recoiled in pain, the whole body finally moving as one, as the face began to steam and blister. It threw its captives. Lucy and Whitehall yelled as they went flying. They crashed painfully into a bookcase, tipping it over with a crunch. The creature was shaking itself wildly like an animal, trying to dislodge the holy water burning through its flesh like acid. None of the other limbs would risk themselves to touch it, but they could sense the pain. With several strangled cries, it turned, flopping and twisting, and took off towards the darkness.

"After it, men!" Whitehall bellowed, staggering to his feet. He held one arm tenderly and winced, but he didn't look badly injured. At his age, Lucy wouldn't have been surprised to find that the hits hurt more.

She scrambled up too and checked her gear. Vincent and Fred moved up either side of her, relief on their faces. Whitehall rounded on all of them.

"You three get out of here," he growled. "This is not your territory. This is not your fight. Fancy bringing a girl into this turmoil." He raced off after his people without another word.

Lucy drew herself up to protest indignantly, but Vincent rested a hand on her shoulder. She met his cautious eyes.

"You're not really going to leave them to that thing, are you?" she asked. "He's lost a quarter of his people already!"

"He told us to leave, and we're going to do what we're told," Vincent replied.

Lucy opened her mouth to protest, and then shut it again. He was her master; there were times to stand your ground, and there were times to obey. He had taught her to pick her fights. A thank you would have been nice though. Vincent kept a firm hand on her back as he directed her towards the door.

"You got that thing running, kid," he said. "They can take it out from here."

"And if they don't?" she retorted.

"Then Tony and Fred seal the building and we burn it to the ground," Vincent replied. "And the Order can blame it on the Romans, like they did last time. Or the Germans. Or the English. Someone European."

Lucy glowered, but did as she was told. She wasn't disappointed to be getting away from the abomination. Everything about it turned her stomach. It was the fabric nightmares were made of. That was why killing it would make her feel better. Then she would know she could beat it. Then she would know it was dead. She wasn't sure she trusted Whitehall and his cronies to finish it off. Besides, they felt no closer to finding Fajr.

9

The sunlight outside was painfully bright after the cursed darkness of the library. Lucy stumbled down the stairs, shielding her eyes. Vincent and Fred flanked her like an honor guard, but she knew they were just keeping an eye on her. As horrifying as it had been in the fight, she couldn't imagine what it must have felt like to watch that thing nearly eat her.

"Where to now, Sir?" Fred asked. "We didn't exactly get any decent intel from that trip."

'We know what she's searching for from her research," Vincent replied. "It's somewhere to start. Knowing the questions that drive her will help to direct us where she is going. We also know she was there in the last twenty four hours."

"How do we know that thing didn't get her?" Lucy asked, shivering at the thought despite the heat.

"There would have been more of a mess," Vincent growled, as though daring anyone to contradict him.

Lucy didn't have the heart for it. She didn't know the girl they were looking for, but she desperately wanted to find her alive. She wouldn't wish a death like that on anyone, not even Whitehall. All thoughts of Fajr were forgotten as she came down the stairs. She looked to the fence, and her mind emptied. Tony was gone. There was no sign of him. Lucy took off, racing across the courtyard to the iron rails. Vincent and Fred followed close behind. She didn't know what she was planning on doing as she reached the fence. There was no sign of Tony. No sign of the handcuffs.

"Do you think you can track him?" Fred asked Vincent as they reached Lucy.

"We can ask around," Vincent nodded his head at the bazaar. Crowds moved through the stalls and shopkeepers kept a sharp eye on everything around them. Some harried and bartered, others lounged around smoking. "Someone will have seen what happened."

"What if he's gone into the library?!" Lucy panicked.

"He's not stupid," Fred insisted. She paused thoughtfully. "He's not that kind of stupid. Nigel's people might have found him out here and gotten him somewhere safe."

"Then why didn't he say anything?"

"Don't borrow trouble, kid," Vincent sighed. "Let's ask someone what they saw, and then we can work out where to direct our concerns."

Vincent took point again and led them across the street. A large stone archway marked the entrance to the bazaar, and a river of people flowed through it. Vincent approached one of the vendors by the entrance, set up in a pink stall that might once have been red. Lucy listened to them talk, but she didn't understand the language and the patient tones of their negotiation irked her. Panic still rose in her chest like a balloon, expanding and taking up space where her lungs used to be.

The thought of the monster in the library was like a cold touch of death down her spine. She hadn't killed it. It wasn't over. Tony was gone. If that thing got him... The thought made her want to cry. Maybe he could destroy it. If it came for him, maybe he could blast it the same way he'd taken out the demons on the ship. His magic was powerful, more so than even Fred seemed to understand. But if he had blasted it, and it hadn't died, he would have collapsed... then it could have eaten him.

The man Vincent was speaking to began to gesture and point down the street. Lucy felt hope swell in her breast. Then, as Vincent was finishing up thanking the man, a sharp whistle sounded behind them.

"Doc!" Tony's familiar voice called.

They turned and Lucy saw him coming through the crowd towards them. He looked better than when they had left him. In the hot sun the shadows of his eyes faded. There was a spark there, cheeky and alive, but his grin was characteristically sheepish. He hurried over to them and Vincent eyeballed him as he approached.

"I see you got yourself free," Vincent commented.

Tony nodded, rummaging in his pocket and pulling the cuffs back out. He handed them to Lucy.

"I believe these are yours, Miss." He dropped them in her hand and kissed her cheek. "The concern is appreciated and it's cute you thought it would work."

"Bloody gangsters..." she muttered under her

breath, dropping the cuffs back into the side pocket of her bag and trying to hide her blush. Of course he'd know how to pick his way out. Sometimes his eyes were so honest and his manner so sweet it was hard to remember this was probably his element, but he was one of Ferro's boys. His family would have taught him how to get out of tougher steel than that. The kiss was new. In public, no less. The behavior was so unusual for Tony it had caught her off guard, but she wasn't displeased.

"How was the library?" he asked.

"Grotesque," Vincent answered. "And not as informative as I had hoped. It was better than nothing though. We know Fajr is looking into the history of the cult and locations of their activities. She must be trying to find them and bring them down at the source."

"Well, I don't know if it will help, but I had a bit of luck myself–" Tony began. He stopped, staring over their heads towards the library. "What are they doing here?"

The other three turned and saw Whitehall lead half a dozen men from the building. The chief Hunter was pointing and ordering the others around.

"That was fast," Lucy commented, remembering where they had left the Chancellor's team.

"Too fast," Fred agreed.

"And they're organizing a barricade and evacuation," Vincent added, already taking off towards the library again. The others hurried after him.

Sure enough, as they moved back towards the gates, Whitehall's people were shooing civilians away and closing off the area.

"Nigel!" Vincent roared, running up to the fence.

"You're still here, Temple?" Whitehall called back. "Make yourself useful and help clear out the market."

Vincent ignored him. "What happened? What did you find? Where's the monster?"

"We lost it," Whitehall replied.

"You what?!"

"We lost it," the Chancellor repeated. "It was dark, the thing ran off–"

"It's as big as a fucking house, Nigel!" Vincent bellowed at him. "How did you lose it?!"

"You don't get to take that tone with me, Temple," Whitehall snapped. "I gave you that pin–"

"Don't threaten me, old man," Vincent hissed through the bars. "I'm on the Council too. If you could remove me, you already would have. You don't have the votes."

"I am still the Chancellor! You do as I say! Now, get these civilians out of here!"

Whitehall's orders were capped by an earth-shaking explosion. Part of the library wall blew out into the courtyard, raining dust and rubble over the cobbles. Out of the dark hole came half a dozen, giant, mismatched hands, grasping at the edges with long, spindly, rotting fingers. They pulled the hideous mutated body out into the daylight. All the heads lifted in unison and screeched at the sky.

The monster swayed and shifted as it looked up at the heavens. Whitehall instantly began barking orders at his team. The crowd outside the bazaar panicked.

People began to scream and flee. Lucy grabbed onto the fence to stop herself being swept away in the press of bodies, as everyone began to race up the street or into the market. The crowd shifted like a wave, made denser by fear. Tony held on around her. He pressed her to the fence, his body held protectively around her. He was warm and tense. His breath felt hot against her cheek, and she could sense his eyes on the monster. It was hard not to look at it.

Fred yelled out in a language Lucy didn't recognize, and red light filled the air behind them. It reminded her of the shield Fred had cast to protect Vincent. This one seemed thinner and less substantial, but significantly bigger. It began to herd people back. Lucy turned her head to watch the crowd start to clear, guided by Fred's light. The mage herself looked strained. Her hands glowed, sweat dripped down the side of her face, and the tendons stood out on her neck.

"*Lignum animarum*," Tony whispered.

Lucy turned to him. She had expected him to ask what the thing was, or rush to help Fred. He did neither. He was still holding on around her, and his eyes stayed on the abomination. The shadow about his gaze had returned. Lucy had expected an expression of terror or disgust. He just looked grim. His lips set in a thin line and his brow furrowed. He hadn't taken his eyes off it since it had appeared. It was probably a healthy survival tactic, but the intensity of it concerned her.

Vincent was kicking the gate in. Whitehall was yelling at him, but he was clearly ignoring anything his old mentor had to say. He had a pistol in one hand and his sword in the other, and he was wearing that all too familiar expression. Lucy called it his 'if you want something done right' expression. He moved faster once he was inside the courtyard, racing down the line of the fence away from the entrance. He began to fire. The creature roared as his bullets struck. Vincent kept moving. He was trying to draw it away from the gate, back towards the library.

Half the creature pulled to follow him. Half of it twisted towards the crowd it could see in the street. The body scrabbled and snaked, straining itself. It bit and snapped as each piece fought for dominance. Whitehall's men positioned themselves defensively and began to fire. Bullets tore across the monster, splattering the ground with its decaying blood. Whatever cognitive processes fought inside it snapped. All the warring brains seemed to process the danger. It bolted.

Vincent's plan to give it a moving target and keep its attention failed. The creature ran from the Hunters and went straight for the crowd. Lucy remembered the ravenous hunger with which it had devoured the men it could get its hands on. They had to keep it away from the bazaar. Fred's shield wouldn't be enough, and she looked out of energy. Lucy tried to shrug Tony away, but he was already moving. She dropped her empty rifle and drew her pistols. There was no way she could stop that colossus with just her handguns, but she had to try.

It loped awkwardly towards the gate. She took aim from where she stood by the fence. Then Tony was there. He stood between the creature and the street.

"Tony!" Lucy screamed at him.

He ignored her. The thing barreled towards him, hunger glistening in its dead eyes. Tony stood his ground and raised his hands. Red lightning erupted around the creature like a storm. The light lifted it off the ground and held it, writhing in the air. Flecks of gold interspersed the red, shooting back and forth. Light covered the boy's hands like gloves. He grimaced, digging his heels in and gritting his teeth.

Fred dropped her barrier. She didn't look like she had the strength to hold it anyway, and she was staring at Tony. Her usual severe glare was tinged with alarm. The creature writhed and twisted, hissing and snarling as though in pain. Tony had all of its attention. The faces warped and bent to look at him. He stared back. He twisted his hands, trying to control the impossible amount of energy binding the monster. More of the streaks of lightning became gold, like an electrical storm. Then they began to dig in.

The heads began to shriek out of sync, until the air rang with a chorus of pain. The lightning pierced the hideous seams of the creature, and began to pull the pieces apart. Green-grey goo splattered across the ground. The monster screamed and struggled, reaching desperately for Tony. The mage was starting to shake, but his focus didn't waver. He pushed back. His hands tightened. A gross Frankenstein arm tore off the body. It hit the cobbles with a splat. Tony grimaced and pulled.

The creature ripped in half. Heads and limbs crashed across the ground. Sinewy arms smeared over the courtyard, and half-rotted skulls cracked open. What was left of the abomination, still standing, staggered back, screeching like a wounded bird. Tony sagged down onto one knee, half collapsed. The light was gone from his hands. The rest of the monster seemed to take this in. With fewer heads it appeared to have more control. It was smaller, but smarter. It lunged. One desperate bony hand clawed for the mage.

Lucy fired. Half the giant fingers exploded. Her holy bullets sank through the decaying flesh and hit rotting bone. They burst through the joints, shredding the fingers. The monster leapt back with a cry. Lucy ran forward, pistols up. Over her dead body was that thing going to eat her fake husband.

It saw her coming and scrambled back. She must have looked dangerous. The monster twisted away. It saw a gap in the Hunters and bolted along the fence line. She couldn't let it escape. Lucy jumped. She leapt up onto the fence and sprinted along the top, firing after the creature. It moved faster than she did. Its giant limbs swung in great loping strides. Lucy didn't miss a shot. She blasted through the limbs on her nearest side. They trembled. The injured arms couldn't support it. The creature tipped. It hit the ground with a splat. Ooze and blood ran out of it, pooling in the gutter of the courtyard.

Lucy ran up, emptying her pistols into the twitching mess. The heels of her boots slotted against the railing. She balanced carefully as she reloaded. The monster swiped for her. Its hands were too injured to support its weight, but they could still grab her. She cursed and leapt. Bullets scattered over the ground. Her nose filled with the sick scent of death as she dodged. A faint breeze brushed against her as the hand missed her by a hair. She hit the cobbles with a grunt and rolled. Another hand came down behind her.

She was in its space now. Too close. She sprinted as she came to her feet. A head strained for her, jaws open and dripping. She yelped and jumped. The only thing on her side was speed. She hadn't been able to finish reloading. Two bullets. She kicked off the monster's forehead, flipping over the face and firing one shot straight into its eye. Her feet squelched into a shoulder. She slipped, but caught her footing, and ran deeper into the creature. Somehow that seemed safer. There were rips deep through the flesh where Tony's magic had torn it. They formed tunnels, with edges burned and blackened. She staggered in where it couldn't reach her and paused, gasping.

An organ pumped beside her, black and glistening. She couldn't place it. Nothing about the creature was normal. Entrails webbed like sticky netting above her. At least she was safe from it in here. She listened to the beating beside her, like a heart. It didn't look like any heart she knew, but that didn't mean it wasn't one.

The body twisted beneath her. Lucy staggered and whimpered. It was rearranging itself. It was finding a new way to stand. She had to finish it before it could get up. She shot the twitching organ. The creature froze. She could feel it pause. Right tactic, last bullet. With a yell she lashed out and kicked as hard as she could. It wasn't enough to take down the monster. The creature spun. Lucy cried out and stumbled. It was like an earthquake.

Gunfire sounded beneath her. She leapt back as bullets ripped up through the flesh around her.

"Vincent!" she called through the gap. Lucy kicked through the perforated tissue, tearing a hole. Her old mentor was down there. He must have run after her. His grizzly face looked up through the remnants of ripped muscle.

"Get it, kid!" he yelled, throwing his sword up.

Lucy caught the weapon. Vincent rushed back, firing towards the other end of the monster and maintaining a moving target. Lucy twirled in, severing the ligaments around the heart. She cut the organ away and kicked it through the hole beside her. The abomination froze. She could feel the different pieces shivering as one. Above her the burnt webbing of one of Tony's seams quivered. She sliced through it and jumped up. If this thing was about to collapse, she'd rather not be inside it. She really hoped Vincent had gotten clear. The twisted corpses began to tilt. Lucy burst out of the top of it, bouncing between broken limbs and flipping out to the ground.

She hit the cobbles feet first, her breath trembling and her hands clenched around the sword handle. The creature hit the ground behind her, pieces tearing apart and slipping across the courtyard like spilt offal. Lucy whirled around. A rough arm caught her around the shoulders and buried her face in familiar tattered fabric.

"You alright, kid?" Vincent asked, pressing her into his shoulder. "You hurt?"

"I'm not hurt," Lucy pulled herself back from his

embrace and shook her head. "I'm okay." She held out the sword and he took it back with a sigh.

"You did good, girl. You did real good," he praised.

She grinned at him, waiting for the admonishment or even the reality to kick in. Neither looked like they were in a hurry to arrive. She shivered, letting a deep sigh move through her skin. Adrenaline still burnt through her body. The fear seemed so far away now. The creature was disgusting, certainly, but it was also vanquished. She turned to the gate.

"Is Tony—" she began.

He was already there. Tony staggered over to her, a handful of her spilt bullets gathered up in his grasp, and his dark eyes giant with awe.

"Miss Lucy, that was the most incredible thing I've ever seen!" he exclaimed breathlessly.

"What was?" she asked, looking behind her and hoping he wasn't talking about the twisted creature.

"You!" he replied. "You running along the fence and shooting and then jumping over it and flipping around and slicing it up! You took that thing down singlehandedly!"

"Tony, you ripped it in half," she reminded him gently.

"That was just magic though," he shrugged, pouring the bullets into her hands. "That thing shouldn't have been put together in the first place. It was a mistake. I was just fixing it."

"It was the most impressive display of magic I've ever seen," she told him. "I had no idea you could do that."

"Yeah," Vincent muttered. "It was on par with the beam of light you shot out of the ship." The Hunter looked down on them gravely, silently impressed. "I think we're going to need to have a talk at some point, boy."

Tony blanched nervously. Lucy moved to stand by him, then she saw Whitehall. He was striding towards them fiercely, his face like a thundercloud. Vincent saw him coming too. He positioned himself between the Chancellor and the children. If possible, his face was darker than his old mentor's.

"What in God's name do you think you're doing?" Whitehall demanded. "Look at this mess!"

"Back down, old man," Vincent warned. "She just saved your ass, so keep walking."

"You have no ground to stand on, Temple," Whitehall retorted. "You think anyone actually believes that girl is your daughter? This wasn't your fight, and you have no place getting involved with an apprentice like that."

"My apprentice is worth more than all of yours combined!" Vincent countered. "She is better than anyone you have trained in the last thirty years! Your rules are archaic, your followers are embarrassing, and your ways are dying! If me and mine weren't here to pick up your slack how many people would have died here today?! How many citizens would have been killed if that thing had gotten into the bazaar?! You think I'm a problem for bending your laws, but your system is broken!" Vincent fell silent as Fred rested a gentle hand on his arm. The look she directed at him was full of warning, although his glare acknowledged that her caution came too late.

"And you finally admit it," Whitehall scowled triumphantly. "We'll see how the Council likes your flagrant disregard and disrespect for everything our Brotherhood has held sacred over the centuries. You may be a fine Hunter, Temple, but you have been a disappointment to me and a thorn in the side of our Order for far too long. Your nuisance outweighs your skills, and your hubris is going to catch up with you."

"May it catch up with us both, Nigel," Vincent finished wearily. "If I have my due coming, I'm eager to know what I've earned. You, I think, have more of a surprise in store for you. You have turned your back on many innocents and their needless deaths. I hope I'm there when their ghosts find you."

Vincent turned away, guiding Lucy and the others with him. He didn't glance back. Lucy did. No one was looking their way anymore. Whitehall seemed content to let Vincent have the last word. The Chancellor looked like he had already won. He began directing his people to send messages and begin the clean-up.

She didn't have the nerve to ask, but Fred's glare told her that something had been said. Something important. Vincent had done something Fred wanted to slap him for. Again. The mage waited until they were up the street and out of sight of the library before she spoke.

"Sir," Fred began cautiously. "I know we just helped to save lives, and I have no regrets on that front, but you just put yourself in a precarious situation, and it feels like we're going in circles. We are no closer to Fajr or the cult she stalks. They are clearly three steps ahead of us. What if the next time they attack we're not so lucky?"

"What would you have me do, Fred?" Vincent sighed.

"Well, not throwing yourself and Miss Lucy into Nigel's firing line might have been a good start," Fred replied.

"Is Miss Lucy in danger from him?" Tony butted in.

Everyone looked to him. He had a serious crease between his brows and a hostile turn to his lips that spoke volumes of threat. The corner of Vincent's mouth gave a slight wry twitch at the sight.

"If you're around, boy, I seriously doubt it," he commented. "How did you do what you did to that thing?"

"I just did it," Tony replied. "I just do the magic like Miss Winifred teaches me."

"That ain't like I teach you, kid," Fred disagreed. "I couldn't do what you did." She gave him a firm look, and Tony's expression slid from ominous to thoughtful.

"I just..." he thought about it. "I just had to pull it apart. It was bad magic. It should never have happened in the first place. I could see what it was, and what had happened to make it, and I just had to undo that. It was like..." he stopped and fear crept across his face. He glanced at Vincent. "It was something from where you found me that time. It was part of that, and I could feel it the same way. Those people are there now..." Tony shook his head. "But I don't think there's any getting them back."

"You knew what made it?" Fred pressed curiously.

Tony nodded. "You couldn't feel it?"

"No," Fred shook her head. "You don't get that ability through my teachings. That's something you brought back with you."

Tony nodded again as though that wasn't really a surprise. "There's a thing in Hell – the Dreamlands, Darkness, whatever you want to call it – a thing at the center that calls life to it. It got me once. It has those people now. They tried to summon something and it didn't work. They got the spell wrong. Maybe they were new mages, young or inexperienced, and they didn't know what they were doing. The magic couldn't pull through what they wanted from the place they were trying to reach, so instead it pulled them through the magic. They were summoned as their own monster wherever they wanted it to be. I could feel them fighting it. I fought too. The best I could do was try and separate them again, after it tried to make them one." He shrugged. "I doubt it will be enough. The center draws all souls to it, to make them one. It's not as nice as it sounds."

"You see enough of things we see, it doesn't sound nice at all," Fred muttered.

"And that's what happened to you?" Lucy implored. "Two years ago? With the book?"

Tony nodded. "The magic that made that creature tried to make me like that too. It took my soul to the place theirs have gone." He hugged himself tightly despite the heat. "It wants me back. I can feel it reaching sometimes…"

Lucy wrapped him tightly in a hug, and nobody cared to stop her.

"Perhaps the cult will slow," Fred mused. "If they just lost a handful of members like that it might give them pause to consider what they are tampering with."

"Maybe," Vincent grimaced. "But unlikely. It may even have been a sacrificial test. Fajr is the only one who may know what they're up to, and we're not much closer to finding her."

"Actually, Doc, we might be," Tony offered, half untangling from Lucy to dig through his satchel. "I was about to give this to you before, but then that thing at the library happened. While you guys were inside I thought I should have a look around, maybe pull off a bit of snooping. I asked around and one of those market vendors told me that a young lady ran out of the library late yesterday like dogs were on her heels. She dropped this." Tony pulled out a small diary bound in blue cloth. "It's all full of funny squiggles, but I figured, Doc Temple, that you could read it." He handed it over to Vincent, eyes characteristically wide and begging approval. "At least, I hope so. I hope it's what he said it was, because he stiffed me for it. Cheeky rip-off bastard."

Vincent took the diary and began to leaf through it. His eyes traced the Arabic quickly, skimming through pages of roughly scribbled notes.

"How much do I owe you for this?" he asked Tony. The boy shrugged.

"It's no worries, Doc, as long as it's helpful. If it's a fake I'll be having words with that *rompicoglioni* though."

"It's not a fake," Vincent assured. "This is Fajr's. This is how we find her."

10

They returned to the house and Vincent spent the afternoon reading. The sun was getting low and the sky was on fire when Fred came and found him. He sat reclined in an armchair on a balcony overlooking the city, his research illuminated by the fading light. He looked up from the pages as she approached.

"You've had your nose in that thing for a while," she commented, sitting down in the chair opposite him.

"My Arabic isn't as good as it used to be," he replied, rubbing his weary eyes. "How are Anwar and Anisa?"

"They're alright," Fred answered. "They're more injured than they want to pretend, and they're worried for their daughter. You could go and speak to them yourself, you know."

Vincent sighed and closed the diary gently over his hand, using it as a bookmark. He leant back in his chair and looked to the darkening sky.

"I don't know what I'd say." He drummed the fingers of his free hand on the fabric cover. "They gave her all her uncle's old journals. She read them all. Naeem is a great source of inspiration to her. She learnt so much from his writing – I'd wager she's better than any of Nigel's people, hence all the grief she's given them. I don't know what Anisa was thinking, but she let the girl pursue this path and there were always going to be consequences to that." He pressed his lips together and let Fred wait. He could feel her looking at him expectantly. She knew there was more on his mind. He tried to find the words. "He trained her... from beyond the grave. The way she writes... it's Naeem all over again. She learnt what he learnt. I feel... I feel like I trained this girl, like I'm responsible for her now."

"We've got enough children to worry about, Vincent, without you picking up more strays," Fred commented. "I know it's your calling, but it's dragging me down too. I have Helen and Toby to worry about. Instead, I'm halfway around the world looking after a Mafia kid you got us entangled with."

"You're worried about his powers?" Vincent looked to her.

"You're not?" Fred raised an eyebrow.

"I've never met a mage like him," Vincent admitted. "That doesn't have to be a bad thing. He has a gift."

"He absolutely does," Fred concurred. "Which is why I agreed to train him. However, I don't know what his gift is. I don't recognize it, and I don't know where it came from. I don't know that it isn't just a curse. That kind of raw power, that limitless energy he channels, it's not his. It's coming from somewhere else. Directing it is putting him in the ground. You saw him faint after the attack on the ship."

"But he held his own today," Vincent countered. "You saw what he did outside the library. He was reversing black magic, undoing the darkness the cultists had unleashed."

"All magic is black magic, Vincent," Fred scoffed. "Witchcraft, eldritch sorcery, whatever you want to call it, it's all the same. There is no good or evil magic. There is only power, and the choice to use it as the caster sees fit."

"Then why does his look different from every other mage we've ever seen?"

"I have no idea," Fred replied. "That's why it frightens me."

"There are things we don't understand," Vincent sighed and rubbed his face. "There will always be things we don't understand. Hopefully Tony can help us learn something new, help us better understand the darkness we navigate. He found his gift in a place no one has ever returned from. A place so twisted and alien to all that the sane hold dear I'm surprised we managed to save him. Perhaps, as he untangles himself from it, we can untangle his gift and find out how right you are about the singularity of magic."

Fred rolled her eyes. Vincent grinned at her. He knew she thought him delusional when it came to magic. She was his expert, after all, and he trusted her judgement. If she was worried about Tony, then he needed to heed that warning, but he knew the boy's heart was in the right place. They wouldn't have been as successful as they were today without his gift.

"He saved a lot of people this afternoon, Fred," Vincent smiled. "Be gentle with him."

"I'm not being anything with him," she countered. "You want someone to be gentle with him, you tell your harlot."

"That's uncalled for," Vincent criticized her language, then considered her tone. "What are the kids up to?"

"Getting in trouble."

"Do we need to intervene?"

"Be my guest," Fred offered. "I'm not touching it."

"Do they have separate rooms...?" Vincent mused, sitting up straight. "We never told Anisa they're not actually married."

"We are actually married and we got separate rooms," Fred pointed out.

"Yes, but they know us," Vincent smiled. He sat back again with a sigh. "I suppose you're going to tell me it's too late to worry about it now."

"A little bit," Fred confirmed. "But what were you going to do? Yours can break down doors and mine can pick locks."

"Mine can pick locks too," he sighed. "I taught her well."

"That you did," Fred smiled. A grim severity settled in her expression as she watched him. When she spoke again her voice was soft, but the humor was gone from her tone. "You did something incredibly stupid today, Vincent."

"You're talking about losing my temper with Chancellor Whitehall?" he checked.

"You told him you broke Hunter laws," Fred reminded. "You're not allowed to train her. Women can't join the Brotherhood. You threw that back in his face and he will take it to the Council. It was a stupid and unnecessary risk."

"Let him do his worst," Vincent scoffed angrily.

"You say that, Vincent, but I'm worried he will," Fred pressed. "This is the same Council that excommunicated Stuart. They threw him from the Brotherhood and expected him to keep fighting without their aid until it got him killed. You said he was a better Hunter than you and that skill didn't protect him. They would have let him die or sent him to the rope themselves. He's only getting by now because you make sure he gets help behind everyone's back."

"I'm not sure sending him a Mafia apprentice can be called help," Vincent replied.

"It absolutely can, but that's not the only help you've given him," Fred argued. "You were the only one of the Council who voted to keep him. You knew he didn't deserve expulsion, and you've been looking out for him ever since. Your kind are quick to turn on each other in the face of tradition, Sir. I know you know this." She paused and a deep concern settled in the crease of her brows. "You always told me that you couldn't save Stuart because, right or wrong, he made a stupid mistake. He got caught because he was an idiot who did something he could easily have avoided. Vincent, I feel like I just watched you get caught doing something unbelievably stupid. You told Nigel, to his face, that you had taken on an apprentice against Hunter law. The lie was working. They could never have proven that you weren't just making sure the girl knew how to defend herself. For you to have committed a crime you had to admit that you did, and you fucking did. I couldn't believe my ears when I heard you say it. Sir, you endanger not only yourself, but everyone who finds shelter under your roof, and especially Lucy. You just threw her under a cart, and she doesn't even know you did it."

Vincent rubbed his chin as he let Fred rant. She was right. He didn't want to admit that out loud, but they both knew it anyway. He didn't have many friends left in the Order. He'd never had that many friends to begin with. But he had allies. Stuart Owens had been an ally, and he felt a small begrudging niggle at being compared to him. Stuart's mistake had been unbelievably stupid and costly, but it sounded like he was doing alright with Tony's cousin. Vincent didn't want to compare mistakes, but that was exactly why Fred had done it. He grimaced.

"Nigel will take it to the Council," he agreed. "I will have to deal with that. But perhaps it is time. We've talked about it before. I was never allowed to train you as an official apprentice. The law against women is stupid and dangerous. The darkness that plagues the world has never been more deadly than it is now, and we need warm able bodies like we needed them for the war. If anyone with the skill and passion of my girl wants to step up and help, I'm not going to turn them away."

"You did it on purpose," Fred growled him. "You want this fight."

Vincent glared at the sunset like it had personally offended him. "I've never understood why it matters so much what people have between their legs," he muttered. "We all bleed just the same when we're injured."

"You know I support your cause," Fred sighed. "But you're risking a lot."

"I'm not afraid of Nigel," Vincent stated. "The man's only lived this long because he's a coward. He's a coward who trains up others to die in his place. That spinelessness was the reason he wouldn't help me find the man who shot Naeem. He rolled over because it was easier to bury the issue than stand up for what was right. He will go crying to the Council about my broken law, and they will rebuke me, but I will plead my case and I will use Lucy as an example to all of them. My girl can best any of the old men at that table, and when she does, we will change the way they see the world."

"That's a lot of pressure to put on her," Fred warned. "Especially without telling her you're doing it."

"I will tell her when the issue arises," Vincent promised. "But until then she can just continue as she is. She won't let me down. I don't think she can."

"And what if you're wrong?" Fred pressed. "What if they cast you both out and come for her?"

"Let me deal with the Hunters, Fred," Vincent sighed. "I have the situation under control, whether or not you believe me. It may not have been a calculated move this afternoon, but I can use it to my advantage now." His eyes scoured the horizon. "I lost this fight once. I won't lose it again."

He could feel Fred watching him warily. She was concerned for him, and he appreciated it, but he didn't need it. Not right now. Right now he needed to finish reading the diary and continue their mission. Fajr had written of snippets of history she had found on the *Alshifaq Alfidiyu* cult and various places they had based themselves over the years. She spoke of an oasis in the desert that had once contained the key to their lair – the tomb of a pharaoh.

* * *

The bedroom was large and light and spacious, like seemingly every room in the house. A sizable, solitary bed stood in the middle of the room against the back wall, but there was still space to cartwheel around it, if one felt so inclined. Right now that didn't feel like a priority. Right now was tranquil and beautiful and Lucy didn't want to disturb the moment.

She stood at the window and watched the late afternoon sun stretch deep shadows across the city. The air was still hot and a gentle breeze drifted in like a warm breath against her. She had bathed and changed after her fight at the library. Her buttoned shirt and long trousers were a light linen that brushed softly against her skin. The view was so different from anything she knew. Everything about this moment gave her a yearning to travel she had never known before. The world felt bigger and freer. So did she.

She heard the door open behind her and turned. Tony froze when he saw her standing there. She smiled at him. He didn't smile back. His hair was still damp and uncombed from the bath, and he wore only a towel around his waist. He clutched it awkwardly to his body as panic consumed him.

"Uh, Miss Lucy–! Um, y-you... you shouldn't be here..." he stammered.

"It's our room," she shrugged.

"It's what?" he replied, looking like he was about to run back into the bathroom and hide.

She laughed at him. It was hard not to when he got like this, but part of her wasn't laughing. As adorable as his blush was, his discomfort echoed back to her. She stepped away from the window, moving towards him and exacerbating his panic.

"Tony–" she started slowly.

"Um, if you just let me get my things I can change in here," he replied quickly, the words tumbling over themselves as he gestured to the bathroom. His eyes stayed on the floor like he was scanning for snakes and he refused to look at her. He moved towards his bag, but she was already in the way. He hesitated, unsure where to flee. Lucy approached him, unbuttoning the front of her shirt.

"I thought we could pick up where we left off on the ship..." she suggested.

"I don't think that's a good idea," he shook his head.

"Tony, why does it always seem like you're more terrified of me than any of the monsters?" she asked quietly.

"It's not like that–" He looked up defensively. His eyes snapped shut and she watched his lips form a silent curse as he glimpsed her bare chest. "Miss Lucy... this... this isn't a good idea," he muttered.

"Why not?" she asked, stopping right in front of him.

"You know why," he protested. "I... I'm trying so hard to be decent... you make it so difficult."

She slid her top from her shoulders and discarded it on the floor. Tony seemed unaware with his eyes squeezed shut. He didn't budge. She slid her arms around his shoulders, pressing her skin to his and tiptoeing to kiss him. He didn't resist, but he didn't cave either. She held her lips to his mouth, breathing in the scent of him and letting her chest rise and fall against his. She willed him to surrender, but he stayed like a statue.

"I love you," she whispered onto his lips. "I love the way you try and do right by me, but we're not like normal people, Tony. We're not living by the rules of everyone else, so why pretend?" She took a gentle breath and brushed her lips down the side of his neck. Her whole body felt tight and pained. She wanted him so badly. "I know you think you're protecting me, but I live every day in much greater danger than you can put me in. If tomorrow kills me, I'll regret not doing this."

"Don't talk like that." His eyes snapped open. He looked down at her seriously, all traces of embarrassment gone. Tony raised his hands and traced her cheeks softly with his fingers. "You'll be fine, Lucy. I won't let anything happen to you."

She smiled and kissed his chest. He was still hot from the bath. His skin tasted clean and he smelled like soap as she drew her lips down his torso, kissing as she went.

"Lucy!" he exclaimed, panic returning. She stopped and lifted her face to his.

"Kiss me," she requested.

He obliged, maybe just to stop her from doing anything else, but she'd make the most of it. She latched on around his neck, gluing her lips to his. Her fingers tangled in his wet hair. He opened his mouth to her kiss and let her inside. Her whole body felt like fire. She kissed him fiercely, her breath turning to gasps against his tongue. His arms tightened around her, crushing her to him.

"Tony," she moaned onto his lips.

She turned him around and guided him back towards the bed. He hit the edge and sat down, pulling her with him. She straddled his lap. His towel was damp beneath her, but she worried he'd panic again if she tried to remove it. His lips moved down her neck and he squeezed her breasts. She wondered if she had him yet. He was easy to spook, but it was worth a try. She reached down between her legs, trying to feel under the towel.

Tony froze. Every muscle in his body seemed to tighten. He caught her wrist with an iron-like grip. Her fingers brushed the hard lump beneath his towel. His breath crashed rhythmically against her chest in panicked gasps. She kissed the top of his damp hair.

"Can I touch it?" she whispered. He stayed frozen. She couldn't pull her hand free. "Tony…?"

Slowly, inch by inch, he almost managed to relax. He let her wrist go, burying his face in her chest, his eyes squeezed shut.

"I ain't ever seen you lose a fight," he muttered. "Can't imagine I'll win this one."

"If you really don't want me to, just say," she

insisted.

He didn't respond. He just stayed, holding her, breathing heavily with his face buried between her breasts. She took his silence as an answer, carefully moving the towel and reaching down. She began to stroke him gently. Her fingers tightened around his erection, caressing it. It wasn't like she'd thought it would be, but she didn't really know what she'd been expecting. His arms held her tightly against his body as she played with him. He kissed her skin where his head rested. She could feel his breath, hot and heavy. His kisses became hungrier. She rubbed him harder. This was what she sought, to feel like he wanted her as much as she wanted him.

"Stop... stop!" he ordered. He pulled her hand away.

"What's wrong?" she asked.

He didn't answer. She brushed her lips against his forehead curiously, but he wouldn't look up. She kissed him again, adjusting herself over him. She wrapped her arms around him, holding him gently and running her fingers through his hair.

"Tony...?" she whispered.

He didn't speak, but his fingers found the drawstring of her trousers. Lucy felt her breath catch. Tony patiently unlaced the bow. He kissed her neck as he slid his hand under the fabric. She gasped as he touched her, clinging to him tightly. He started rubbing gently between her legs. She buried her face against his neck, moaning with pleasure. He pressed harder.

"Wait!" she gasped. "Gently."

"Like this?" He lightened his touch again.

"Yes," she moaned. "Tony… oh god…" She pressed her lips to his to silence herself, but it wasn't enough. She was gasping. "You…" she muttered. "I want you…"

Whatever resistance he had been attempting was foiled. He tipped her back onto the mattress and surrendered completely. They both did. She didn't know how much time dissolved in a haze of passion. It was clumsy but intoxicating. Everything she'd tried to learn in the past two years failed to prepare her for the reality. The raw sensuality of it.

The sun set over them as they moved together, tangling across the bed. Sometimes it felt like nothing could sate the fire of yearning in her, but she had him. It was all she'd wanted for so long. She let him take her first, but eventually curiosity got the better of her. She rode him now, moving exactly how she needed to. He moved beneath her, feeding her fire. The sensation built, the way she'd known it should. She could barely keep back a cry. She kept going until she felt like she might faint, until her body shook and trembled from the intensity of her orgasm. She could hear herself breathing. She sounded like she was crying. Finally, she slowed.

She didn't know how long it had taken. Time had lost meaning, but the last of the daylight was a sharp orange. Tony was staring up at her in complete awe. She groaned, sagging over him and letting her hair fall in her face. With a whimper, she pulled herself off him and collapsed at his side.

"Lucy..." he whispered. He rolled to face her and cupped her cheek in one hand. "Lucy? *Bella*...? ...How are you feeling?"

"Like I can fight God," she grinned, her face half-buried in the blankets. She gave a content giggle and nuzzled deeper into the bed.

Tony chuckled lovingly. "You probably could..."

"Good," Lucy muttered, rolling back slightly to face him better. "Vincent is probably going to tell us that's tomorrow's mission. I wouldn't be surprised."

Tony was still holding her. She raised a hand and traced a finger down his cheek, smiling at the look on his face. There was something so sweet about him.

"Thank you," she murmured.

He laughed. He clearly didn't think she was the one who should be doing the thanking. He leant over her and kissed her gently.

"You're the most amazing person I've ever met," he whispered.

"And don't you forget it," she teased.

"I won't," he promised earnestly. "Lucy... will you marry me?"

She laughed. He didn't.

"Oh Tony." She kissed his hand, still resting by her face. "You don't have to ask just because we did this."

"I'm not."

"It feels like you are... No, it's okay. Wait–"

He rolled away from her. She sat up, following him.

"No, Tony, I'm sorry–"

He rummaged over the side of the bed where his clothes had been dumped on the floor and turned back to her. She fell instantly silent. God, his face was so earnest. He held a small gold ring, intricately engraved with flowers. It was beautiful. Her mind went blank. She had no idea what to say. Fortunately, he began to answer without her having to ask.

"I talked to Doc Temple on the boat," he admitted nervously. "He said it would be okay... Well, he said that your opinion mattered more than his, and he didn't have any objections. I... Miss Lucy, I've loved you since I met you. I think you know that. It took me a long time to get up the courage, and I was worried the Doc wouldn't approve, being that you deserve better, but then... then when he said it was okay... and then when you cuffed me outside today, I just thought... I'm never going to find another girl who'll chain me to a fence to keep me out of a library."

Lucy covered her face with her hands as she dissolved into quiet laughter. She didn't mean to, but she was unusually high-strung in this particular moment, and it was such a Tony thing to say. She knew what he meant, but the way he'd said it was ridiculous.

"I mean you were looking out for me," he muttered. "I've never had anyone who cared like that before. You're the kindest, fiercest, most beautiful girl in the world. When I got myself free I just knew... I had to say something, do something. The diary was a fluke. I was looking for this. I thought I'd get it and say something maybe on the way home... maybe once all the chaos was over, maybe I'd be able to ask, but now..." he trailed off, pressing his lips together anxiously. He was a bundle of nerves, eyes downcast, fingers trembling.

Lucy watched as he steeled himself and met her eye again.

"This wasn't how I thought it would go," he admitted. "But Lucy Phillips, will you marry me?"

She reached out, closing her hand over his and the ring, and leaning forward over her knees. She planted a soft kiss on his lips.

"Is that a yes?" he asked nervously.

"Yes, Tony," she chuckled. "I didn't realize you'd been thinking about it seriously. I thought you were just worried about doing right by me."

"That's been on my mind for a couple of years now," he admitted. "I just... with my family and my ghosts..."

She cut him off with another kiss. This one lingered. She took her hand from his to touch his face, pulling him to her. He responded in kind, drawing her back into his arms. Her fingers traced his jawline and she curled up against his naked body.

"You're just perfect," she told him. "I'm not worried about your family or your ghosts. I'm tougher than they are."

"That you are," Tony smiled.

"Can I see the ring again?" she inquired cheekily.

"You can keep it," he grinned, offering it to her again. "It's yours."

Lucy inspected it curiously. It was very pretty. Tony slid it onto her finger in place of the fake she had borrowed from Fred. It fit better.

"How did you know?" she asked.

"I guessed," he grinned. "You have little hands."

"*Petite*," she countered.

"*Piccola*," he replied, linking his fingers in hers and kissing her again. "*Bella*."

The room was growing darker still and the last light of the day stained everything like iodine. Lucy reclined back against the bed, pulling Tony down over her. He followed willingly, without letting his lips leave hers. They didn't have anywhere else to go tonight, and there was nowhere else in the world she wanted to be.

* * *

A lone palm tree rose towards a turbulent sky. Stars chased each other in dizzying spirals towards nothing. Vincent stumbled towards the tree. Its fronds waved gently in a non-existent breeze. He couldn't remember how he'd gotten here or what he was looking for. Beneath the tree stretched an oasis. It glowed with a comforting light, but it was surrounded by death. Plant life stretched back from the small pool and gathered near the base of the tree, but it was littered with bones. The empty sockets of various skulls stared up at Vincent, and he stared back.

He staggered across the sand onto the soft grass beneath the tree, and he sank to his knees. It was comfortable here. It was peaceful. This was a place of knowledge and victory. Though whose he could not say. It felt like his, yet, as he rested back against the tree, he knew he was waiting here for death. Perhaps his death would prove to be victorious. He closed his eyes against the strange ghostly grey of the world and let himself drift.

A hand ran through his hair. It was a soothing touch, familiar and intimate in a way he wasn't used to. He wondered if it was Fred. It wasn't like her, but he couldn't think of anyone else it could be. He opened his eyes to the blank face of the Prince gazing at him like a dark mirror.

"You've been looking for me," the Prince said in his deep voice.

"I have, "Vincent agreed, feeling his body sag with the weight of his relief.

"I'm not that hard to find," the Prince told him. "If you need me, you just have to ask. I'll always come back to you."

"We have a deal…" Vincent recalled.

"We do," the Prince smiled. "Whatever you need, Doctor Temple. Your friends have been distracting you. You keep running off after humans. You don't really want them, but I understand your distraction. They are fascinating." His icy black fingers traced Vincent's cheek. "It's time to come home now."

Vincent nodded. That made sense. It was time to go back. He had found what he had come for, his purpose. It wasn't the people. It wasn't…

He blinked. This wasn't right. Not quite. He reached out a hand towards the Prince.

"What are you doing?" the Prince asked, his deep voice echoing as if from far away.

Vincent touched his face, or the space where his face would have been if he had one. His action mirrored the Prince's own gesture. The oily black visage rippled, the ripples cascading down his entire body and shifting his form. A face took shape, became real, a face so familiar it made Vincent's chest ache.

"You've been looking for me," Naeem said. He crouched by Vincent's crumpled form, his stance patient and his eyes sad.

"Yes," Vincent breathed, finally realizing the truth. "Yes, I have. I... I couldn't remember... but I do now! I've been looking for you!"

Naeem glanced over his shoulder, looking around the desolate oasis. He turned back to Vincent. There was a regret in his eyes that Vincent felt haunting his soul.

"Now you know where to find me," Naeem confirmed.

Vincent felt the hand move through his hair again. He started and woke. He was lying in a bed. The air was cool and the room was dark. He didn't know where he was. It took him a moment to recognize the room, the house. Anisa and Anwar's place. His guest room. Fred stood beside the bed, her fingers only just pulling away from his hair.

"I could hear you dreaming," she said.

"I wasn't using," he muttered. "Maybe something left in my system, but I didn't take more."

"What are you looking for, Vincent?" she asked.

"I'm not sure..." he replied. "Something... someone..."

"Who?"

He tried to blink, but he couldn't keep his eyes open. His lids were so heavy. He could feel her there still. He didn't want her to go.

"You..." he answered. "I'm looking for you..." His

voice was little more than a whisper, trailing into nothing as sleep took him again.

11

Vincent was used to waking before the sun, but this morning dawn rose before he did. He woke feeling exhausted and sickly. His dreams still plagued him. That was the trouble with the tonic, regular use made a restful night's sleep impossible. There was only work. Only exhaustion. Always answers. Knowledge was the poison and the antidote.

He bathed and dressed before heading to see Anwar, who was propped up in bed with his leg bandaged. He looked as tired as Vincent felt.

"Winifred told us what happened yesterday," he announced. "Your family are downstairs breakfasting with my wife."

"Good," Vincent sighed. "I'll need to get them packed again."

"You're leaving already?"

"Not properly," Vincent replied. "We'll need a boat and a guide, if you can arrange it. I have a lead."

"Consider it done," Anwar nodded. "I'll get my best people on it."

"Thank you," Vincent said.

"Just find my daughter, Doctor Temple," Anwar sighed. "Bring her home."

Vincent nodded and left him to rest. He staggered down to breakfast, letting his body explain all of yesterday's aches and pains in detail. When he reached the dining room there was an atmosphere around the table he didn't want to disturb, lest it try and draw him in. Fred was talking with Anisa, and the kids were steadfastly looking at their food. Presumably that had something to do with Fred's innuendos last night, and he didn't want to know. Unfortunately, his very presence drew attention.

"How are we feeling this morning, Sir?" Fred inquired.

Vincent grunted in reply as he sat down. It was a standard reply. Words were overrated. However, in company it felt rude, so he sought to add a light elaboration.

"Slightly better than when you checked on me in the night, but not by much."

Fred's brows knotted in confusion. She looked like she had no idea what he was talking about, but Anisa spoke first.

"Help yourself to breakfast, Vincent," their hostess invited. "If you need any help with the journal, I would be happy to assist."

"I've already spoken to your husband," Vincent nodded to her. "I have a lead and he is speaking to your staff about getting us a boat. We will leave as soon as transport allows."

"You're not going to tell me more than that, are you?" she accused.

"No," Vincent replied. "The deeper into this you go,

the greater the danger to your family. I do not want to bring Fajr home only to find that she is in more danger here than she was in the cult's shadow. Your home has already been attacked once. I don't want to draw further danger here."

"If we have already been attacked once, surely leaving us in the dark cannot protect us from future threats," Anisa argued.

"She has a point, Vincent," Fred chipped in. The gaze she directed at him was cautionary.

"I don't know as much about magic as you do," Vincent conceded. "But I do know more about hunting cults and their monsters. I've been thinking about the two attacks we've encountered since landing here. I was assuming, because of the attack on the ship, that the monsters were being summoned on us – on me – but what if they're not? The first attack was on the house, but we had only just arrived. The second was on the library, but that began a day before we got there. Everywhere I go is merely following a trail. What if they're targeting Fajr?"

"Then that is even more of a reason to involve me in my daughter's affairs!" Anisa exclaimed.

"Except I intend to find her, bring her home, and put an end to this mess," Vincent countered. "If nothing else I want to make sure the cult stops hunting your daughter. If I can convince them I am the threat and stamp them out, then she can come home safely."

"Good luck, Doctor Temple, but you don't know my daughter," Anisa huffed.

Vincent ignored that. He had a feeling he did know

Fajr now, quite well, especially given that he had never met her. If he could handle her uncle, he could handle her. Besides, he'd had a lot more practice managing unruly girls since then. Speaking of, his ward was sporting a new ring on her left hand. If that was all the trouble Fred had been referring to last night, then they were doing just fine. Still, it wasn't like Fred to misjudge her warnings. She was still glaring at the far wall like it had offended her. Her eyes were full of deep contemplation as she gazed over the rim of her teacup.

"A penny for your thoughts, Fred?" Vincent asked as he helped himself to breakfast.

"For someone who's never taken to the magical arts, Sir, you might be onto something with that theory," she commented.

"You don't always have to know how the machine works to see the pattern in its functions," Vincent shrugged.

"Yeah…" Fred mused, sipping her tea. "I don't have any experience with summoning spells, but I have studied them with regard to reversing them. It is possible that, without any physical object to tie their magic to Fajr, the cult is attempting to summon creatures to her location. That could be why their magic is going wrong. Summoning an entity to kill someone, without a physical object to direct the magic to that person, should be difficult bordering on impossible. Especially if all the direction they can give is something like 'the one who hunts us'. In that case, between Fajr, ourselves, and Nigel's people, those poor ugly devils wouldn't know which way was up. It might explain why that thing in the library was basically dormant until we arrived."

"It's as sound a theory as anything, until we get more evidence," Vincent accepted.

"Tony, what do you think?" Fred asked him.

Upon being addressed, Tony choked on his coffee and tried to look anywhere but at people. An answer did not appear to be forthcoming, and Fred glared at Lucy.

"You broke him," she accused.

"I did not!" Lucy protested.

"Segreti," Vincent raised an eyebrow at him.

Tony looked like he was on the verge of discovering invisibility magic in order to avoid the conversation, and he would not meet Vincent's eye.

"Any snippets of wisdom regarding summoning spells, Tony?" Vincent pressed.

"No, Sir," Tony squeaked. "I don't know nothing about summoning."

"The first magic you ever performed was to reverse a summoning," Fred reminded him.

"That was the book, Miss Winifred," Tony muttered. "I didn't do nothing."

"Tony," Lucy said his name as kindly as she could. "Your use of double negatives implies that you do know something and that you did do something."

Tony stared into his coffee like it contained an escape hatch. He blinked.

"You know what I mean though," he muttered. "All I know is that something went real wrong when they did their library magic. It's possible that they didn't know what they were doing or where they were directing it and they ended up sucking themselves through the spell." He grimaced. "That's terrible practice though. Amateur work. I... I expected the cult to be more of a threat... If that was really what happened... they're as much a danger to themselves as anyone else."

"Long may it stay that way," Vincent replied. "I'd rather have things go wrong for them than us. Perhaps such a mistake will put them off another attempt for a while." He paused. "Or perhaps they made a decision to sacrifice some of their younger, weaker members on a spell they were unsure about, presenting it as a test."

Silence reigned beneath his dark conjecture. There was only one way to find out. The road beckoned.

* * *

The day was hot and bright. Tony sat smoking a cigarette in the bow of the felucca as they sailed up the Nile. The cool breeze coming off the water ruffled his hair. Lucy was nestled beside him, resting under his arm and toying with her ring. It made him smile. He couldn't remember the last time he'd been this relaxed. It was possible he never had been. The strip of eternal blue ran endlessly before them, and the golden desert rose up either side. Distant hills and cliffs of tan, where sand and stone merged seamlessly, were all that separated the river from cloudless blue sky. He kept waiting for the gunfire to start, for some great and hideous monster to rise up and eat the boat, for the fight to find him. It always had before. Yet, the perfect warmth of the day seemed impenetrable to horror.

Vincent and Fred hadn't said anything about the ring. Tony knew they knew about it. Lucy had been all but flaunting it. He was glad she liked it. When the shopkeeper had shown it to him he had been sure it was right, but that hadn't made him less nervous. Fred was sitting halfway down the felucca, on the other side of the sail, and Tony could see a book on her lap. Everything above her waist was hidden. He was grateful they didn't have to avoid looking at each other. Vincent was down the back talking to their skipper. He was the man with the plan, and he could speak the language. The rest of them were just doing as they were told.

It was afternoon when Vincent finally asked him to help. He'd been starting to feel lazy, just lounging around the boat, but he'd never been much for sailing. He was very good at following orders, however. Vincent made the most of that and gave him brief but specific instructions. He was five minutes into adjusting the sails when he noticed Fred had taken his spot to converse with Lucy. Panic gripped him.

"Segreti!" Vincent called him.

Tony turned to him meekly. Vincent's long strides brought him off the bench at the side and down to Tony's level.

"You doing alright, kid?" he asked.

"I just saw Fred with, um, Miss Lucy..." Tony muttered.

"Miss Lucy, huh?" Vincent smirked. "You worried

about the ladies having a chat?"

"No, Sir," Tony blushed. "Just... Miss Winifred... y'know, she can be a bit..."

"Well, maybe Lucy needs someone to put their foot down with her," Vincent reasoned.

"She didn't do anything wrong!" Tony defended, knowing full well that having no regrets didn't make their behavior above reproach. Vincent gave him a long look and Tony felt himself shrinking under it.

"Boy, you are a terrible liar," the old Hunter commented. "How did you ever make it in the Mafia?"

Tony shrugged. "Uncle Elia keeps me out of the big stuff. He just gets me to do a little magic here and there."

"He ever get you to use magic to kill anyone?" Vincent asked.

Tony shook his head. "No, Sir. I wouldn't do nothing like that, unless I was helping Hunters. Fred would have my guts if I did. Mister Ferro's not a bad man, Doc. He wouldn't ask me to."

"Elia Ferro is a very bad man, Tony," Vincent countered. "He is as criminal as they come. However, I think he might be a little afraid of you..."

"Afraid of me?" Tony was too bewildered to maintain his embarrassment. "No way, Doc. *Capo* ain't afraid of me."

"You have a naïve view of your uncle, boy," Vincent sighed. "You are a gentle and delicate person capable of incredible violence. You have a power and morality Ferro knows he can't comprehend. The only reason he isn't bullying you into taking down his enemies is because he's scared of you, and he doesn't know what he might end up unleashing."

Tony's face fell and he gazed down at the water. Of course the day had been too beautiful to stay that way.

"He's scared I'll turn into a monster 'cause of all the ghosts..." Tony muttered.

"No, boy. He's wary, not stupid," Vincent corrected. "He knows you're not a killer, not really. Not unless forced. He doesn't want to force you, not because he's kind, but because you might decide to save lives by turning on him."

"I would never!" Tony protested.

"Never say never, kid," Vincent warned. "What if he told you to kill innocent people?"

"I wouldn't do that either..."

"I would hope not," Vincent replied. He sat back down on the bench and stretched his legs out stiffly in front of him. The old man squinted up at Tony through the daylight. "But if you're going to marry Lucy, I need to know you can make the right call when things get tough. I am not having Ferro drag her into his business just because she's marrying into your family."

"That won't happen," Tony swore. "I... I'm not sure what being a mage is going to mean for me, Doc. I don't know what the future is going to look like... but I ain't letting Lucy get dragged into my family's business. No Sir. No way."

"Then we're good," Vincent grinned into the sun, leaning back. "I'm glad we had this talk, Segreti. When we last spoke I knew you were serious, I just didn't realize you were so proactive. But like I said on the last boat – as long as she's happy. I suppose congratulations are in order."

"Thanks, Doc," Tony smiled. "For the approval and the chat." His expression shifted to a grimace as he gazed at the river and remembered their conversation on the ship. "God I hope demons don't start attacking us this time…"

Vincent threw his head back and laughed. Tony did not join in. He was serious. That was probably what the old man found so funny.

Further up the felucca, Lucy was sitting with her elbows on her knees and a glare on her face. She was aware she had adopted a 'fight me' stance when Fred had come her way, but she felt she needed an aggressive defense. Being that it was Fred, the odds of this being a polite conversation were not high.

"Cute ring," Fred commented as she sat down.

"Thanks," Lucy replied. "Tony gave it to me."

"That much I had deduced," Fred smiled, crossing her legs and setting her closed book on her lap. She gave Lucy a very serious look. "Are you being careful?"

"What do you mean 'careful'?" Lucy asked. "I'm always careful."

"Brushing aside the gross hyperbole in that," Fred dismissed. "I'm asking if there's a chance you're pregnant. Are you taking any precautions? He might have given you a ring, but you ain't married yet, and I don't know how long we're going to be away for. Are we going to need a shotgun wedding on the banks of the Nile?"

Lucy paled. "Our papers already say we're

married."

"I'm not worried about your papers, girl," Fred sighed. "I'm worried about you and Tony. I'm worried that you're pushing. I'm worried…" Fred gave another deep sigh.

"You sound like Vincent…" Lucy muttered.

"No surprises there," Fred smiled ruefully. "Look, Lucy, what I'm trying to say is… I know your father tried to use you as a virgin sacrifice – twice. I can't imagine how horrible that was, and how many different ways it must haunt you. Tell me that isn't why you're pushing Tony. Tell me that isn't why you did it."

"It isn't," Lucy sniped coldly. "I guess it's just a lucky side effect."

"Then why are you pushing him without implementing any measures to keep yourself safe?" Fred asked.

Lucy met her eye, unafraid, and gave her a long look. Her expression settled into scorn.

"You're not worried about me," she snapped. "You're worried about him. You think I'm some kind of floozie who's going to get bored and ditch him."

"I can be worried about both of you," Fred retorted. "And don't put words in my mouth. Listen hon, you're not the first girl I've been around this tree with. Hell, when I was your age, I made some terrible decisions. I know how alluring it can be to have someone like you, to have someone love you, especially when it feels like the rest of your life is falling apart. But, yeah, Tony is a delicate kid. He's sensitive, and I do worry. Comparatively, you're confident and bold and you can push him around. I need to know you're not going to bully him under the guise of affection. I need to know you're not going to get bored of him and drop him once you grow up, especially if you don't take care of yourself and end up with kids."

Lucy stayed silent for a long time. Fred didn't push for a response or act like Lucy was ignoring her. She was happy to give the girl time to process. By now Lucy was hugging her knees and she looked troubled. Finally, she spoke.

"I love him," she muttered. "I do love him. I'm not trying to get myself in trouble. Fred... how... how do I know if..." Her face screwed up in fear. "I wasn't careful. I didn't– and we did–" She blushed scarlet. "How do I know if I'm pregnant?" she whispered, full of dread.

Fred smiled at her. "You're not pregnant, Lucy."

"But how do you know?!" Lucy hissed. "It was only last night! I can't possibly tell so quickly! What if I am?!"

Fred rolled her eyes. "I'm a witch. I can tell. You ain't pregnant. Just because you haven't got yourself in trouble doesn't mean you can't though. I want to make sure you two are being careful. I don't want to end up raising your kids just yet."

Lucy took a deep breath and looked out over the water. Her eyes were still worried.

"How do I do it, Fred?" Lucy whispered. "What do I do to stay safe?"

"Well, there are some obvious options," Fred replied. "But you're a teenager with the survival instinct of a lemming, so maybe we rule those out."

Lucy poked her tongue out at Fred. Fred grinned at the rude gesture.

"You knew what you were doing was reckless," Fred warned. "You don't get to be sour with me just because reality is hitting now. You're a wild child, Lucy. I imagine that's one of the things Tony admires about you, but he was worried about this – you can't convince me he wasn't. In his own timid way he's trying to be responsible and you smashed straight through that like a sledgehammer. He doesn't have the nerve to stand up to you."

"That's not true," Lucy protested. She shirked as soon as she said it and her blush deepened. "I don't mean to bully him. I just... I like him..."

"And he likes you," Fred agreed. "Thing is, Tony's good at doing what he's told, and he's scared of messing up. In his family, you screw up bad enough, you get shot. Your father gave you free rein before he went evil, and Vincent is probably worse. Everything you've learnt about consequences you seem to have learnt the hard way. I'd really like to change that for you, if you want to listen. I don't want this to turn into another tough lesson."

"Thanks Fred..." Lucy muttered bashfully.

"No worries, hon," Fred replied, placing an arm around Lucy's shoulders and kissing her hair.

Lucy felt like she was going to cry. Tears stung her eyes. Her chest hurt. No one had really treated her like this since her mother had died. The closest person would be Helen, Fred's lover, who played mother to Lucy sometimes, usually when she was mothering her own son Toby anyway. The thought of Helen and Toby helped settle Lucy's grief.

"I suppose you never had to worry much about such things," she sighed to Fred.

"Not so much," Fred agreed. "But you're not the first girl I've looked out for."

"Is Vincent discussing the exact same thing with Tony?" Lucy asked, watching her mentor having words with her fiancé down the boat.

"Possibly," Fred shrugged. "You never know with Vincent. He might just be threatening the boy's life. Y'know, making sure he's put the fear of God in him before he lets the kid marry you."

"Tony said Vincent gave him permission to ask on the boat over here," Lucy admitted.

"He what?" Fred stared at her.

"Tony said Vincent gave him permission before we arrived in Egypt," Lucy repeated. "He said that Vincent said he had his blessing, as long as it was what we both wanted. As long as I was happy. He wouldn't lie about that."

"No," Fred agreed through clenched teeth. "Your boy is too stupid to lie."

"He is not!" Lucy protested. "He's too honest to lie, there is a very important difference!"

"Write that down," Fred ordered as she stood up. "I want to be able to show it to you in five years."

"Are you going to go and beat up Vincent?" Lucy inquired.

"We'll see..." Fred replied.

"How do you expect me to learn to be gentler with

Tony if this is how you treat your husband?" Lucy pressed.

Fred glared down at her. "Don't push it, kid."

Lucy sighed and sat back. Vincent could handle himself, and he wasn't going to let himself be bullied by Fred if he wasn't wrong. She watched the mage stalk down the side of the felucca towards the men. The notion Fred had planted that she bullied Tony stung. She hoped that wasn't the case. She never meant to bully him, she was just trying to get him to let go a bit, live a little.

She watched Fred reach the others, but they were too far away and speaking too quietly for her to hear anything. Vincent's expression didn't change. He stared Fred down with those sharp dark eyes that told her she wasn't going to win this one. Yet, it wasn't his victory to be had. Whatever Fred was saying, it had an effect on Tony. His expression became utterly imploring. She began to falter under his wide innocent eyes. Lucy grinned. She giggled to herself as she watched Fred reluctantly soften against Tony's kind face. He was so sweet. So earnest. All hers. She started toying with her ring again. It was beautiful. So was he. She promised herself she would be a good wife, provided she was still allowed to slay monsters, and it wasn't bullying to insist on that.

* * *

They sailed the river for three days. The second day took them past Cairo. Vincent smiled as he watched the kids behold the pyramids for the first time. He had forgotten what wonder felt like. Too many years had been spent in the dark, fighting for what felt like the last vestiges of light. This strange found family he had ended up with gave him hope again. Those kids, for all the trouble they posed, were an anchor for good in his life. A reminder of what he fought for.

But the shadows in the back of his mind lingered. No beautiful world could shift them. He knew why he was out here. Why they were all out here. He had his family to protect, and that extended to Fajr. She had a day's head start on them, but they were making good time up the river. He had her notes. They would find her. They had to.

Dusk was a pale gold stain on the inky twilight of the third day. It sapped the color from the world and turned the desert grey. Their guide had been pestering Vincent to let them stop. He didn't want to be sailing after dark this far up the river, and he didn't want to end up in crocodile territory. Vincent didn't want to agree, but he was reluctantly starting to admit to himself that he might have to. He had been watching the landscape slide by and nothing had marked the trail from his dreams. In the dark he would be lost.

Just as he was reconciling himself to halt, he saw it. The lone tree atop the bank, stark against the last of the light. Vincent directed their guide to the area and told him to pull up. Excitement sparked the old Hunter's chest. After days of rest he could still pursue the trail. The Darkness would not hinder his mission.

There were weak protests as he rallied the others,

about scorpions and snakes and the dangers of the desert at night. Vincent brushed them away. There was nothing out there that could kill them faster than they could kill it. Besides, they were so close. He could feel it. The darker the desert became, the closer to the other world he felt. Almost as if the guiding hand of the Prince drew him where he needed to be.

Vincent bade their guide wait with the boat. He had supplies fit for a two day stop, and that was what he would do. If they hadn't found Fajr by then, he shouldn't keep lingering for them.

They pulled up on white sand and Vincent led his crew ashore. The tree stood tall on the bank above them, with greenery cascading down to the water. Everything but the silver earth was stained black by the night. Vincent started the climb. He could feel the other world calling him. The dream hadn't finished. It had been left incomplete. He had to resolve it. He had to know how it ended.

He clambered to the top and didn't wait for the others. The stars were spinning in the dark sky. He could see them swirl. It was making him dizzy. He stumbled to the tree. The bark was rough between his hands. This wasn't right. Not yet. Someone was calling to him. A voice on the wind. He turned, collapsing back against the tree. A hand struck him sharply across the face.

"Vincent!"

He blinked as Fred's face swam into view. She was glaring at him.

"Vincent, what is going on?!" she demanded.

"You're scaring me."

"I..." he winced and pinched the bridge of his nose. Everything was so hazy. "I think... I think I was dreaming..." he muttered. "Or half dreaming..."

"Where are we? What is happening?" Fred pressed.

"We're in the desert, looking for Fajr," he sighed. "I'm... I'm following something..."

"What, Vincent? What are you following? Because I am not following you for another step if you're just running into the desert like a madman, and I'm not letting the kids follow you either," Fred warned. "We don't have enough water to survive getting lost out here." She nudged the heavy satchel slung across his shoulders that rested beside him. "If I go through your bag, am I going to find vials of that poison you snuck with you? Are you high on it now?"

Vincent shook his head. "No... no, Fred. Not since the house."

"Are you sure?"

"Go ahead and look," he invited, safe in the knowledge that she hadn't threatened to check his pockets. He couldn't afford to be stuck without it if he needed it, whatever Fred might think. He looked past her to the sky. The darkness was bright with stars, scattered like a spray of paint across the heavens. They didn't move, not fast enough for him to see. He slowly pulled himself back to reality.

This was not the oasis. The tree was still the marker from his dream, he was sure of it, but the oasis he was searching for wasn't attached to it. Behind them stretched the canyon of the Nile, and before them lay endless rolling desert. It dipped and rose in silver waves, but there was no sign of his path. He opened his satchel and dug inside for Fajr's journal. She had sketched maps of where she intended to travel, where her research had directed her to the cult. Unfortunately, her sketches weren't easy to read. His team appeared to have come far enough up the river to be the right area. After that, things got a bit messy.

"*Atabae altalu almaksur,*" Vincent read under his breath. "*Atajih ymynan...*" He pulled a face, as though he wasn't sure he was reading it right. The light was faint, her scrawls were clearly hurried, and his Arabic was far from perfect. He looked up again and traced the horizon under the stars. In the tumbling sand and stone stood a jagged outcrop that looked as though it was missing a corner. A broken hill.

Vincent pushed himself wearily to his feet. Fred leant over to help him up. Her anger had burnt out with her fear, now that she knew he was alright. He staggered upright, still holding the journal, and pointed towards the hill.

"We go that way," he instructed.

No one argued. Vincent steeled himself and led on. The others followed carefully behind. He knew they were all watching him, watching for any sign he was slipping, but perhaps that wasn't a bad thing. His throat stung with the need for the tonic, and only his absolute certainty that a sip now could prove fatal was keeping him from it. Back home he never took it on missions. He drank it so carefully he had hidden his using from Fred. Here that wasn't an option.

The moon rose as they travelled. It crested the landscape like a halo, shining over them with a holy white light. Vincent followed the journal as best he could, but the river was well out of sight when the clues ran out. If he'd taken a wrong turn somewhere...

He sighed. At least he could find his way back.

"Are you alright, Sir?" Fred asked.

"Just getting my bearings, Fred," Vincent replied. He gazed across the moonlit desert. It was beautiful. It was a shame all his adventures were forced by rising evils. It would have been nice to just explore the wonders of the earth for the sake of it. "We've been walking a while. Maybe take five if you need to, just while I work out where to go next."

"Do you need some help?" she checked.

"How's your Arabic?" Vincent asked.

"*Touché*," she nodded.

Fred sat herself carefully in the sand and took a sip of water. Lucy and Tony followed suit, curling up together. It was cold out here at night, but the walk kept them warm, and when the sun rose it would get hot fast. Vincent was lost in the depths of the journal when he heard Tony speak up.

"Hey, look, there's someone out there," the boy pointed. "No way..."

"It can't be..." Lucy added.

Vincent looked up. A small figure in the distance looked his way, and then disappeared over the rise. Vincent recognized them instantly.

"Naeem..." he breathed. He took an involuntary step forward. A hand grabbed his arm. He looked back.

Fred had a tight hold on him and she looked grim. He hadn't even heard her stand again. She held her other arm out to the kids, who were half-risen from the ground, biding them stay.

"Tony, what did you see?" she demanded. "As much detail as possible."

"Oh, uh..." He looked around, but no one was going to answer for him. "I saw a man, over there on the ridge. He, um, was wearing blue... Uh... I think... I think he looked like the merchant that gave me the diary... but it's dark, I'm not sure..."

"Lucy," Fred cut in. "What did you see?"

"I saw a man there too," she answered. "I didn't realize he was wearing blue though–"

"I didn't ask you to corroborate," Fred interrupted. "I asked what you saw."

She gave the girl a firm look, and her hold on Vincent didn't falter. Lucy bit her lip and looked between them all before continuing uncertainly.

"I, uh... I saw... I saw a man in a suit. He, um, he looked... well, he reminded me of... Y'know that last mission, Vincent? The one before we left? There was a servant who set my shoulder... I thought it looked like him..."

Fred looked back to Vincent. He could tell by her eyes she had heard him, even though it had barely been a whisper.

"Who did you see?" he asked.

"No one," Fred replied. "You all started looking away when Tony pointed, and I didn't see a soul." She paused and the serious look between them lingered.

"You know it's a trap, right?"

"Then it would be rude not to spring it," Vincent smiled grimly.

Fred looked like she wanted to protest, but she held her tongue. Vincent gave her a nod. He knew what she wanted to say, and it deserved acknowledgement, but this was their only lead. If someone was going out of their way to guide him, it was only fair he take the hint. At least they had the benefit of knowing it was a trap. Slowly, Fred's fingers relaxed and she let her hand drop from his arm. No more holding back.

The kids picked themselves up and put away the water. They watched Vincent expectantly, even though they too had seen the direction of the stranger.

Vincent took point again and led them deeper into the desert. The sand shifted under his feet and slowed his pace, but he stalked persistently onward. As he crested the rise where he had seen the shadow of Naeem, he saw the oasis. It was small and sat nestled in the valley. He searched the ground at the rise and found no trace of footprints. Nothing to suggest someone had actually been here. That meant an illusion. Strange. Strange and powerful.

There was nothing to hide their approach, nothing to use for cover. He motioned to Fred and she nodded. If something attacked them coming down the dune, she was all the defense they had. She knew it, and she showed no fear at the thought. They started down, slipping and sliding their way through the sand. Vincent felt like the ground was shivering. It was unsteady, and sand cascaded down the bank as they shuffled forward. The sensation eased out as they neared the oasis. Vincent kept his eyes peeled, but everywhere looked deserted. This was a source of water in the desert. He expected wildlife, if nothing else. The only living things seemed to be the plants. As he reached the edge of the grass he felt it. That chilling darkness. Something bad had happened here. He stood, closed his eyes, and breathed deeply, trying to get a feel for the evil.

A loud thump broke his concentration. He turned to the sound, and saw a cloaked figure climbing from a hole in the ground. They had flipped a stone slab into the sand like a trapdoor. Vincent drew his pistol, but didn't raise it. He heard a rough feminine grunt as the slight figure hauled themselves up and onto the grass. They were almost completely covered in an abaya and niqab, but he caught the dark eyes of the girl staring at him as she came to her feet. She drew her blades from beneath her robes, and had a sword in each hand before he could react. He knew exactly who she was. She didn't know he'd been searching for her though, and demanded his identity in Arabic.

"Vincent Temple," he answered her.

"You should not have come, Vincent Temple," she warned, abandoning her fighting stance but keeping her weapons ready. "You have no business in my country."

"Your mother asked me to find you."

"I know," she snapped. "And she was wrong. She never should have contacted you. Leave. Now."

"I can't do that, Fajr," Vincent sighed. "I promised

your parents I would bring you home. I can't break that promise."

"You would drag me kicking and screaming to my home and leave the world to the hands of sorcerers and madmen?" she snarled. "You would let them test their magic here?"

"Nope," Vincent shook his head. "I'm going to stop them too."

"You and your English Council have no business in Egypt anymore," she warned. "You have killed enough of us. Get out. Get out before you get me killed like you did my uncle!"

Fred stepped forward, but Vincent threw an arm out to keep her back. He knew Fred would want to defend him from those words, but as far as he was concerned Fajr had a point. It was fair, even if it hurt. Even if it seared.

"I don't want you to get hurt, Fajr. I don't want anyone to. That's why I'm here."

"Tell that to the beasts they unleashed on me at the library!" she retorted.

Vincent took a deep breath. He could feel the sand shivering again. He was tired. His throat burned. He didn't want to fight her on this, not when he agreed with her. She should be allowed to fight the cult herself. He should have to answer to her for Naeem's death. But right now he had a promise to keep, and he needed her to be safe. Women weren't allowed to be trained as Hunters, not in either of their cultures. She would have no support and no blessing if she continued down this path, and she wasn't experienced enough to take down an entire cult herself. He had served with men who had died for that lesson.

"We killed that thing," he told her. "Fajr, child, I can't let you do this alone. Put down your weapons and talk to us."

"I'm not disarming myself in the presence of my uncle's murderer," she snapped.

Fred broke. She shoved through and Vincent was forced to grab her by the arm. Her hands had begun to glow. It wasn't strong, but in the darkness of the moonlit desert it looked bright. The red glow was like firelight in the oasis.

Fajr's face was covered, but Vincent could see the girl flinch at the sight of magic. His hand tightened like a vice on Fred's arm. She wasn't going to show her anger here. Not against a child. A sharp click sounded behind them. Vincent turned his head and saw Lucy raising her rifle.

"Lucy!" he snapped.

"Sorry, Vincent," she replied, taking aim. "But we've got bigger problems right now."

He followed the line of her shot. She was aiming just shy of the trees. The sand was shifting. Something was moving through it. That was what kept making the ground shiver. It was tunnelling straight at them.

"Crap," he muttered. He released Fred's arm and drew his sword just as the sand erupted like a geyser before them.

TOMB OF ENDLESS NIGHT

12

The desert exploded. A wave of sand sprayed across the oasis. The creature was massive. A giant snake ribbed with thick plates of armor shook free of the earth. Its wide elongated head stared down, bearing multiple eyes on either side. It had a long thin mouth, like a snout, which stretched open to expose vicious fangs.

Lucy fired. So did the creature. Sickly green sludge sprayed from its mouth. The group dove apart as one. Vincent heard the sizzle as the sludge hit the sand and caught the edge of his coat. Sure enough, when he looked back, one corner of the tattered hem was dissolving, and the sand was melting to glass.

"Acid!" he bellowed the warning.

Lucy's shot had gone wide when she jumped. At least she hadn't been hit. Vincent leapt up and dove for the beast. His sword slashed uselessly against the carapace. He fired his pistol. The bullet left a spiderweb crack and ricocheted off. Not good. It was too big to escape from. Vincent raced away as fast as he could, but it wasn't fast enough. His feet slipped in the sand. The creature towered above him, acid dripping from its jaws. It snapped at him. Vincent tried to dodge. It was futile.

A loud crack echoed through the desert. The beast smashed its face against a dome of red light. Vincent glanced through the magic shield to Fred, who stood braced to hold her spell. The monster shook its head, trying to comprehend what had gotten in its way.

Then Fajr raced in. She rushed the monster's body near the grass, where it protruded from the sand. Her swords flashed. One blade drove under an armored plate. The monster shrieked and thrashed. The sword stuck fast. It was ripped from Fajr's hand. She bolted back into the garden. The worm roared. Spines unfolded down its back, quivering in rage. It lunged for the running girl.

A bullet ripped into one eye. The thing shrieked as it was knocked back by the blow. Lucy was crouched in the sand with her rifle poised. The monster turned its snarling head, trying to find her. Tony stood with his hands out. An arcane circle kept trying to flicker into life before him. The flashing light attracted the creature. It opened its mouth wide.

"Tony!" Lucy cried, tackling him out of the way of the acid.

It splattered harmlessly in the sand, which smoked as it melted. Beside them, Fred unleashed her power.

"Not the time to be trying new spells, Segreti!" Fred yelled.

Tony muttered something, but the sound was lost in the sizzling of Fred's magic. Red lightning crackled across the worm's body, trying to penetrate the gaps in the carapace. The monster twitched and flailed. It was hard to know if the magic had hurt it. It reared back.

Vincent took another shot at it. It screeched and sprayed a band of acid across them. Tony yelped and threw up a shield. It blazed red for a moment, stretching across all four of them, before gold light crackled across it. The acid sloshed over the barrier and hissed, but the magic held strong. Tony threw it back, splashing acid across the creature's armor. It smoked and spat, but the carapace took little damage.

The snake shied away from the onslaught, squirming back through the sand. These people weren't the reason it was here anyway. It dove for the oasis. Fajr, hiding in the bushes, was down to one sword. The creature's nostrils flared as it sniffed her out. She dove before it struck. It gave chase. Vincent rushed after them. He couldn't let it hurt the girl.

Fajr raced through the grass. She dodged around the pool of the oasis, weaving between the trees. The worm ploughed ahead. Its body rose to the surface, avoiding the roots below, and snaked across the ground. It opened its mouth to spray. Another of Lucy's bullets smashed it in the back of the head. Its acid sprayed off target. The burning sludge cut through trees and scarred the greenery. Fajr yelped and jumped as the felled trees crashed before her. She pounced onto a falling tree. It hurtled towards the earth. Fajr kicked off it. She leapt across the tumbling trees. Her boots barely touched the bark as she sprung lithely through the carnage. Momentum propelled her as she hit an upright tree and ran straight up the side, flipping back off the top. She lashed out with her sword. The blade caught in the spines. She drove it further, spearing the back of the monster's neck. It tried to throw her off. Fajr clutched the handle with both hands, hanging on for dear life.

The snake writhed. It thrashed violently, trying to shake her free. Vincent was still racing up behind them. The creature's tail smashed him in the side. He went flying. Vincent hit the sand with a grunt. His bag flew off. The vials in his pockets scattered. Everything was strewn across the patch of desert, but the soft sand eased the landing. Vincent grimaced and took aim from where he lay.

Then Tony was there, still trying the same spell from before. Vincent could see the circle flickering. The boy focused, sweat dripping down his cheek as he directed his magic. His eyes flashed black. The circle held. Everything went white.

Vincent could hear the snake screaming. Its agonized shrieks echoed through the entire desert. He blinked rapidly as the world came back into focus. Tony was half slumped in the sand. The kid swore helplessly.

"It didn't work..." he groaned, weakly staggering and tripping.

Vincent saw the snake. A massive chunk of its armor was missing from its back. He didn't know what Tony had been trying to do, but that looked like it had worked in Vincent's book. Fajr was already crawling to the naked patch, blade free. She drove her sword into the creature's exposed flesh, tearing down. The worm screamed like it had never known pain before.

Vincent finished lining up his shot and fired three times. Each bullet struck true, burying themselves in the body of the monster and exploding with holy runes.

Fajr drove her blade deeper into the creature as Lucy's bullets followed Vincent's. The holy bullets ripped the monster apart as Fajr shoved her sword up into the spine. The entire worm shuddered. Its body gave one last death twitch and fell to the ground.

Nothing moved. Vincent felt there was great wisdom in not moving. His ribs felt tender where the worm had smacked him. He just wanted to lie in the soft sand and not do anything for a bit. A gentle clinking brought him back to reality. Fred was picking up the vials.

"Wait... Fred..." Vincent muttered, trying to roll onto his side and crawl up.

Fred popped the cork out of a vial with her thumb and tipped the contents into the sand.

"STOP!" Vincent's voice cracked like a whip.

Fred completely upended the vial, but she didn't move to empty the next one. Vincent glared murderously at her. He could feel his temple throbbing. More clinking came from behind him. Lucy was helping Tony up, so that left Fajr. The girl had retrieved her swords and pulled the front of her niqab under her chin, exposing her face. She had picked up some of the vials and was inspecting them.

"What is this?" she asked, raising one at him.

"Medicine I take," Vincent stretched the truth. "Fajr, child, are you alright?"

"What do you care, colonizer?" she retorted, still studying the vial. "You know your kind can leave now, yes? We won our independence years ago, and still you come and mess up our lives."

"I'm American," Vincent clarified. "Not British."

Fajr laughed at him openly. "Good for you, white man." Her tone was scathing at the notion Vincent's distinction might matter. She held up a vial and shook it. "This is the drug, yes? The one my uncle wrote about. Your gateway magic."

"It's poison," Lucy answered, walking over with Tony's arm around her shoulder. The boy looked gaunt, but he could walk. Fajr gave them a grudging look.

"You are his daughter?" she asked.

"His apprentice," Lucy replied coolly.

Fajr eyed them all up. There was deep suspicion in her gaze, but less aggression than her words. Something about the group wasn't adding up for her. Vincent wanted to know what, but there was a time and a place, and perhaps this was neither.

"We need to get you home," Vincent sighed and held out his hand. "The vials, please."

"I don't think so," Fajr disagreed, stowing the vials inside her abaya. "I have worked too hard to get here, and I will not let the likes of you ruin it."

"Where is here?" Tony asked, looking around. The oasis was half destroyed, and everything looked silver and black in the moonlight.

"This is an ancient base for the cult I'm tracking," Fajr answered. "I managed to..." she sought for the word in English. "Join...? I joined the clues."

"Combined the information?" Lucy offered.

Fajr nodded. "Yes, combined. I put all the pieces together. The clues led me here. It doesn't look like it has been used in a while."

"How did you find this place in the middle of a desert?" Tony asked incredulously.

"How did you?" she retorted.

Tony pointed at Vincent. Vincent sighed. He had found it faster because he cheated, but Fajr's long head start had required him to cheat to find her in time. Still, he had used a portion of the girl's old clues to get there. She was thorough and talented. If the world was different she would make an excellent Hunter. Once again, Vincent found himself begrudging his archaic institution.

"Fajr–" he began again.

"No, Temple," she shook her head. "If half of what my uncle wrote about you is true, then you are a Hunter – first and foremost. The cult must be stopped, and I will not turn back. I will not. You know I am right. I have seen what your help does to my family, so I warn you, stay out of my way."

"I can't do that," Vincent sighed. "My job is to eliminate the threat and get you home safe. If I have to drag you kicking and screaming... so be it."

Fajr snatched one of the vials from inside her clothes and held it up threateningly, as though to destroy it.

"I wouldn't," Vincent warned dangerously.

"Okay, hold up," Tony interrupted. He stumbled off Lucy's shoulder and planted himself in the middle, holding his hands out either side. "This feels like it's getting outta hand. Doc, I didn't sign up to go kidnapping ladies. Also, Miss, I'd swear on my life Doc Temple means you no harm, even if he's talking like a punk. You did mighty fine with those swords. Why don't we just team up to beat this freakshow?"

"Vincent Temple is the one who got my Uncle Naeem killed," Fajr snapped. "I will not work with the likes of him."

"You have no idea what you're talking about!" Fred spat.

"Vincent didn't get anyone killed," Lucy agreed. "He wouldn't. One of the other Hunters killed Naeem. Vincent was devastated."

"Is that what he told you?" Fajr retorted. "How many of you knew him back then? How many of you were even alive back then? You think you know what happened? Were you there?"

"I didn't know him then," Fred admitted. "But I have always seen the cross he bears from it on his soul. You speak so cruelly, kid, yet you weren't born back then either. You're an ignorant child spouting anger. I dealt with plenty like you in my time, but you best believe I won't stand for this kind of talk about Master Vincent. You keep that dirty mouth shut, or I'll shut it."

"Fred!" Vincent snapped.

"I'm dealing with it my way, Sir," Fred replied. "You had your chance."

"Oh, you're dealing with me?" Fajr snarled. "How exactly is that going for you?"

"Better than it will go for you, kid," Fred warned. A small glow crept up her fingers.

"Enough!" Tony ordered. Golden light flared in a patterned circle around him, disrupting the sand before fading to nothing. "*Smettila!* Everyone cool it, or I'm finishing it."

Vincent watched silence fall across them all. If Fajr's words hadn't been so cutting he might even have smiled. He could almost hear Elia Ferro in Tony's warning. The boy had undoubtedly seen his uncle end enough arguments that way. It was funny to see him emulate it. It was funnier that it had worked.

"Thank you, Tony," Vincent gave him a nod.

Tony returned the nod, grateful at the affirmation.

"You're his sorcerer...?" Fajr asked, her expression wary of Tony and his magic.

"He's my sorcerer," Lucy grinned before anyone could say otherwise.

Tony smiled sheepishly. His challenge still hung in the air, especially after the impressive show of magic he had displayed against the snake, but he couldn't hold it. Now that he had everyone's attention, he didn't know what to do with it.

"Fajr..." Vincent began again softly. "What did you find in the hideout?"

She glared like she wanted to snap again, but held her retorts back. Perhaps she knew she it would be easier to stop the cult with help, or perhaps she knew it would be easier for the cult to kill them if they fought amongst themselves.

"Nothing useful," she answered finally. "The texts that led me here were ancient. This place has not been used since before my lifetime, I think. It is too old."

"Is there anything that talks about where else they might be? Sometimes the old temples reference each other."

"The texts on the walls are not legible," she retorted.

"The water has been in before. It is drier now, but it was damaged once." She gave him a sharp look and teased the vial in his direction. "Why not take your gateway magic and find out where they are?"

"It's not that simple," Vincent replied.

"Also," Fred cut in. "If I see him using that poison I'll box his ears."

"Winifred's threats aside," Vincent brushed over that, "using the tonic is not a magic fix for anything. It is extremely dangerous. There is no guarantee that you will find the help you seek, but there is a guarantee that it will hurt you, possibly kill you. I've been using it for years to cheat fate, but I am under no illusions that it is killing me."

"You're not cheating fate," Fred growled. "You're addicted."

"I'm not addicted," Vincent lied, fighting the itch in his throat. "Being a Hunter is dangerous. You have to be faster, stronger, and wiser than what you hunt. Some of those creatures have existed longer than time. If winning those fights isn't cheating fate, then I don't know what is."

Fajr sighed as she listened to them bicker. She reached into her clothes and pulled out another couple of vials, then she held them out to Vincent. He approached her slowly and took them. She handed them over without threat of leverage.

"You can check the bunker," she relented. "But I will not leave until we have found an answer. It is my home and my people in danger. If I do not fight for them, no one will."

Vincent took the vials with a grateful nod and pocketed them. Fajr indicated the hole in the ground, before stalking to a tree and sitting down in the grass beside it. Vincent felt a weight fall from his shoulders. It was a blessing to have reached this understanding, at least. He still had a fight with Fred to go, but Fajr wasn't going to stab him in the back if he turned around, and he might as well search the bunker for clues. Walking away to focus on the mission was a good way of convincing Fred he was fine. Besides, he had his vials back from Fajr. That was something.

He started across the grass. It felt good to have solid earth beneath his feet again. The others were following him. He had a strong feeling that Fajr knew better than to try and run off while they weren't looking. Even if she did, he could follow her trail now. She wouldn't get far, and he was pretty sure she knew that. He reached the edge of the hole and looked down. The darkness was absolute. Given the proximity to the water, it was easy to believe the place had flooded before. Perhaps it had been built long ago when the land was different. So many of the dark places had been.

Lucy brought over a torch, and Tony hovered at her shoulder as she handed it to Vincent. Fred watched them all seriously. She also had not forgotten that Vincent owed her a fight, but she was keeping her vials until the appropriate moment. The scent of evil washed out of the hole as Vincent shone the light down and leant over the edge. It was still strong here. The drop down wasn't far. He was about to climb in when Tony whirled and cried out.

"No! Stop!" he yelled.

Vincent turned, and realized Tony wasn't looking at him. The boy was looking at Fajr. The girl sat with her legs crossed, leaning back against the tree where they had left her. Her eyes rolled back. An empty vial rolled across the grass from her limp fingers.

13

Vincent rushed to the slumped girl, but it was too late. Even as he took her by the shoulders he could feel her body go limp with the drug. He pressed an eyelid up, but her eyes were black. The same black his went when he ventured into the Dreamlands. The same black Tony's went when he channeled his dangerous magic. He set her gently back against the tree and started to rummage in his pocket.

"Don't you dare!" Fred yelled, hurrying up behind him with the children in tow.

"I have to!" Vincent retorted. "She's never done this before, she doesn't know what she's doing, she has no guiding light to come back to! If I don't get her out she could die in there!"

Fred stopped, towering over him as he knelt on the grass. Vincent glared stubbornly up at her as he pulled out a vial.

"You know I'm right," he finished.

He could see the resentment in the set of Fred's lips. She wanted to push back. She wanted to argue. But he was right about this and Fajr's life hung in the balance.

"How do we help?" Lucy asked.

"Keep a light for me to come home to," he replied.

They both glanced at the torch he had returned to her and she nodded. Vincent sat himself down opposite Fajr and popped the cork of another vial. Fajr was already beginning to shiver. He tipped the vial back, swallowing the contents and letting the cool, bitter liquid sooth his throat. It only took a few seconds for the soothing to become burning, and then reality warped.

Vincent woke to the muffled sound of crying. He opened his eyes and found his starry gaze directed at the twisting earth. The ground beneath him was soft. The same bone dust he had fallen through before. Except now it moved. It swirled gently beneath him as though being drawn into a massive vortex. Vincent raised his eyes to see the swirling center on the horizon. It was far away, but it would reach them. It would reach all things. One day.

Trees of bone and tendon roped up around him in a sick mirror of the oasis. A black lake of blood, decaying and ancient, filled the acidic air with an overpoweringly putrid odor. In front of him sat Fajr, shivering on her knees. The Prince stood over her. One inky black hand rested over her face, and it had begun to melt. Dark ooze completely coated her face and dripped down her chin, sliding down her neck. She twitched repeatedly and the sound came again, sobbing or choking.

"Let her go," Vincent rasped, struggling to his feet.

"You do not give orders here, Doctor Temple," the Prince replied soothingly in his deep rich voice. His other hand rested on Fajr's back, and he pushed her deeper into the ooze of himself, spreading down her body. "She asked for this. Would you deny her what you so often claim?"

Vincent stared. He had let the Prince's wisdom wash generously over him so many times... but he had never seen it happen before. It had always seemed so soothing, so peaceful. The culmination of endless searches finally finding a deeper understanding. A connection with something other. This... This looked horrifying, like a nightmare. She looked like she was dying.

"Where is she?" Vincent asked.

"A place you would not seek to go," he replied.

"Send me anyway," Vincent demanded, striding forward and kneeling before the girl.

"Always the hero, Temple," the Prince smiled fondly at him. His faceless head had already turned from the girl. He'd been gazing at Vincent through absent eyes since the old Hunter arrived. "It would be imprudent of me not to warn you against the action, but you already know that..."

"Just do it," Vincent gritted his teeth. He didn't need a lecture, especially not one he'd had before. The Prince was his friend, and always warned him, but Vincent made his own choices. It was why he always came back.

The Prince smiled facelessly, as he always did, and reached out to Vincent with his other hand. Vincent closed his eyes against the swirling madness of the heavens. He felt the Prince's fingers caress his face delicately. The touch was cold and soft, like refreshing cool water. It washed over his head like a fountain of life. He couldn't fathom what about it made Fajr twitch and writhe. The sensation was a peaceful one. Then the

Darkness swallowed him whole.

* * *

Lucy clutched the torch as she watched Fred standing over Vincent. The beam of bright light exacerbated the darkness. Fred looked exhausted. She looked resigned. Her frustration had nowhere to go, and it just seemed to fizzle out as she stood over the slumped old Hunter.

A match flared as Tony lit a cigarette. He always needed something to fidget with, especially when things got tense. The glow from the end illuminated his face in the night and brought out the dark shadows around his eyes. He sighed a pillar of smoke into the sky and ran his fingers through his slicked hair.

"I'm gonna need that torch," Fred commented.

Lucy started from her contemplation of Tony to meet Fred's eye. The woman was looking at her shrewdly.

"This torch?" Lucy replied. "But... but what about Vincent? He said he needed a light to come back to."

"Then we're just gonna have to move them too," Fred shrugged. "I want to check out that old cult lair. Tony, if I grab the girl, can you carry Vincent?"

Tony pulled a face. Vincent was heavy, and carrying him was dubious, but Tony could certainly try and drag him over the grass.

"I can get his feet if you get his shoulders," Lucy offered.

Tony nodded. He stubbed his cigarette out on the hard carapace of the dead snake nearby and tucked the butt behind his ear. Lucy propped the torch in the side of her bag and helped Tony haul Vincent off the ground and to the edge of the pit. Fred followed with Fajr in her arms. They went down carefully, but the drop wasn't dangerous. Fred went first, and Lucy passed Fajr to her before following them. Tony struggled to pass Vincent down for the women to catch before bringing up the rear.

It was cold in the underground space. A cave-in had left only a single rectangular room accessible. The walls were lined with ancient stone, and sunlight hadn't seen this place in centuries. Still, the preservation was poor. Fajr had been right about the water damage. It ran in obvious trickles around the walls, and tide marks drew themselves along the stone like a height chart for bygone floods. Sand had made it in and sat thick and compact around the edges where the water had drained into the ground.

Lucy pressed on the sand with her fingers. It felt cold, but it wasn't damp. She felt better about leaving Vincent and Fajr lying on it, although she was still anxious about having moved them. Fred knew more about such magic than she did, and Lucy trusted her, but there was something about the tonic and what it did that made her afraid to mess with it. It made her skin crawl. So did this place. She missed the sky intensely. Something was haunted down here. The kind of haunting her own home had once suffered from.

"This is an evil place," Tony muttered, relighting his cigarette. "What do you want to do, Fred?"

"I want to investigate it," she replied, taking the torch from Lucy and scanning the walls.

"I thought you didn't read Arabic," Lucy commented.

"I don't," Fred smiled. "But this isn't in Arabic." Sure enough, as Fred narrowed in on snippets of preserved carvings, lines of hieroglyphics peaked out from the damage. She held out a hand and traced some of them gently. "This is an ancient arcane language. The mystics of a time forgotten by ours used it."

"Can you read it?" Lucy asked curiously, peeking around her shoulder.

"I can try and translate it," Fred nodded. "It would be remiss of me not to." She steadied the torch and began to make her way methodically down the side of the room.

Lucy hung at her shoulder and followed her inquisitively, but as soon as it became clear that Fred wasn't translating out loud she lost interest. Tony was sitting on the cold, clumped sand with their unconscious friends. He smoked his cigarette and watched them lie there. Lucy felt her chest tighten. The last thing she wanted was something to drag him back into dark memories. This place had a bad air about it. Evil lingered. She didn't know what Tony had seen in the Darkness, but she worried at the way his eyes lingered on the sleeping figures. What could he see in their faces?

He rubbed his tired eyes, unaware of her watching. His gaze stayed down, roaming the floor. Lucy blinked. She wasn't sure if he was focused on the tonic users after all, but he was definitely avoiding looking at the walls.

"Tony...?" she moved over and sat beside him. "Are you alright?"

"Yeah, of course," he replied, perking up.

"You're allowed to be tired."

"You never seem to be," he smiled. The shadows on his face were as dark as ever, but there was a cheeky spark in his eye when he looked at her. The usual squeak of nerves didn't make it into his voice, and the deep ease with which he spoke was reassuring. "I'm doin' okay, Lucy."

She sat down beside him and slipped an arm around his back. He returned the gesture and pulled her close, turning his face away to breathe smoke towards the hole in the roof.

"I trust you, but you should tell us if you're wearing thin," she commented. "That spell you did out there must have taken a lot of energy. I can't imagine what pulling through that much magic would do to someone."

"It ain't so bad," Tony shrugged. He tapped ash into the sand. "I'm getting better at it. Besides, the spell didn't actually work."

"It looked like it worked pretty well from where I was standing," Lucy replied.

"I was trying to banish the monster," Tony confessed.

"You what?!" Fred broke her concentration from the wall to turn on him.

Tony flinched when he looked up at her, but whether it was at Fred or at the sight of the walls was hard to tell.

"I was thinking about what you said earlier, Fred," he admitted. "About how my magic is different from yours – how we don't know what it is or how it works. I thought... well, maybe I should focus on what I know how to do. The first thing I ever did with magic was banish something. I thought I'd try and copy that power again."

Fred stared at him so intensely Lucy began to cower, but Tony stared back calmly.

"Segreti," Fred began through clenched teeth. "Do you remember what that magic did to you?"

"Of course, Fred," he replied solemnly. His eyes glazed as they traced over the walls, and he blinked rapidly to focus himself. "I know what it did, but... but maybe that was more the book than the magic? Or it was the book's magic? Either way... I feel like I know the theory, y'know? I can't explain it. I told you I felt like something came back with me. There is something in me, maybe a part of myself that was in the tree, it knows things I can't explain, but I do know them."

"Tony, experimenting with knowledge and power you can't control isn't something I'm going to support," Fred warned. "It's too dangerous. What if it hadn't blown the creature apart? What if it had blown you up instead?"

Tony shook his head. "It wouldn't do that, Fred. I know what I'm doing."

"Really?" she raised her eyebrow with characteristic suspicion.

"I didn't know I knew until this talk, but yeah, now that I have to defend it, I do know what I'm doing," he insisted. "This ain't some parlor trick, Fred. I know my onions. You spent the last few years teaching me the basics. I got that down. I keep trying to hold the power back and rein it in to make it do your spells... but the best things I do with it I do when I let go."

"I'm not saying I ain't grateful for all the things you and your power have done, Tony," Fred sighed. "But that magic came from a dark place. I've seen power manipulate people before. Just make sure it's not trying to get you to do something that will send you back."

Tony paused at her warning. He tore his eyes from the walls and looked down at the sand again, scuffing the heel of his boot where he sat. Lucy snuggled in closer and Fred turned back to the carvings.

"You were in a tree...?" Lucy whispered.

Tony nodded. He didn't say anything more. Fred had shot his confidence, and Lucy wasn't even sure she was mad about it. The mage had done it with Tony's best interests at heart. None of them wanted to see what happened when he was pushed to breaking point. No one wanted to see what would happen if the magic ate him.

Lucy sat with him in the sand, watching Vincent lie completely still. It was impossible to know what was happening with them. She half expected twitching or screaming – like a nightmare – but there was nothing. At least they were both still breathing.

Further down the room, Fred began to mutter curses as she dragged the light over a large picture painted on the wall. It was ancient and the water had eroded it until more than half the paint was missing.

"What's wrong?" Lucy called to her.

"This is exactly what we're looking for," Fred muttered. "But I can't read it."

"I can," Tony offered, stubbing his cigarette out in the sand. He stood and walked to the wall. Lucy hurried to follow him, and saw Fred start when she beheld his face.

"Tony!" Fred exclaimed.

Lucy caught up. Tony's eyes were completely black. He held out a hand and placed it on the wall. Light spread out under his palm, restoring the painting and filling in the gaps. Lucy grabbed him, but his hand didn't budge and the work was already complete. He blinked a few times, clearing the darkness from his eyes, and looked down at Lucy with her arms wrapped around his chest.

"What?" he asked curiously. "I told you, I know what I'm doing." He let his hand drop from the wall and slid it casually into his pocket, draping his other arm around Lucy as she clung to him.

Fred was watching them like a hawk. Lucy knew something was wrong, but just like Fred, couldn't prove it. Tony was using his power to help. That was what Fred had been training him for this whole time. Maybe he really was learning how to use his power to do things Fred didn't know. Maybe he was getting a handle on the different magic. But it was dark magic...

Tony was unfazed. He raised his hand again to point at the image as he described it.

"It's an ancient map of the region, back when it looked different," he offered. "These little symbols everywhere, they're the locations the cult would hide. All the different hideouts could find each other."

"And you know this because..." Fred coaxed in a tone of voice that suggested she knew his statement to be true.

"Magic," Tony shrugged. "You know this because you studied, Fred. I guess... I guess I just went to the school of hard knocks, if you can apply that here. I know because... because the roots know, and they share that."

"The roots know...?" Lucy echoed.

"Alright. Okay," Fred muttered under her breath. "Okay. Sure. Let's... look, let's just take a copy of it so that when the others wake we can show them and be ready to go."

Lucy obediently took a small notebook and a pencil from her bag. She didn't like this, but she didn't have a better idea.

* * *

Vincent stumbled into the cave. He knew where he was the instant he arrived. He didn't need the toxic air of the Dreamlands or the poison in his veins to feel pain here. He had been to this place so many times it felt like he never left. He didn't understand how he hadn't become desensitized to it over the years, how it felt fresh and real and raw every single time.

Echoes of gunfire ricocheted off the walls. Bullets sprayed the room. Vincent sank to his knees. It was already happening. Silence began to fall. Somewhere in this room his past self was clutching the still warm body of the boy he had been responsible for. The friend he had promised to look after. Vincent stayed where he knelt, grief fresh and sharp, and wiped the tears from his eyes. He had no desire to look.

A hand touched his shoulder. He looked up, expecting some wraith, some ghost of Naeem come to torture him further, as he so often found. It nearly was, but not quite. Fajr still had her niqab under her chin and the resemblance to her uncle was not lost on Vincent, but there was nothing aggressive in her eyes anymore. It felt like another trick, but somehow Vincent knew it wasn't. She had seen something here…

"Did you see him?" Vincent demanded, suddenly desperate. "Did you see the man who shot him? Every time I came here searching… I… I could never make it out. I could never be sure. Did you see the man who shot Naeem?"

"No," she shook her head, then slowly knelt by his side. "But I saw you."

The way she was looking at him was alien. It reminded him of Fred's look sometimes. He didn't understand the why, but he could comprehend the what. She had seen his grief. He could see it in her eyes. Decades of his own pain shone back at him. It was hideous and tragic. Like drops of blood washed into a gutter, lost and hopeless, still full of the life they had been, but could no longer be. Vincent could see the conception of his endless grief in Fajr, and she held no grudges now that she knew his pain. None of that made sense. He had done nothing to earn her forgiveness. This was not a place to come to be forgiven. This was a place of torture. You had to earn knowledge.

It was possible the Dreamlands had shown her Vincent's pain to hurt her, to make her feel as he did, but why return her to him if she would attempt to cleanse his conscience? His brain made the connection a second before he heard the sound. Vincent lunged. He shoved Fajr to the ground, holding her down and shielding her with his body. He felt the bullet tear through his side. He'd had worse. It was only a single shot. This world was simply trying to replicate an event. It was simulating real fears.

Vincent rolled back with a grunt. He pushed Fajr into cover behind a lumpy rise of stone. She held tight and dragged him with her. He hissed with pain. A trail of blood smeared across the rocky ground. Sound rose up behind them, some sickening inhuman wail. It grew in volume and pitch. Vincent shivered at the noise and dragged himself after Fajr. He pressed a hand to his side. Blood gushed sticky and wet through his coat. His nausea rose, though from the sound or the wound he wasn't sure.

Something slithered heavy and wet across the ground. He groaned. Fajr squeezed his hand. He squeezed back. With a grunt of pain, he raised himself up to look over their rocky cover. The center of the cave shimmered. A gateway to an astral plane sparked and twisted like the soul of a midnight nebula. Monstrous black tentacles slid out of the starry cluster as though some hideous harbinger sought to pull itself through.

"At least we know what the cult is trying to do," Vincent muttered.

"I don't have my swords," Fajr stressed.

"No," Vincent sighed, well aware that he had none of his own weapons either. "This realm does not belong to us." He struggled up, blood dripping between his fingers. "To venture here is to surrender your mind to all that time and space will allow."

Fajr stood carefully and helped Vincent up. She pulled his arm around her shoulders. The cave began to crack and crumble around them as the portal drew bigger. The wailing intensified. Vincent winced at the sound. He winced at his pain. And he watched the birth of an apocalypse with patience.

"What is it to look at the heart of a dark star come to devour our world, and feel awe over madness?" Fajr asked softly.

"It is its own madness," Vincent replied in kind. They stood, arm-in-arm, and watched the void stretch as the creature inside it sought to come through. He could sense her deep contemplation at his side, and he felt completely calm as the darkness came for them. It was almost as though he stood with the Prince himself, the soothing company of the shadowy figure easing his pain and absorbing his terror. The warm comfort of the Darkness bestowing its love.

With a stubborn huff, Fajr shifted Vincent's weight on her shoulders. He gasped in pain as his wound pulled, and his hand tightened over the bullet hole.

"I am not mad," Fajr stated boldly. "And I will not die here."

She moved for the rough stone tunnel behind them, half-dragging Vincent with her. He stumbled along at her side, wincing with every step. She kept a tight hold on him. He knew his fear should be deeper. He knew the threat was real. He knew this world was trying to kill Fajr and make him watch. With every step they took that fear grew. Deep in the cave was the sweet safety of death. Fajr was adamant it wasn't his time. She was going to make him live.

They staggered through the tunnel. The pain in his side stabbed violently. It felt like it was tearing. It felt like the bullet was scorching. His chest tightened. His breath caught. The pain and the fear kept growing. His boots scuffed the rocky ground. The sound of the wail grew behind them. It was joined by a rising slither.

"Come on, Vincent!" Fajr huffed, dragging him faster.

"Leave me," he ordered.

"And abandon the opportunity to shoot you myself?" she gasped. "Unlikely."

Vincent smiled. It was an alien action in this torturous world. Reality nearly split. No one should smile here, save for the hot grip of madness. Vincent's smile was not insane. The only part of him that wasn't, in this place. He didn't know if he had a type, or if he just brought attitude out in people. Lucy spoke to him like that. Fred had been doing it for nearly two decades. Naeem used to rib him with the same dry, sarcastic wit. Fajr was just like her uncle, even though she had never met him. The thought was a spark of bright inspiration, so sharp and real it took its own form.

"Vincent?" Fajr panicked as the air began to glow.

"We're near the door," he replied. Newfound

strength surged through him. He took his weight from her and hurried forward, keeping his arm around her shoulder.

The wail turned into a full-blown scream. The sound made him dizzy and he stumbled again. He pressed forward, holding tight to the girl, the two of them guiding each other. His head protested the noise. It felt like his brain was throbbing, his ears bleeding. This thing knew he was escaping. It didn't want him to go. The light kept growing. He felt like he was coated in black tar. It oozed across his body, but he was pulling free. The tension across his skin became stringy. It began to tear. He ripped himself free, pulling Fajr with him.

They both fell, gasping, into the sand. The air still burnt, but now it was bright. Walls of rock rose up around them like a massive chasm. The sky was alive with screaming chaos. Vincent and Fajr sprawled apart as they fell. She looked up in abject terror at the hellscape before them. Vincent looked back to the path they had come from.

"There!" he pointed.

She looked. There was a crack of a doorway in the rock wall. It had been carved, ornate and monstrous. Tentacles of stone sucked hungrily around the frame, groping for the world, birthed from a deadly symbol in the center of the structure. That was it. That was their goal. The end of the world. That was where the cult was hiding.

The world was already warping. Vincent grabbed Fajr again, holding her protectively.

"This is where things get bad," he warned her, as the last of the Dreamland's hold washed away.

* * *

Vincent woke in sand and worried he was still dreaming. Everything hurt. He felt like he'd swallowed fire. Even his eyes burned. He couldn't bring himself to open them. Fajr screamed. The sound broke him from his personal torture. He rolled onto his side and vomited blood and ooze onto the grainy earth beside him. Hands grabbed his shoulders.

"Vincent!"

The familiar sound, scent, and feel of Fred pulled him back into reality. He blinked up at her. It was dark and cold. The stone walls around them and sandy floor beneath them felt like a tomb. Panic gripped his heart.

"You're okay, Vincent," Fred soothed him. She hushed him as he scrabbled frantically in the sand. Her calm eased his agitation and proved his panic unfounded. There was a dark concern in her eyes, but Vincent recognized the judgement. That wasn't something to fear.

Beside him Lucy was calming Fajr, who pressed her sleeves to her weeping eyes. The girl's breath trembled and shook as her outburst subsided. Leaving the Dreamlands hurt. The Darkness got under your skin, and it tried to come back with you. Those who could slip in by accident while dreaming found it easy enough to slip away again with only a troubled mind. Those who took the tonic and broke down the door to enter had to battle to leave. Leaving the Dreamlands could be fatal.

Vincent took deep, gasping breaths as he pulled himself back to reality. They were underground in a room full of strange carvings. He remembered collapsing on the grass of the oasis. The women were gathered around him, while Tony stood away looking curiously at Lucy's journal. At least everyone was accounted for.

"Where are we?" he grunted, trying to sit up.

"Inside the lair," Fred answered. "We thought we'd investigate while you two were out. A lot of it's caved in, but Tony's getting us somewhere."

Of course, the pit Fajr had been inspecting when they'd arrived. He'd meant to take a look himself before she'd thrown him off track. His brain was addled from his time dreaming. It would take a moment to straighten everything out. He sat with his head in his hands and his elbows on his knees, steadying his breath. The fleshy, bloody taste in the back of his throat made him feel sick, but nothing else came up.

Once he'd taken some deep breaths his heart began to slow. His mind began to steady. He looked up and squinted at the room. The carvings were incredibly well preserved given the state of the space. He was marveling at them when Fajr composed herself.

"It's different," she announced. "What did you do? It didn't look like this before."

"Tony did it," Lucy admitted, still holding the girl and rubbing her back soothingly.

Vincent saw the trepidation in Lucy's eyes. It was

possible she was consoling Fajr to comfort herself. He glared at Tony. The boy noticed and blinked curiously at him, but he didn't look all there. His expression settled into helpfulness as he brought the journal over and held it out for Vincent to look at. The markings from the wall had been copied down.

"We took notes," Tony showed them dutifully. "It's an ancient map of the region. These little symbols are locations of different lairs the cult used to hide in."

"We're in this one," Fajr pointed to one of the symbols. "And this..." she began slowly, tailing off as she dragged her finger to a nearby symbol.

"... is where we need to go," Vincent finished. He recognized the symbol too. The death mark above the doorway from the Dreamlands. It always cost an awful price, but the Dreamlands had never failed to keep him on his path. Once again it had given him the key and shown him where to go.

"Are you sure?" Fred asked.

"Is it even to scale?" Lucy added. "Are we sure the map is right?"

Fajr bit her lip uncertainly. Even Tony's eyebrows creased in contemplation. Vincent watched them. The relentless drive that had brought Fajr this far was wavering under the horror of the Dreamlands. The sensation was unholy and violating, and she was rightfully shaken by it. Tony's eyes were vacant despite the furrow of concentration in his brow. The lost magic of the room was trying to use him as a conduit, and it was taking all his unconscious concentration to fight it. They were right to be cautious. The cult was trying to keep them out, trying to kill them, and they hadn't been doing this long enough to lose their fear of death.

Vincent had one foot out the door already. He knew he had seen not just the past, but the future, in that cave where the world was ending. He knew he was right because he'd already been right. Somewhere across time he had been there before and already done it. Already suffered for it. He knew what was coming.

"The map is right," he stated. "It will lead us to the current lair. If we leave now we can get there before dawn."

14

The moonlight lit their way across the desert. Vincent could feel his limbs trembling, but he steeled himself. That trip to the Dreamlands after Fajr was starting to feel like one too many. He was awake and everything still hurt. His lungs burned. He felt poisoned. Fred was watching him with suspicion, but he tried not to let anything show. Fajr was watching him with an uncertainty that was making him paranoid. She had been so filled with righteous indignation when he had shown up. Now the deference she showed him made him uncomfortable. He couldn't help but wonder if she had seen something in the other world she hadn't told him about.

Lucy was bringing up the rear with Tony. Vincent didn't begrudge her that, but part of him wished he had his apprentice at his side. He was worried about her. About both of them. Tony was vulnerable here. In the depths of night, in the heart of the desert, it was dangerous for someone with his gifts. Night always blurred the lines between magic and reality, and out here, in the world where man had yet to dominate the land, nature reigned supreme. He had done something in the lair they had left behind, or it had done something to him. Vincent had a horrible feeling that not even Fred knew which had occurred.

The sand was soft underfoot as they came over the top of a dune. Stretching before them the sand became rock and opened gently into a deepening crevasse in the desert floor. Vincent stared down at the haunting silver landscape. Moonlight stained the earth and glowed so brightly in the sky that Vincent had to squint. There it was – somewhere in that fissure was the door to the cave. The door to the cult's current lair.

Vincent started down the slope, leading the way. There was nothing they could do about the trail they left, they just had to be careful. He kept his eyes peeled for any sign of the cult. They would have watchers and scouts, surely. Vincent didn't know how deep or far the doorway was. It was possible they weren't quite in cultist territory yet, but in his heart he didn't believe that.

They began down the narrow path into the ravine, travelling deeper into the darkness of the abyss. The moonlight left harsh shadows and alien highlights on the stone walls. No matter what his eyes told him, Vincent knew they were in danger here. Every hair prickled on the back of his neck. His nostrils filled with the cold dark scent of realms beyond. The canyon was haunted, deeply and powerfully. Every nerve in Vincent's body fizzed. He was waiting for it. That moment. The echo of a monster stirring. The glint and grate of a cultist's blade or a creature's claw.

The sound that finally met his ears was not that sound. A vehicle engine growled into sharp silence as it was shut off. There were voices. Vincent peeked around the corner. Soldiers. A whole troop of British soldiers. The company was parked up and unloading gear right in front of the carved doorway. It rose up behind the trucks like a grotesque, foreboding scar in the cliff face.

Vincent watched the men gear up, wondering what in all hell the British Army were doing getting involved in something like this. Then he saw him. Whitehall. The Chancellor walked around from behind one of the trucks, stark in his pristine linen suit. It was almost luminous in the moonlight. He was always dressed for business, but never for work. This time he'd brought soldiers to do the dying for him.

Vincent stepped out from behind the cliff and started forward. His footsteps crunched beneath him on the sandy earth. A hundred guns and torches turned on him. It was brighter than the sun, but he barely shielded his eyes. His squint exacerbated the deep scowl across his face. He waited.

"Temple!" Whitehall snorted. "I should have known."

Darkness returned as the lights and weapons were lowered. Vincent blinked back hallucinations as he waited for his vision to return. The others were coming up behind him, and Whitehall had the group in his sights now. The old Chancellor stormed their way. His white moustache bristled with irritation.

"What the blazes are you doing here, Temple?" he demanded. "How many times do I have to tell you to keep out?!"

Vincent met the man's eye has he reached them. He

couldn't be sure who was the most irate, but he would have put money on himself. He was certainly the scarier of the two. Vincent was as dirty as Whitehall was tidy. He was filthy and unshaven, his ragged coat was spattered with blood and slime. He looked like a man who did the work. Whitehall looked like a man who paid others. Vincent met his eye unrelentingly and he could see the deep, almost imperceptible flinch in Whitehall's soul. The Chancellor knew it too.

"What's the British Army doing here, Nigel?" he growled.

Whitehall's expression was scathing. "We've been outsourcing help, which you'd know if you ever attended the Council meetings or consulted the minutes like you're supposed to. Things are changing, Temple. The world is changing. Nothing went back to normal after the war. If we want to stay ahead of the fight, we've got to keep on top of things."

Vincent scoured their surroundings through narrowed eyes. The soldiers were packing holy bullets, no doubt about it. Morally, Vincent couldn't take a stand against that. He'd given the recipe to gangsters to get the help he needed back home. But Whitehall didn't know that. He could have tried to play the old game, press the Chancellor on tradition, but there were more immediate concerns.

"They're gearing up for a massacre," Vincent nodded his head at the soldiers.

Whitehall's expression hardened. "How many years have we done this, Vincent?" he asked quietly. "How long have our people fought to protect this world, storming lairs like this and giving their lives to stop this evil? Our teams, trained to their peak, burst in on apocalyptic rituals performed by mad cults – bullets flying, monsters thrashing, everyone screaming. There're always good men who die. There's always some robed lunatic who escapes in the chaos. They get away and build up the cult again. Twenty years later we're back trying to stop the same madmen all over again. Wouldn't it be easier to take in enough people, surprise them, and gun them all down in one hit? No survivors. No escaped remnants of evil. I thought you of all people would understand."

"That's how you kill innocents!" Vincent growled. "Hostages! Hunters! Our people! Going in all guns blazing to kill everything in a room is how you end up with spies alerted early, utter chaos, escaped cultists, and friendly fire deaths!"

"And once again we are at the impasse of simply agreeing to disagree," Whitehall sighed. "I understand why you're so sensitive to this, Vincent. I really do–"

"My last apprentice was killed on one of your missions!" Vincent exploded. "Do any of those men know what they are getting into?"

"They are an elite specialist force," Whitehall replied. "They know what they're doing."

"But they're not Hunters," Vincent shook his head. "They're not trained. Not for this."

"Your opinion isn't warranted, Temple," Whitehall retorted. "This is my mission. Not yours. You and your people aren't welcome here. My people will take care of the mess–"

"Like you did at the library?"

Whitehall looked furious enough to strike him, but he held back. Vincent kept pushing, clawing for any inch of ground he could take. He edged into Whitehall's space with all the intimidation he could muster.

"You need Hunters in there," he warned. "You need someone who knows what they're doing. I'm going in with you."

"I already told you to get lost," Whitehall snarled. "I'm not telling you again. I've started drafting a review of your behavior for the Council. The fact that we haven't kicked you out yet is a walking bloody miracle. Leave now, take your collection of little girls with you, and I will add it as a reference of eventual cooperation to an otherwise damning report."

"Your report can kiss my ass," Vincent replied. "The men sitting on your Council might not want to cross you, but they want even less to pick up the slack I would leave behind. How many jobs get pushed onto me because you lot run into something you don't want to touch?"

Whitehall scoffed at him. "You are the job no one wants to touch! Or were you trying to imply what happened in Boston wasn't a disaster? How about the creature in New York? What about when you went down to cover New Orleans?" Whitehall sneered, his moustache twitching in disgust. "I suppose you mean that catastrophe with Owens. Believe me, Vincent, your opinions on that matter were less welcome than usual. We only asked you to step in because we needed the whole story and we knew you were the only one he'd give it to. If we let you loose you'd throw in our lot with the criminal and depraved. Save your breath and leave me in peace."

Now Vincent was the one who felt like he'd been slapped. None of it was new information. He knew how other people thought. Still, hearing it laid out like that, knowing what he was keeping from the Council, it lit a flicker of self-doubt. The moment was short lived. Like all the old orders, the Council of the Brotherhood of Hunters had become a bureaucracy of self-interest. They were interested in what kept them safe. If that meant saving the world, they'd do it. If it just meant saving their own skins and letting others fall, they'd do that too.

"You do it your way, Nigel," Vincent relented. "Me and my people will be waiting in the wings to clean up your mess. When the Darkness is done picking its teeth with your bones, we'll do what needs to be done."

Whitehall paused, his sudden hesitation evident.

"Like you said," Vincent shrugged. "No escaped remnants. Take them all down. We can wait and make sure that happens. You take those inexperienced boys in and do the hard yards, if you really believe that's what's right."

Whitehall didn't move. Vincent watched him through narrowed eyes and hoped his satisfaction wasn't obvious. He was calling the old man's bluff, and he knew it. The real question was, did Nigel?

"Fine," Whitehall snapped. "You can come too. The more we have on our side the better, obviously. Gather up your lot, we're commencing presently."

"Just me," Vincent replied. "I can't trust the safety of my people in a room with yours – so you only get me."

Whitehall looked like he was about to fight him again, but the angry retort died on his lips and he shrugged it away. The look he gave Vincent was weary and relenting.

"You do whatever you think is right, Temple," he surrendered. "I've agreed that we should put aside our differences for the sake of this mission – for the sake of the world. Bring your people or don't, but I need all hands on deck from everyone coming into that lair with me." Whitehall turned away and walked back to his troop.

Vincent watched him go. He waited for the Chancellor to glance back, but he never did. Vincent returned to the others who were waiting patiently for him. His eyes fell on Lucy. His apprentice was watching him expectantly, as though awaiting orders. Fred and Fajr were far less deferential in their gaze. They had been watching the men argue with an old anger in their eyes and the air of women who didn't wait for permission to do what they pleased. Tony wasn't watching him. The boy had that glazed, distant look in his eyes and his expression was troubled.

"There's something in there, Doc," he warned as Vincent returned to them.

"I know," Vincent nodded. "I can feel the darkness. That's why I'm going with them. I need the rest of you to wait here. You know cultists. You know demons. Nothing evil gets out of that cave under your watch – got it?"

"You're leaving us behind because you don't want Nigel's people to shoot us," Fred accused.

"It's safer," Vincent nodded.

"For whom?" Fajr retorted. "This is my mission, Vincent. This is my country and my people in danger. You want me to let the English dictate our fate? Again?!"

"The fate of the entire world could be at stake in that cave, girl," Vincent sighed. "Our work goes beyond borders. It always has. That's why I'm here. You gotta let me do my job." His tired dark eyes met hers and his look was direct. "I can't carry your body from their lair like I did your uncle's. I just can't. Whitehall's worried about escapees – or so he claims – hence the army. He wants to blow the cave to kingdom come to avoid a future resurgence. Our compromise is to have you lot on the door. Whatever tries to escape, I know you'll stop it."

Lucy and Fajr shared a look. The girls were fighters and they didn't like the idea of sitting out the action. Both of them turned their gaze to Fred. Vincent felt his heart sink. Apparently everyone knew who the real boss was. Still, Fred didn't flinch. She was watching Vincent resolutely with her sharp eyebrows narrowed.

"Vincent..." she finally sighed. "If you die in there, Sir, I swear I'll kill you."

"I'll keep that in mind," he smiled, and kissed her brow.

The girls had settled at Fred's declaration. They weren't going to fight both the adults on this, and Fred would make sure Vincent's orders were obeyed as long as she agreed with them. Vincent gave them both a nod.

"I'm counting on you two," he said.

"Don't worry," Fajr glared. "You're the only thing I'm letting out that door alive."

Vincent glowered, but Lucy put a hand on Fajr's arm and gave Vincent a nod.

"We won't let anyone on our side get hurt," she promised.

Fajr didn't argue. She'd probably only said it to get a rise out of him because he was pushing her out. That was a frustration he understood, but he was grateful she was heeding him. He trusted them, and he couldn't risk bringing Fajr inside. He had learnt that lesson the hardest way he could. It wasn't a mistake he would make again.

Finally, he turned to Tony. The boy had a pained tightness at his temples, but his distracted eyes met Vincent's this time. There was an urgency in his gaze. Vincent placed a hand on his shoulder.

"You're going to look after the ladies for me, aren't you, kid?"

"Yeah Doc, of course," Tony muttered. His eyes flickered between the old Hunter and the cave squeamishly. "It… it's in there… I can feel it. It's creeping. Not just the Dark. Not just the dogs. I remember this feeling. I know what he feels like. He's in there. The one with hungry eyes. He's waiting for you."

Vincent felt his mouth set in a hard line. Half of him wanted to ask what Tony meant, but he got the impression the boy was already conveying what he felt to the best of his ability. If Vincent wanted to know more, he was going to have to go inside and shoot it in the face to find out. He patted Tony's shoulder.

"Thanks for the warning, boy." Vincent turned and left them. He strode over to join Whitehall, who gave him a nod as they took point. The squads fell in behind. Vincent eyed up the soldiers armed and in formation behind him. That was a lot of men with guns on his back... if Whitehall wanted to get rid of him...

But if Whitehall had really wanted to get rid of him, he would have done it a long time ago. It didn't do to dwell on the distrust now. He glanced at his old mentor. Whitehall gave him a confident nod. Vincent returned the gesture. They started into the cave.

Above them the stone tentacles seemed to reach from the arch, groping over their heads. A haunting dread filled the air beyond the doorway. The darkness was thick and cloying. It pressed in tighter than the walls. Light had to be kept to a minimum so as not to alert the cult, but it left the passage frighteningly claustrophobic.

Vincent could hear his own ragged breath mingling with anxious panting behind him. Muffled footsteps scuffed the earth. The clinking of metal and rattle of pebbles echoed in the dark. He could feel his suppressed memories of the war creeping to the surface. He remembered what it was like to work with soldiers. It wasn't the same as hunting. The responsibility of other lives was constricting. He could imagine that Whitehall found it comforting to have others around to help. Vincent found it was more common to have others around to die.

Even as he wrestled with these thoughts, he could sense something was wrong. He had his sword in one hand and a pistol in the other. His shotgun was slung over his back. He tensed his sword hand, waiting. He didn't want to make a noise if he could help it, but he could sense danger. Fierce. Immediate. Like a creeping hunger. Something cold and disturbing brushed against the side of his face. He lashed out.

Vincent whirled. His blade whipped up and sliced something above him. Whitehall started at his side.

"Temple!" he hissed. He turned his shaded torch up. In the weak beam of light thin tentacles curled down from the ceiling. Vincent grabbed Whitehall's hand and directed the light across their men. The tentacles covered the whole ceiling, raining down over people. Many of the thin tendrils had suckered themselves to the necks of soldiers, squeezing like tar under their clothes and down their spines. The suckered men flinched from the light, their eyes grey and clouded, jaws slack. They looked at their companions hungrily.

"Fu–" Vincent's curse was drowned out as bullets started flying. Soldiers opened fire on the mass above them. Some shot the possessed. Screams echoed in the darkness. The suckered soldiers attacked their comrades, lunging and biting.

Vincent leapt away as everyone turned on each other. Chaos erupted behind him. Screams of horror became shrieks of pain. Flashes of gunfire lit the panic. In the erratic light Vincent could see tentacles lunging for him. He slashed his sword up. Wriggling drips gushed across him. He bolted. The writhing limbs dripped from his clothes. He kept his sword raised, slashing overhead. He couldn't let it get him. The thing moved fast. If even one sucker caught him...

He could feel black blood splatter his coat and hat. Slicing a path through the tentacles would only do so much good. He had to find the heart. A creature like this had a central mass, they always did. But the path was dark. Vincent stumbled. He crashed against the rock wall. His shoulder hurt where he had thumped it. The darkness made him feel dizzy. When nothing was anywhere, everywhere spun. He groaned, clenching his teeth. Something cold and wet slithered down the side of his neck. He roared and lashed out. The wormy appendage flopped beside him.

Vincent rummaged in his bag. He ripped out an old-fashioned oil-rag torch and lit the end with a match. Flames roared into blinding life before him. The ceiling reared back. The horrific monstrosity stretched on in the darkness, but it shied away from the flames. Vincent gathered himself and his things. He held the torch high in one hand, and kept a tight hold of his sword in the other. Shouts and gunfire still echoed loudly from the other direction. The best way to help those men now was to kill this thing.

Blood pounding, heart racing, Vincent took off. He waved the torch above him as high as he could. Perhaps if he could burn the monster that would weaken it. But the ceiling was growing further away. There was a sudden horrible sucking. Something must have worked. Vincent could see the mass of tentacles rush back above him. He gave chase. Anything to keep it off the soldiers.

The tunnel ended in a jagged crack ahead. Vincent didn't even slow. He burst through the gap into the cavern beyond.

15

Vincent stopped dead. He stood on the precipice of a small ledge. The cavern stretched out, massive and twisted, ahead of him. Torches had been rigged to pillars and stalactites, casting atmospheric shadows through the deep cave. A waterfall trickled and splashed down one side wall, its small pool reflecting fire. The cult had cleared the stalagmites in the center to create a space for their worship. There they gathered before a dais erected with a large throne upon it. Vincent recoiled as he saw the remains of the tentacled mass rushing back to its master. It was not a beast like he had thought. Not completely. The cloaked figure on the throne raised his arms, which returned to humanoid shape from the dark writhing ooze they had become.

All eyes in the room were on the stranger at their door. Vincent recognized humans and demons among the throng. All looked at him, even the figure on the throne. His face was cast in shadow, completely hidden, and yet Vincent was sure he knew him somehow. He was sure the man was smiling.

"Hello, Doctor Temple," the leader greeted him in perfect English, his deep voice carrying across the cavern.

Vincent stood stunned. It was everything he'd been expecting, and yet somehow it wasn't. Something was throwing him. His mind felt hazy, like it had been wrapped in cotton wool. Victory burned in his chest. He had done it. He had found what he had been searching for this entire time. What he had really been searching for. If only he could remember what it was...

Noise erupted behind him and Whitehall burst into the cavern at his side. Vincent could hear the surviving soldiers rushing the gap.

"Kill them," the leader ordered.

As one, the cultists drew blades and clubs from their robes. The demons screeched and lunged. Vincent didn't have time to think. He jumped the gap. His knees protested the landing, and he tossed his torch away as he rolled to spare them. He came up swinging, drawing his pistol in his other hand. Something sailed overhead.

"Grenade!" Whitehall bellowed.

Vincent dove behind a pillar. The explosion was pierced by screams. Demonic snarling drowned out the other noises. Then the gunfire started. Enough of Whitehall's soldiers had made it through the gap; none of the cultists had guns. The Chancellor was getting his massacre. But the other side had demons. Vincent snuck out of cover as the imps hit the front line. The soldiers' bayonetted rifles might could shoot holy bullets, but the blades were useless against demons.

Behind the demons came the cultists. Vincent took one out as he swung around the pillar. His bullet ripped half the man's head away. Two more were running up to take his place. One wielded a cruel sacrificial knife, and the other a sharp sickle. Their eyes were insane with religious ecstasy. Vincent could make out screaming on both sides. Some in agony, some in homicidal rage. The cultists were declaring their actions for their chosen one, their messiah. A glance to the throne was a mistake. He couldn't help it. He felt compelled to look. It gave the cultists time.

The one with the dagger lunged him. Vincent dodged at the last second, but the sickle was coming for his throat. He twisted, snarling as his back pulled. The tip of the blade caught his cheek. He fired his pistol. The bullet caught the dagger-wielding cultist full in the chest and knocked him back. Vincent drew his sword up with the other hand. The sickle blocked it, catching his blade in its curve. He brought his other hand up and shot the man, shoving his blade back. The cultist fell.

A demon swooped in. Vincent fired. The bullet smashed into the rocky ceiling, raining dust. Vincent swung his sword to block the creature's claws. It screeched at him. Blood dripped from its fangs. The red death of a soldier stained its mouth. Vincent fired again. His bullet tore through the monster's arm. It screamed and flailed. Vincent's sword couldn't hold it off. It shoved him back against a pillar, its one twisted arm pinning him down as it lowered its snout to him.

Vincent struggled. The creature's hot breath prickled his skin. The stench heaved his stomach. He couldn't get free. Suddenly, the creature howled. It threw back its head and lurched. A bullet struck its side. He took his chance. With a roar, Vincent lashed back, slicing through its torso in a thick spray of demon blood. He turned and fired his pistol, aiming straight for the throne. His bullet exploded into the side of the headrest. It missed the cloaked man's head by less than an inch. The cult leader didn't even flinch. He sat, reposed, in his chair, his face still in darkness, but his grin apparent in his posture.

Vincent took aim again. He had one more bullet. That was all he needed. He lined up the shot. His finger tightened. Claws snatched him. With lung-crushing force, Vincent was hauled from his feet. A demon grabbed him and tossed him into the air. He smashed into a stalactite, knocking his head. Then the ground came rushing back.

* * *

Outside the cave the cold of the darkness was seeping into the ravine. Lucy rubbed her shoulders and shivered. They had heard gunfire and yelling earlier. The fight had already begun and they weren't allowed to go and join it. She was perched on the back of one of the army trucks with Fred. Tony leant against the side near them and Fajr paced in irritation. Lucy felt the cold ease as Tony draped his jacket around her. She smiled at him. He smiled back and tapped the ash from his cigarette into the sand.

"Well," he announced to the uncomfortable silence in the wake of the gunfire. "This is fucking ominous."

"It's infuriating," Fajr countered, but no one called him on his language. They all felt it.

It was Tony's turn to shiver. Lucy looked up at him.

"Take the coat back," she offered.

He shook his head, placing an arm around her and kissing her hair.

"Ain't that kinda cold," he muttered.

Fred watched them closely. She had good reason to look more dour than normal, but even the shadows in her eyes were exacerbated.

"You feel it, don't ya, kid?" She gave him a look.

Tony nodded. "Something's wrong. Real wrong. You know I ain't ever left the States before, but there is something in that cave that I know. Something I've met before. That means I know it from somewhere else. Somewhere worse."

"That's what we expected though," Lucy reminded them, slipping her arms into the sleeves of the jacket and pulling it snug around her. "We knew there would be some great evil darkness in there."

"Na, Lucy," Tony shook his head, reluctant, but compelled to disagree. He took a drag on his cigarette and they all looked at the black doorway. More screams and gunfire echoed out. "There is something in that cave that doesn't want us dead... it just wants us here. Somehow, that's worse. It... it loves us."

Fred grimaced. Lucy looked between them.

"Loves us?" she echoed. "Wait... then... is it even bad...?"

"Yes," everyone answered her unequivocally.

"I think, perhaps," Fajr began, "when you say 'love', you mean this thing sees us as we might see *basbousa*?"

"That's a pretty good analogy," Fred nodded. "I might like cake, but that doesn't mean the cake's going to be happy about it."

"Is it like the thing in the library?" Lucy asked nervously. "That abomination that ate people?"

"It's worse," Tony muttered.

A tense silence settled over them all. Muffled echoes of violence bouncing from the cave didn't improve the atmosphere. Lucy stood from the back of the truck and grabbed her rifle.

"Lucy!" Fred snapped at her.

"He's in trouble, Fred," Lucy insisted. "He's in big trouble. We can't just sit here and do nothing."

"I agree." Fajr drew her blades and gave Lucy a nod. "I'm with you. We have to help them."

"Vincent told us to wait, so we wait," Fred ordered.

"Something is wrong, Missus Temple," Fajr insisted. "Your husband is probably dying – fighting to remove the poison from my land! This has to be our fight if we have any chance of keeping our country safe from its own radicals. It cannot be up to others to swoop in to save us. Not when it is so clearly a trap for those outsiders."

"You realize it's you he's worried about?" Fred pressed her. "You realize he's making us wait out here because he's afraid that you'll get hurt? He promised your mother he would bring you home safely."

"He's not bringing anyone home if he dies," Fajr argued.

"And they got no magic," Tony chipped in. Everyone looked to him. He finished his cigarette and pulled out his pistol, checking the bullets as he elaborated. "We're in the middle of a desert, hundred leagues from anywhere, and you and I are the only magic this side of evil," he told Fred. "Those Brits don't got none. The cult will have some, but those army boys sure don't."

"That boorish old man wanted a massacre," Fajr reminded. "He might be getting one, but those are British screams I hear."

In the wake of her statement they could all hear it. The screams were faint from the depths of the cave, but they were distinctive.

"Fuck," Fred swore. She climbed off the truck and checked her satchel and her pistol. "Fine. Let's do this. If he asks I didn't okay this and, Lucy, you watch Fajr's back."

"Of course," Lucy agreed.

Fajr knew better than to protest the help. She and Lucy shared a nod. Fred looked over at Tony.

"Alright, boy. Let's go keep these girls safe."

"Yes Ma'am," he nodded.

Fajr and Lucy took point with the mages keeping close behind them. With the darkness looming and the dread growing, they started into the cave.

TOMB OF ENDLESS NIGHT

16

Vincent hit the ground with a grunt. His head pounded and his vision swam. He tried to push himself up, but his arms trembled and he stayed down. Hot breath tickled the back of his neck. A growl rumbled in his ears. He shifted. Not fast enough. Claws raked his shoulder. Imp drool splattered his cheek. He couldn't lift his gun.

The imp's head exploded. Blood and brain burst out in a fine mist. Its body slumped sideways. Vincent struggled up, leaning on his elbow.

"That's my girl..." he muttered, glimpsing Lucy across the way, staring down the barrel of her rifle. His vision wavered and it looked like there were two of her. There she was, saving his bacon. She crept low as she slunk from the doorway, and dropped down beside Whitehall.

Shit! Whitehall! Lucy! Fajr! The girls were not supposed to be here! Even as he thought it, Fajr came bounding over, her swords making easy work of cultists and demons alike. She beheaded a man with a single swipe, kicking his robed body away.

A demon lunged at her. She threw her swords up in an X. The imp hit the blades and red light pushed it back. The magic in the swords flared in a seal that kept evil at bay. She drove both blades down into the demon's chest. It flailed. Blood bubbled up through its lungs. It choked, sagging towards the floor. She kicked it off her swords and hurried over.

"Doctor Temple!" she called.

"You're not supposed to be here!" he growled.

"You're welcome," she replied, offering him her hand. Her other hand held both swords carefully away from him. Blood dripped from the blades. Vincent pulled a face, but he was still dizzy. It was a hard blow to the head he'd taken. He took her hand and let her help him up.

As he struggled to his feet, red lightning crackled around them. A cultist had rushed Fajr from behind, but the lightning caught him. He screamed as he began to burn inside it. Vincent shot him in the head. Just as suddenly, Fred appeared at his side. Fajr gave her a nod and leapt back into the fight.

"Don't worry, Sir," she consoled him. "I've got her back, and we've got yours."

"None of you should be here, Fred," he groaned. "She shouldn't be."

Fred shrugged. "That's what you get for springing the enemies' traps, Vincent." She reached into her bag and brought out a disc. It was time to dust some demons. Fred threw the disc above the battle. Vincent braced himself for the glow. It never came. The man on the throne stood quickly, throwing out a hand. His arm twisted and warped, stretching to the roof of the cave and snatching the disc from the air. The black writhing ooze consumed it. It contained the explosion. At least, it seemed to.

Then golden lightning erupted from it. Small sparks at first, but the forks arced in and out of the twisted limb. Tony stood by the cave wall with his hands raised and his eyes focused. He pushed. The cloaked man let out a cry as his mutated flesh burned. He ripped his hand back, destroying the disc and letting the ooze revert to flesh. Charred patterns marked his skin.

Tony went for him. The boy threw golden lightning across the room. The battle froze as they watched. An arc of light crackled across the ceiling. Raw energy lit the room like the brilliance of day.

The man at the throne caught it. With his damaged hand he reached up and snatched it from the air. The force made him stagger, but barely. Just enough to step back. To knock his hood down. His black eyes stared the lightning down as it sparked and flared in his fist. It was like a storm in a bottle. The man looked up at Tony and smiled. The kid froze as he recognized the face.

"You're getting better, boy…" he purred. Then he threw the lightning back. Tony dove sideways. The magic exploded a crater in the rock wall. Chaos resumed. The cultists launched back into the fight. The soldiers were startled by the magic, but their training and weapons were better. They gave as good as they got. The biggest threat was the demons, and the holy bullets were thinning their ranks. Fajr was carving her way through the battlefield. Fred's lightning whipped through the fight, the red glow amplifying the blood painting the room.

Vincent stayed rooted to the spot. He stood, dumbfounded, still staring at Professor Isfet. The cult leader stood regally in his black robes with his cunning smirk. It was impossible. Vincent had killed him. He had gunned the man down rescuing Toby two years ago. Yet, somehow, here he was again.

Lucy aimed her rifle and shot at the man who had just tried to blow up her fiancé. Isfet raised his hands, the ooze spreading before him and soaking the bullets. Her shots didn't seem to hurt him. Whatever he had come back as, it was impervious to holy bullets and solar discs. Still, as Vincent watched him smiling at the carnage, delight apparent on his face, he knew this was the exact same man he had fought on the peak of the spire.

He felt like he was in a dream. The fight was slowing down. Bodies littered the floor in heaps. Both sides had taken massive casualties and neither would stop until the other was destroyed. Isfet had laid the trap and waited. He was enjoying it. Pleasure radiated off him. Vincent could feel it all the way across the cave. The man didn't even care if his side won. He just wanted the fear and the pain.

Vincent reloaded his pistol and aimed it slowly. His mind was in a haze, but he knew what he had to do. He aimed the barrel straight for Isfet's head. If death hadn't kept him the first time, Vincent would just have to kill him again. Isfet turned. He met Vincent's eye. His smile broadened at the sight.

"Come fight me like a man, Temple!" he goaded. His deep rich voice was like a lullaby in Vincent's mind. He couldn't fight it. His hand trembled. His aim dipped. He dropped his sword and raised his other hand to steady the first. He had to take the shot. No matter how foggy his mind felt. He had to end this. He fired.

Isfet's smile flickered for a moment as he dodged the bullet. It hit the back of the throne and sent up a spray of splinters. He whirled back, his grin returning.

"Don't let me distract you from the fun," he warned.

"Vincent!" Lucy yelled. She barged him with her shoulder, knocking him to the side. The claws of a demon tore through the tail of his coat. Both of them seemed to have come from nowhere. Lucy's rifle hung empty from its strap. She had moved onto her handguns. She fired two shots, one from each pistol, straight into the monster's chest. Without stopping, she aimed across the room and took the head off a cultist sneaking up on Whitehall.

The Chancellor looked feral. His white suit was heavily bloodstained. He had his pistol in one hand and a rifle in the other. The bayonet at the front was buried deep in the neck of a dead cultist. Fred and Tony were shredding another demon with magic. The boy let his mentor's spell take the lead as he paused to put a bullet between the monster's eyes.

Vincent staggered upright again. He shook his head to clear it. His vision was fine, but his mind was so hazy. His thoughts felt muddled, like something was messing with them, like the dreams were reaching across to him. He felt he should jump back into the fight, but looking around it seemed like it was over. Half a dozen soldiers were still standing, disemboweling the last of the cultists. The last adversaries were being cut down just like that. He looked to his apprentice. Lucy turned back to him. He reached out to her.

There was a roar of fury and a shot went off. Vincent felt the bullet rip through the bottom of his sleeve, close enough to singe his arm. They both whirled to look. Fajr had kicked Whitehall's gun from his hand. It spun out of his grip and skidded toward the throne. She knocked him back, standing with her sword at his throat and fury blazing in her eyes.

"Fajr!" Lucy called out.

The soldiers saw her holding the Chancellor down and took aim. One called out.

"Ma'am, let the man go," he warned.

Fajr glared daggers over her shoulder at him. Her niqab was tucked around her neck, leaving her face exposed. Her dark hair fell thick around her shoulders and her striking expression dared the men to shoot her. Lucy ran between them.

"Enough!" she ordered. "We're not fighting each other! Everyone, stand down!"

"He just tried to shoot you in the back," Fajr accused, pressing her blade to Whitehall's skin.

"I was aiming for the demon!" Whitehall protested.

"She had already killed it," Fajr retorted. "You were aiming for her... the same way you shot my uncle."

"Slander!" he roared. "She's crazy! Men, take her down!"

"Weapons down or you die!" Vincent ordered, leaping to Fajr's defense. He aimed his pistol at the soldiers. "No one hurts the girl!"

"Of course you're choosing her!" Whitehall spat. "You'd let her kill me just to sate her bloodlust. I should never have let you in here, Temple. You're no better than the monsters."

"We're no better?!" Fajr retorted. "You just tried to kill his apprentice!"

"You're delusional!"

"You're a murderer!"

"I'm a Hunter!" Whitehall roared, pushing himself up. The blade across his neck drew blood as he resisted it. "I'm the best and the last of the line of true Hunters! The kind the world will be without when your kind infiltrate our order!"

"Her kind?" Vincent echoed dangerously. He felt the madness creeping through the back of his brain. Reverberations of Whitehall's defense of Naeem's murder were crashing to the front. It had never occurred to Vincent his mentor could have been the one to pull the trigger... but if Fajr was right... if Whitehall really had taken the shot that nearly took Vincent's hand off...

"Spare me, Vincent," Whitehall snarled. "You know well what I mean and you flout my laws deliberately. We are supposed to be a pure order! Incorruptible! The Light that banishes the Darkness! You consistently throw our lot in with women and negros and homosexuals – the weak and criminal – and then you have the nerve to act like you're in the right! You don't want your apprentices removed before they can stain us? Pick some appropriate ones."

Vincent's blood ran cold. He felt like he'd been shot.

Fajr had been waiting for it. She'd worked it out before he had. She knew Whitehall had murdered Naeem. Vincent had never believed his own teacher could have done such a thing. A cover up? Certainly. But the actual murder...

"STOP!" Lucy threw herself between Fajr and the soldiers and grabbed Fajr's arm. "You can't kill him! Not here! Not like this!"

"This is justice!" Fajr cried.

"This is vengeance," Lucy argued. "It's vengeance, plain and simple, and you have every right to want it, but we have to do better, Fajr. We have to be better. Otherwise we're no different than him." She looked over her shoulder and met Vincent's eye before turning back to the other girl. "Vincent taught me that. We can't just be killers. We have to represent the best of humanity. Tie him up. We'll take him back and he can stand trial for what he's done. That's justice."

Everyone held their breath as Lucy talked them down. Slowly, they all began to lower their weapons. Whitehall staggered to his feet, touching the shallow cut at his throat. His expression was a mask of homicidal rage and disgust. It was impossible to know who offended him more; the women or the soldiers who had refused to shoot them. He opened his mouth to speak, but the words never made it out. A bullet ripped through his forehead. Brains splattered the ground behind him. His body collapsed over them. Lucy whirled around to stare down the barrel of Vincent's smoking pistol.

A small giggle escaped from the throne where Isfet

sat, watching the entire proceedings with relish. He had all but merged with the background until his delight was too much to contain. Lucy's attention was fixed on her mentor.

"Vincent!" she cried in despair.

He holstered his pistol and raised his hands in surrender. The soldiers had aimed their weapons at him, but all seemed hesitant to shoot. He stepped forward. Lucy stared at him with the eyes of one betrayed. He laid his hands on her shoulders and kissed her head.

"You were right," he told her simply, with a peace in his voice that had never been there before. "I will face whatever comes my way, but that was justice. There is no court in the world that would have convicted him. What he did was evil, but society is on his side. I taught you once that we must resist humanity's evils, and we should, but we also have to right the ones we can. This was an evil I could right. Forgive me."

Lucy looked torn, but she could see in his eyes he had made the right call, even if it was only the right call for him. She nodded and stepped back.

A gunshot blasted through the cave. The sound exploded through the silence. Vincent whirled on the soldiers, but they all looked as shocked as he did.

Lucy was blown off her feet. She hit the ground hard. Blood quickly soaked across her thin shirt. She didn't move. Her eyes were closed, her body limp. The blood stained through Tony's jacket, flooding from the bullet hole in her chest. Fajr cried out and fell to her knees beside her. Fred rushed to them with a yell of outrage.

Vincent turned on Isfet. The cultist checked the chamber of Whitehall's pistol, the gun he had just retrieved from the floor at his feet. He sighed at its emptiness, but his work was already done.

"If you want something done right, eh?" he smiled at Vincent.

Vincent lifted his weapon with a roar. His anguish was beyond words. He bellowed in pure fury as he unloaded all his bullets into the man before the throne. He wasn't the only one. The soldiers shot with him. Isfet laughed manically as he sank all the bullets. They splattered harmlessly across his body, oozing dark goo. Nothing stopped him. Nothing even hurt him.

"Oh, I am sorry, Vincent..." he chuckled. "She was just too good an anchor for you. She had to go."

Vincent was still pulling the trigger compulsively, even though his bullets had run out. He was too enraged to reply. Words utterly failed him. He took up his sword and charged.

"I suppose it is that time again..." Isfet smiled. His dark viscous body shifted as Vincent charged him. His face smoothed over. Vincent recognized him even as he ran. His memories came flooding back. That was how Isfet was still alive! He hadn't been a real man to begin with. He had been the Prince. Always the Prince. Vincent remembered the battle on the spire. He remembered all the battles before. He had found his quarry – the one he had searched for all his life. The Darkness all Hunters sought. The one he had found and forgotten so many times before. The one who took his memories so that he could keep playing with him. Keep tricking him. Keep drawing him back to the Dreamlands. He knew what was coming, knew the horror of his inevitable amnesia, and still he couldn't stop himself. He was running right into it. Then something happened.

The Prince turned. His head snapped quickly, spotting something across the room. Somehow, the same way that Vincent knew the creature was usually smiling, he knew that the smile had faltered. It returned as the Prince looked back to him.

"You can't save them both," he taunted.

Vincent looked. Tony. The boy's eyes had gone black, the Darkness staining his veins the instant Lucy had been shot. He was walking towards them slowly. Patiently. He was in no hurry. Golden light poured from him. It exploded. The light burst out of him in a beam, blasting the Prince before Vincent could get to him. Vincent staggered and fell, throwing an arm over his eyes. It was brighter than the sun. Then it was over.

TOMB OF ENDLESS NIGHT

17

Vincent shivered blindly on his hands and knees. He couldn't see anything. He realized he was gasping. But he was alive. He was breathing. He still had his memories. That hadn't been part of the Prince's plan. Slowly, painstakingly, his vision began to return to the dim cave. The torches glowed from the ceiling above him.

"Vincent!" Fajr's voice called to him. Her hands grabbed his shoulders.

"The... children..." he muttered weakly. As his sight came back he could see Tony collapsed on the ground. The kid was greyer than old snow. He didn't look like he was breathing. He looked like he had back when Vincent had found him in the hallway two years ago. Lucy was lying pale and still in Fred's arms. Blood had soaked through her clothes. Red light burned around her torso and Fred's hands. The soldiers were staggering over with first-aid packs. Everyone looked dazed by the magic. Isfet was nothing more than a sticky black robe at the foot of the throne.

Fajr helped Vincent to Lucy. He sunk to his knees at her side.

"She's alive," Fred announced, as the soldiers joined

them. "It didn't get her lungs. Bullet's shallow..." Fred grimaced, sweat dripping down her cheek as she focused. She had no healing magic, that wasn't how magic worked, but it was still useful. The red light pulled the bullet from Lucy's ribs. Fred was right, it wasn't deep. But the pain was enough to bring her back. Lucy cried out and spasmed.

"How...?" Vincent stared in disbelief. A cotton blazer wasn't exactly bulletproof. Vincent reached down, tossing away the bullet Fred had removed and touching the jacket. Something heavy fell out of the breast pocket. Tony's cigarette case. It had a hole clean through it, but it was sturdy, and two sheets of metal were better at slowing a bullet than human skin.

"She's not outta the woods, Vincent," Fred panted. "I need you to stitch her up."

"I have to get Tony," Vincent replied. He dug into his satchel and dumped his medical supplies on Fred. Then he pulled out a bottle of tonic.

"No!" Fred ordered. "Vincent, that shit will kill you! How much have you had in the last few days?! I want to save him too... but you puked blood a few hours ago after drinking that... you do it now and you might die!"

"There's no other way, Fred," Vincent sighed, kissing her hair. "Take care of Lucy for me."

Before he could do anything else the vial was pulled neatly from his fingers. Vincent turned to meet eyes darker and more serious than his own.

"Stitch up your apprentice, Doctor Temple," Fajr ordered him coolly. "I will retrieve the boy."

Vincent opened his mouth to argue, and then

realized she was the one making the right decision. It was the strangest realization he'd ever come to in his life, but he felt like his brain was working properly again – or starting to – for the first time in many decades. He had all his memories back. All the stolen ones. He hadn't even known they'd been missing. All the years of tonic abuse, chasing his abuser...

He nodded to Fajr. "Thank you."

"She's still bleeding," Fajr reminded, before settling herself comfortably on the cavern floor. She uncorked the vial.

"Are you sure you know what you're doing?" he asked.

"I remember," she assured him, and downed the vial.

Vincent turned straight to Lucy. One of the soldiers was on his knees by Fred, bandages in hand, helping to mop the blood. Vincent gave him a grateful nod and then took his gear back from the mage, who was still using magic to keep the girl as stable as she could. The old Hunter glanced up at the other soldiers.

"You keep that girl protected," he ordered.

"Yes Sir," they agreed. If any of them wondered what they were supposed to protect her from, they didn't ask. Vincent sympathized with the lads. Those boys had just survived the darkest night they were ever likely to encounter. They'd been led into a trap lined with demons and watched most of their troop die. Maybe that was the reason they were still prepared to follow the orders of the man who had shot their leader. Or perhaps what had just transpired was more than most people could deal with, and they were happy enough to do what they were told in order to survive.

Vincent got to work on Lucy's wound. Before the bullet had been removed it had been lodged in a rib. The injury was messy, but not fatal as he had first feared. Lucy whimpered as he cleaned her wound and began to patch her up. He muttered soothing nothings as he worked, and Fred helped him comfort her. The girl had more than earned her right to cry for a bit. She was still bleeding profusely. Her body began to shiver as she started to go into shock.

"Get her to bite down on this," Vincent ordered Fred, handing over a wad of spare bandaging. "I'm going to need you to cauterize here," he pointed.

Fred did as she was told, using magic to burn the area. Lucy screamed through the muffling fabric and promptly fainted. She wasn't bleeding so badly anymore though, and that was something. Vincent could feel his knees buckling under him, but he tried to keep the trembling from his hands. There was still room to mess this up. She wasn't safe yet.

He was so focused in his work he didn't hear the soldiers startle. He only heard the gunshot. The sound jolted him. He nicked something. Panic flared as Lucy began to bleed again. Fred was watching. Her magic lit up, cauterizing the nick and trying to draw the blood away from pooling where it shouldn't.

"Vincent..." she muttered warningly, but it wasn't about his work.

He glanced over his shoulder. The ooze that had been Isfet was rising from the cloak. The men had shot at it and now they were panicking. That had been their last bullet.

"Which one of you is the best shot?" he called to them.

The unanimous conclusion was Jason. Vincent called him over.

"Jason, take my pistol out of the holster. Reload it from the pack. Then space the bullets as evenly as you can through that thing."

"It's getting bigger, Sir!" he replied.

"Then do it fast," Vincent grated.

"It's going for the girl!" one of the others yelled as Jason reloaded as fast as he could.

"Don't let it near her!" Vincent bellowed.

"Take Lucy," Fred ordered the man with the bandages beside her.

Vincent didn't have time to grumble. Fred left him to it and stood. He could see her shaking with the effort. The room lit up red with the glow of her magic. He could feel it holding back the darkness behind him.

"Now, soldier!" Fred yelled.

Jason stood and fired.

* * *

Moonlight bathed the darkness. A sky of infinite horrors stretched on forever, each star a whirling mass of devouring tentacles, reaching out with boundless hunger. Fajr stood beneath the sky, waiting for the end. She remembered this. She remembered the pain and the fear. The way the air stung her skin and burned her throat. The cold and the whispers and the thick scent of death.

But it was not the same. Something was different.

She stood inside a ring of pillars, in a place she'd never been, a place she'd never seen, that was somehow still hauntingly familiar. A place all souls knew. Figures stood in the shadows between the pillars, looking down on her. She looked back. The seven guardians. She knew of them. They served the Prince. They ruled the Dreamland. They were children of the Darkness. Everyone who had studied this path knew of the Lords that awaited those who walked it. Fajr couldn't see their faces. Just their silhouettes between the pillars. The circle that ran atop the pillars cast those beneath in shadow. She didn't look. She knew she shouldn't. More than that – she didn't want to know. If she saw the guardians she could never choose to unsee them.

Instead, she turned to the center. She turned to the difference distorting the Dreamland. Inside the center grew the altar. The giant tree of flesh. Fajr had never seen anything like it before. Skin and muscle and tendon twisted and throbbed and pulsed together, growing and stretching up like a trunk, and then branching out in thick, ropy tendrils. Roots had cracked through the stone that had otherwise been polished smooth within the circle. It was a mark of recycled pain and existence so visceral she recoiled from it.

Standing at the bottom of the tree was Tony. He had the Prince by the throat, and held him pressed against the trunk. The tree had begun to devour them both. It did not care at all that the ruler of its realm was its nourishment. It relished in it. The fleshy substance of the trunk had merged with Tony's arms, sucking him inside it, and oozing around the Prince. It embraced the dark one, slowly pulling him deeper. Tony didn't falter as he melted into them both.

"Tony!" Fajr grabbed him by the shoulder. "What are you doing?"

The boy turned his head to look at her. His large dark eyes were glassy, but there was a resolve in those depths that was as familiar to her as a mirror.

"He shot Lucy," Tony replied like it was an answer.

"I know," she nodded. "The Temples are fixing her as we speak. She'll make it. She's a fighter."

"I can't let him hurt her again," Tony insisted, turning back and tightening his grip. The fleshy mass oozed further up his arms as his fingers tensed. "I can't let him hurt anyone. I can keep him here. I can hold him."

"But not forever," Fajr warned. "Could it really be worth it? Being eaten by this thing?"

Tony was silent a long time. He let it slowly seep further.

"I... I always knew I'd come back here..." he muttered. "One day. It always said... it told me I would..."

"That doesn't mean you have to," she stipulated.

"If I let him go we'll never escape his evil," Tony argued. "He will keep coming back, over and over—"

"Yes," Fajr agreed. "That's what evil does. It always finds a way. Even if you bind him here and sacrifice yourself, he will find a way. That's why there are

Hunters. That's why we do what we do. It's why the order was created. It's why the mages help us."

Tony paused. Frozen. Conflicted. His emotions chased each other across his face. Fajr tightened her grip on his shoulder and pressed him back gently.

"Tony, there will always be evil. Our job is to make sure there is always someone to beat it." She looked him dead in the eye. "Your Hunter needs you."

He let go. His hands released the Prince's throat, and he pulled himself from the tree. It clutched desperately at him, but he hauled himself loose, untangling from the thick viscous mess that had begun to coat him. It flopped helplessly, groping for him, but he staggered away.

With an awful sucking sound, the Prince slithered free. He laughed deliciously as he slipped from the mess, his faceless head grinning back at them. Fajr wanted to run, but she couldn't bring herself to turn her back on him.

"Such big words for someone with so much fear wafting off them..." he taunted.

"You ain't as frightening as you think," Tony challenged.

"Not to someone with stolen magic...?" the Prince smiled and leant closer. "What if I'd killed her?" he whispered.

Fajr saw Tony's jaw clench and a vein throbbed in his neck. The Prince laughed. He looked up at the sky with his absent eyes, as though seeing something only he could.

"That's the bell, my little fighters. I can't wait for the

next round," He swung back suddenly, grabbing them both before they could bolt. His touch was freezing as his arms pulled them in tightly, like the embrace of something worse than death. The world spun, until he was holding them above the sky. Above forever. "Give Vincent my *undying* love…"

Tony lashed out, trying to struggle, but the Prince had already let them go.

* * *

The bullets hit the rising goo as evenly as Jason could fire them. Each one struck true and exploded where it connected with the Darkness. Spacing them slowly ripped the thing apart. It wasn't as powerful as it had been when it had been Isfet. Still, no one wanted to tango with it. It never stopped trying to creep towards Fajr. Fred's barrier was wilting. She was running out of steam. Jason's well-placed shots had cut it down to a third its previous size, but it wasn't slowing.

He cursed, trying to reload the pistol again. Fred staggered. Her barrier slipped. The thing lunged. It dove straight for Fajr, as though it could feel the Dreamlands in her.

Fajr's eyes flashed open. She raised her swords, crossed in front of her. The goo smashed into the barrier of the magical blades. She sliced outwards, rolling to her feet and driving it back.

Everything went bright.

A beam of golden light disintegrated the Darkness, turning it to flakes of ash. Tony was on his feet again, hand out. The beam burst from his palm, a golden arcane circle glowing through his fingers. He walked forward, pushing the light deeper into the ooze. When he was satisfied the threat was reduced to dust, the magic went out. Everyone stared at the angry teenager.

"Well, damn son," Jason gave him a look.

"What is that kid…?" another solider muttered.

"The best damn mage I've ever seen," Fred replied.

"Fred!" Tony rushed to help her off her knees. She was exhausted and struggling to stand. He pulled her up and held onto her, but his eyes were busy elsewhere.

"How's it going, Vincent?" Fred asked.

The old Hunter sat back. His hands were trembling now, and they were covered in blood. Lucy was whimpering again.

"We should get her to a hospital," he replied. "She's safe to travel now. For a bit."

"We can take her in the trucks," Jason volunteered. "I know the way back. We can get there quickly."

Vincent nodded his thanks. He staggered to his feet. His legs were barely holding him.

"I… I need one of you to carry her," he requested.

"I can–" Tony began.

"Not on your life, boy," Vincent disagreed. "I'm surprised you haven't fallen over already. I need someone I know won't collapse on me on the way out."

Tony looked disgruntled, but he didn't fight it. He wanted Lucy to get the best care too. The magic he had burnt was not lost on anyone. Indignation alone seemed to be propping him up. Vincent took his weapons back and approached them. He kissed Fred's forehead again.

She gave him a rueful smile.

Finally, Vincent turned to Fajr. She held her head high and met his gaze. They had done it. They had stopped *Alshifaq Alfidiyu*. They had avenged Naeem and found justice. With jerky, bloodied fingers, Vincent pulled the Hunter's pin from his lapel. He dropped it in her palm.

"Welcome to the Order," he told her. "You've more than proven yourself in your mission to stop this cult and bring safety to your people."

The room held its breath. Fajr stared at the pin in her hand, tipping it back and forward and letting the firelight gleam off its tarnished surface. She sighed.

"I cannot take this, Vincent," she replied. "I'm honored you think I'm worthy, but your Brotherhood has never sworn in a woman. They killed my uncle for being a colored person – what do you think they would do to me? It is not your place to make this call. Your Council would condemn us both."

Vincent looked at her for a long time, but he did not take the pin back. Eventually, he blinked and turned away. He crossed to Whitehall's body, knelt, and ripped the Chancellor's pin from his old mentor. He placed it in his lapel in the position of his old one.

"It is my call," he decreed. "If you don't want it, I would never insist you take it. However, Whitehall's actions have driven the Order down a corrupt and bigoted path. If we have any hope of building ourselves up to be worthy of our legacy again, we will need the skills and voices of you and those like you. I aim to see our mission restored. As for the Council… anyone who doesn't like it can go through me."

The entire room watched his threat hang in the air. It wasn't directed at them, but it still managed to be terrifying. There was a very good reason the rest of the Hunters feared Vincent, and this didn't look like a point he was going to budge on. The future was here, and tradition was just going to have to get used to that. Glances bounced between the British soldiers in the wake of Vincent's self-declared elevation. That was certainly one way to make a King – or a Chancellor.

Jason cleared his throat. He had scooped Lucy up, per Vincent's instructions, and stood holding the girl cradled in his arms. Her pale face, half-conscious, rested against his shoulder.

"For whatever it's worth, Ma'am," he offered to Fajr. "The lass here says you should take it. Change the system from the inside and whatnot."

Lucy tried to give Fajr a smile, but she looked like she was about to faint again. Fajr returned the gesture with more conviction. She gave Lucy a nod and fixed the pin to her abaya. Jason returned the nod on Lucy's behalf. He adjusted his hold on her.

"I'm going to get this wee lady out to the trucks," he told them, heading for the tunnel. His comrades looked about the battleground grimly.

"It's going to take a long time to dig enough graves, even just for our own," one commented bleakly. "Especially considering the men back down the tunnel."

"We don't have that kind of time," Vincent sighed. "And we certainly don't have the strength. You all look like you need medical attention, and so do we. I'll say a prayer for the ones who need it, and then we seal the tomb behind us. Permanently."

His declaration met no argument. Everyone knew he was right.

TOMB OF ENDLESS NIGHT

18

Anisa and Aswan were overwhelmed with relief when Fajr returned home. However, they were less than impressed by her initiation into the Order of Hunters. By the time Fajr, Vincent, and the others arrived back, Fajr had adjusted to the idea, and she was starting to like it. Her parents' disapproval seemed to cement her resolve. It didn't have any power to sway Vincent either. His serious eyes could see the reversal of opinion Anisa and Fajr had gone through with regard to his involvement in the situation. As far as he was concerned that was their business. He had chosen the girl with absolute faith in her abilities. She had proven herself to him, and she could prove herself to anyone else in time.

His greatest concern now was the wellbeing of the children. Lucy had been taken straight to hospital, and Tony, who had passed out in the back of the truck, had slept for eighteen hours. The air of displeasure that radiated from Fajr's parents had Vincent eager to avoid outstaying his welcome, if such a thing were even possible at this point. While he didn't want to hand Fajr a badge and abandon her, he was also ready to leave as soon as Lucy and Tony were well enough to travel.

Fortunately, his latest recruit understood. She didn't need any handholding; he knew that, even if he couldn't seem to help himself. As a fully-fledged Hunter she would communicate regularly with the Council, especially their new Chancellor. They'd be alright.

Fajr saw them off at the docks the morning they left. Lucy was walking again, and trying to wave away everyone that wanted to fuss over her – which was everyone she knew. Fajr embraced her very gently in farewell, and the girls promised to write to each other. Vincent had a feeling he was going to end up keeping tabs on Fajr through Lucy far more effectively than any official channels. So he was surprised to find himself caught in his own goodbye hug. Fajr squeezed him tightly around the ribs, with all the force she hadn't used on Lucy.

"Thank you, Doctor Temple," she whispered to him.

"Thank you, kid," he replied gruffly, kissing her cheek. "Don't be a stranger."

"Of course not," she promised.

They said their farewells and set sail for home. Fred set Lucy up in the cabin to rest. Vincent stayed topside, letting the ocean breeze wash over him as they cut through the waves. His shoulders settled as he watched the Egyptian coast disappear behind them. A weightlessness such as he had never felt before rose from the soles of his feet all the way to his scalp. A strange peace tingled through his nerves. The darkness that had plagued his last twenty years was gone. He had finally buried it in the tomb, deep in the canyon of some distant land.

Down the railing, Tony was lighting a cigarette from a paper packet. He looked tired and disheveled, but the shadows around his eyes had eased. Vincent wasn't the only one who had been able to bury his darkness, it seemed. The old Hunter sidled his way toward the boy, who looked up at his approach. There was a confidence in his eyes that was almost startling to behold. It was an alien look on the kid.

"Doc." He gave Vincent a nod and blew out a thick cloud of smoke.

"Tony." Vincent returned the nod. He leant on the railing and gazed out at the ocean. "I've been meaning to ask you..." he started carefully, not wanting to spook the boy. "How did Fajr find you so fast? Bringing you back from the Dreamlands was one of the hardest and most dangerous things you and I ever did. How did she get you back so quickly, and in such fine form?"

Tony gave the waves a sardonic grimace.

"It wasn't the same, Doc," he shook his head. "When you had to get me back... you came to the party late. You had to do all this magic and play it safe. You didn't know what had happened to me. I didn't know what had happened to me. I got snatched. Fajr followed me in as soon as I left, she went in at exactly the same place I did, and... y'know, she didn't bring any of your baggage..."

Vincent shot him a look, but Tony didn't meet it. Vincent grinned at the boy's audacity. Tony tapped ash over the railing.

"I didn't get snatched this time," he sighed. "I went

back on my own. I knew exactly what I was doing and where I was going. I didn't need rescuing, not really. Not like last time. I just needed a little intervention. Girl's pretty good at those hard talks when you need 'em."

"That she is," Vincent smiled.

"The first time I went I didn't know what I was doing," Tony continued. "The book just used me as fuel to make the magic happen. This time I was the one in control. I knew what spell I was using and I used it all on my own. I might have learnt it the hard way, but I know what I'm doing now."

"You sure?" Vincent pressed him gravely. "I don't mean to undermine you, boy, but this is extremely dangerous stuff. What you can do... lad, in all my years I've never seen anyone else who can do what you do. Not even on their side. The Prince called what you were using 'stolen magic' and I can't help but wonder–"

"The thing about stolen property, Doc," Tony interrupted, "is that it's all about a questionable shift in ownership. Possession is nine tenths of the law, and the King of Hell can bitch and moan 'til the cows come home." Tony met his eye. "But it's my magic now."

Vincent gave him a long look. Tony didn't flinch. It was the Hunter who looked away first. The boy had watched the love of his very young life get shot, and had decided the best course of action was a throwdown with the ultimate force of Darkness. But he'd won. That was a story Vincent had seen cost many other people their lives. Tony was the only person he had seen come out the other side, and he'd come out the other side more confident than Vincent would have thought possible. The kid had balls of steel, and the power to back it. Vincent wasn't going to challenge that. Not when it was on his side, and not when it was in defense of his little girl.

"Lord spare the men who cross you," he muttered wryly.

"Only if they deserve it," Tony replied, puffing away.

Vincent wasn't going to contest that either. He was, however, extremely intrigued to see how Ferro and the Mafia were going to contend with the kid once they got him home.

* * *

The two weeks it took them to sail back were the most peaceful time Vincent felt he'd ever lived, and he had all his memories back to reinforce that. They gave new color to the world. The itch for the tonic that had plagued the back of his throat for years was gone. Half his addiction had been his amnesia. Now, finally, he knew he'd been manipulated into a loop of dependence and violence. The Prince's hold on him had been released. He was free.

It was late morning on a grey and overcast day that brought them to the docks of home. Lucy was doing considerably better. She would accept only minor coddling, and only from Tony. Vincent was allowed to carry her bag from the ship, after a brief staring match that ended with Fred laughing at them. As they disembarked from the ship, Vincent could feel the tension rising. She was getting ready to start a fight. He decided to head it off.

"Where do you think you're going, Miss?" he asked.

Lucy turned to him. Her brows narrowed. She knew he knew. She hadn't even started heading in a different direction yet.

"I'm going to see Elia Ferro," she answered coolly. "Tony got some telegrams on the ship. Sounds like they've had it rough in our absence."

"And that's your problem because…?" Vincent pressed.

"Because you asked them to cover for us!" Of course she had known what 'other arrangements' meant.

"Which they are perfectly capable of doing and have been compensated for," Vincent replied. He gave her a look. "If you want to talk to Ferro that's your business, but don't lie to me about it."

She glared. Tony stood nervously at her side. Vincent could tell the boy was waiting for him to lay down the law and drag Lucy back home. However, if the kids were going to get married they needed to know what that was going to look like. Vincent set one of the bags down to cup Lucy's cheek and kiss her forehead.

"I trust you, kid," he told her. "Don't get mixed up in something you can't get out of, and don't hurt yourself, or I'm blaming your boy."

"I'll keep her safe," Tony promised.

"You better," Vincent warned. "Don't think I don't know you were hoping I'd pull rank on her. She's going to be your wife, Segreti. You'll be the one wrangling her soon enough."

"Excuse me?!" Lucy demanded. "I do not need wrangling!"

Vincent gave Tony a direct look. The boy had pinched his lips together anxiously.

"Don't let her walk all over you," he advised. "We'll make sure there's lunch at the house later." He picked up the bags again, gave them a nod, and headed for his car. Fred fell into step beside him and they walked in silence most of the way. Once they were well out of earshot, she gave him a sly glance.

"What on earth was that, Sir?"

"They need to learn what married life will be like," Vincent replied. "They're going to have to make decisions together, and they can't grow up if I'm constantly overruling everything they do. Besides, they'll be far more cautious if I put the onus on them and they have to concern themselves with my disappointment rather than my anger."

He unlocked the trunk and dumped the bags in the back of the car, pretending to ignore the admiring look Fred threw his way.

"That's rather Machiavellian of you, Sir," she grinned.

"Mm," he agreed, closing the packed trunk. "It's nice to have all my faculties back. It's been so long... and I'm going to have to get better at managing people. Those two seem like a good place to start. My head is so much clearer now that I'm not gowed up on toxic waste – who would have thought?"

"Who indeed..." Fred commented drily.

Vincent laughed at her as he unlocked the car.

"It does seem as though this holiday was the best thing we've ever done for you," she added sincerely. "Maybe the girl was right all along. Going back to Anisa and her family was what you needed."

"So it would seem," Vincent agreed, neither of them verbally acknowledging the murder, magic, and chaos that had freed him. They climbed into the car and Vincent settled behind the wheel. "God it's good to be going home though," he sighed as he turned over the engine.

Fred grinned in agreement.

* * *

The gunfire had started before the yelling. A point of professionalism Ferro always appreciated. Still, when the door to his office started to buckle, he knew he was in trouble. Cane in hand, he ducked down behind his desk, curled up tight. The gangster snatched the pistol from his desk drawer. The only weapons firing out there sounded like their own. Something was sure banging an awful racket though.

The latch on the door gave and it burst open. Ferro fired over his desk. He also cursed in several languages. Sure enough it was another goddamn monster. This thing had the upper body of a skeletal ghoulish woman. Her jaw hung agape below soulless eyes and her thin arms clawed out hungrily. From the waist down she was a mass of writhing giant snakes. The creatures pulled this way and that, their splotchy scales rustling like a paper storm. All hissing and baring their fangs.

Ferro fired at the first head to make it through the doorway. The thing was nearly too wide. Unfortunately it could just get in. Ferro took out an eye. That only made it angry. It thrashed and heaved, jerking itself further into the office. Ferro emptied his pistol into it. Didn't even slow it down. There wasn't time to reload. More heads writhed into the room. Two smashed into his desk, knocking it away. Ferro leapt back. He shoved a filing cabinet at them. Snake fangs ripped it in half.

He paled. One of the heads lunged for him. He snatched his sword cane. There wasn't time to draw the weapon. He threw it up, blocking the fangs seeking to shred him. The force of the bite smacked him back into the wall. He slumped. His arms buckled, straining to hold the cane tangled in the giant fangs. Those things were as long as his forearm. If he couldn't hold them back...

But it was stronger than him. More heads were rearing around him. He was about to be mincemeat. He couldn't even draw his sword.

It smashed away from him with a bang. He didn't even know what had happened, but the pressure eased. The heads hit the floor. Ferro struggled to his feet. His whole body trembled. His grip on his cane was slack. The monster was pinned to the floor in the doorway. Glowing golden ropes pinned it like a burning net against the carpet. It struggled weakly, but couldn't budge an inch. A slight figure appeared in the doorway, standing over it.

The girl drew a pistol, aimed it at the gaunt woman,

and fired head and heart. The holy bullets ripped massive holes, exploding and destroying the upper body. The entire creature went limp with death. Lucy stood still, looking down on it curiously. The golden lights over it vanished. Tony walked up behind her, the darkness that filled his eyes dissipating.

Ferro staggered towards them. They looked up from the monster's corpse in unison, concerned inquiry in their eyes. He gave them a nod.

"Tony!" the cry came from the other room. One of the men grabbed the boy in a bear hug. "*Oddio mio!* You and your lady are a sight for sore eyes!"

Tony hugged his friend back and greeted him warmly, looking around the carnage, as the other injured gangsters composed themselves. Ferro stepped carefully around the body to join the others outside his office.

"*Che macello!*" Tony commented. "What happened?"

"We've seen the what," Lucy commented darkly. "I'm more interested in the why." She holstered her pistol again.

Ferro watched the girl. She wore her coat hung on her shoulders, and one hand tenderly touched her ribs. She was injured. Sleeves were a strain she was doing without, but she'd still shot his problem. He took out a handkerchief and mopped the sweat from his scarred face.

"O'Malley," he answered. "We've been having problems with him the last couple of weeks. Been sorting out some of your work and he thinks we're muscling in on his territory."

"*Davvero?*" Tony raised an eyebrow. "He wants to start a war and he's resorted to summoning monsters?"

"*Si,*" Ferro nodded to him. "So much for the God-fearing Irish."

Lucy grimaced and tightened her hand on her ribs again. Tony caught the expression. He quickly pulled up a chair for her and bade her sit. She did. Ferro could see the rest of the room holding its breath as she sat in his presence, but the girl was injured, and she was an esteemed guest. More than. She looked up at him grimly.

"You can tell the gangs, Mister Ferro, that Vincent and I are back in town. We're grateful for your service in our absence, and will let it be known, if you can advise them that any steps into occult territory will be met by the sharp end of my bullets." Lucy voice was tempered by pain, and it sounded like an order.

More air went out of the room, but no one was breathing. Tony noted the atmosphere.

"She's injured," he defended. His hand rested on the back of the chair protectively.

"No one said anything, boy," Ferro smiled at him graciously. "The Hunters are always welcome at our doors, and I would never keep a lady standing." He smiled down at her and tapped his cane on the floor. "If you need someone to take a look–"

"*No grazie comunque.*" She shook her head, and her response earned her approving glances. "Your men need the doctors after dealing with that thing. I took a bullet in Egypt. It's coming right."

Admiring and curious looks were thrown about at

her admission, but everyone knew better than to ask. The girl was an anomaly, but Ferro still controlled the room. Or what was left of it. Still, she was giving him a run for his money without even trying. He knew better than to see her as a threat. Especially when she made such a good ally. There was a ring glinting on her finger he couldn't help but notice, and she noticed him noticing.

"There is another reason I'm here…" she admitted.

"*Si?*" he smiled.

"I would like to ask your permission to marry your nephew," she stated brazenly.

Ferro felt his eyebrows hit his hairline. His surprise was mirrored on the faces of his men. Only Tony and Lucy didn't look incredulous.

"*Davvero?*" Ferro grinned at her.

"Well, Tony asked Vincent for permission," Lucy shrugged. "It's only fair that I ask you."

Ferro laughed heartily. His eyes twinkled with mirth as he gazed down at the girl. She was a strange one, but it was a strange he was coming to admire through Tony's eyes. No woman ever asked permission from the man's family, but if there was going to be a first it would certainly be her. She met everyone's amusement with unwavering conviction.

"*Signorina*, I think we're well past permission." He set his cane under his arm as he took one of her hands in both of his, patting it fondly. "But you can certainly have my blessing."

She gave him a smile and nod of thanks. Ferro turned his eyes up to Tony, still standing diligently at her shoulder.

"*Congratulazioni,*" he bid.

"*Grazie zio,*" Tony nodded.

Ferro eyed him. The boy had grown, even just in his trip away. It was strange how the darkness in him could appear deeper and yet somehow also lighter. As though he knew it better and had let it inside. His fear wasn't as prominent as it had been. If even half of that was the girl's effect on him, Ferro was prepared to marry them himself.

* * *

The afternoon was as cool and grey as the morning. Vincent was out the back of the manor with a small bonfire roaring. Fred was upstairs with Helen and Toby. It was good for her to be home with her family. Toby was at that age where he could talk but couldn't yet be reasoned with. Vincent found it an unsettling period of childhood. Besides, he was fairly sure children were just as unsettled by him. He left the boy's rearing to his mothers.

He hadn't been home for more than an hour before the itch started. It prickled the back of his throat. The sensation sent a panic through his bones.

Of course.

It wasn't over.

It was never truly over. Any other thoughts were foolish. Respite was always temporary. Nothing had been slain. The Darkness still thrived. It was still waiting. Every night darkness crawled across the world. Every time he slept dreams stalked him. Not all of them would be safe. The gateway was always there.

He had retrieved the case of vials he kept in the hut. And the one under the floorboards beneath his bed. And the recipe he kept in the safe in his office. The paper had made good kindling, and the tonic had been a remarkable accelerant soaked into the wood. Every now and again one of the logs would pop, spraying up thick sparks like confetti. Vincent watched it hypnotically, trying not to breathe in the smoke.

When Lucy strode out to join him, he realized she was home. She took one look at the empty cases and bottles by the fire and placed a soft hand on his back.

"I'm proud of you," she stated.

"I guess that makes us even," he replied grimly. A deep sigh escaped his lips. "I had to do it. I had to destroy the temptation. I would have slipped otherwise."

"There's no shame in that," Lucy assured him. "Whatever you need, Fred and I are here for you. Everyone here is."

"Hm," Vincent nodded, wishing he was better at expressing his gratitude. "How are our Mafia acquaintances?"

"Right as rain – or they will be – some of them were a bit beat up," she replied. "They were fighting some kind of Echidna monstrosity when we got there. Tony and I took care of it, but Ferro said it might have been summoned by the Irish who took exception to their work in our absence."

Vincent glowered at the fire. A log exploded,

showering them in sparks. Neither flinched.

"The Greek Echidna not the spiky echidna?" he clarified.

"Yeah," Lucy smiled.

"That won't be the Irish..." he muttered. "Their magic never strays far from home. Goddamnit all! Do I have a bloody gang war on my hands now?!"

"No, Sir," Lucy assured. "I'm taking care of it, and I told Ferro to put word out that we're back in town. They'll quieten down once they have us to deal with."

"They better..." he grumbled, fidgeting with the pin in his lapel. "I've got enough to manage at the moment."

"How did the Council take it?" Lucy asked. "You wrote them before we left Egypt, yes?"

"I did," Vincent nodded. "No one's prepared to oppose me outright. I think some of them suspect I had a hand in Nigel's death, but they won't lay the accusation without proof. Some of them don't even seem to mind."

"Guess we're hitting on all eight then," Lucy approved.

"For now," he agreed.

She gave him that look. She knew it wasn't over too. The girl he'd taken in was certainly a smart one, even if the gangsters she brought home weren't. She kneaded her ribs gently as she turned her gaze back to the fire. This time Vincent watched her.

"It seemed like he was playing with you," she commented softly, massaging her scar. "Isfet. I was so sure the old Professor was dead. At least that mess didn't look like something he could come back from again."

"Don't be so sure…" Vincent sighed. "Professor Isfet is just an alias – in hindsight, a terrible one. One I should have seen if my brain hadn't been so clouded. Monsters like that don't go down easy. Not forever. Not even when your boy dusts them. I've met him more than a dozen times in my years. He always comes back. He always wipes my memories and returns."

"So he is playing with you then?"

"So it would seem…"

"Why?" she queried.

"Why does a mad dog bite?" Vincent shrugged.

They were silent a moment, watching the fire pop.

"So he'll be back then…?" Lucy asked softly.

"Undoubtedly," Vincent admitted, resisting the urge to put a protective arm around her.

"Good." She stuck her hands in her deep pockets and glared at the flames. "I'm gonna kick his ass."

Vincent grinned. The Prince would be back. Always. Ever more dangerous. But so were they, and he couldn't be prouder.

Did you enjoy this book?

Please consider leaving a review for it on Amazon or Goodreads. Every positive review allows me to spend more time writing books for you to enjoy!

Also, don't forget to sign up to the mailing list at www.katehaleyauthor.com for free book deals and new releases!

Other Books By Kate Haley

Gateway to Dark Stars (Vincent Temple Book 1)

Welcome to the Inbetween

The War of the North Saga

Footsteps into the Unfamiliar (short story collection)

1. Steel & Stone

2. Magic in the Marshes

3. Forest of Ghosts

4. Women of the Woods

5. Spirit & Sand

6. The Prince and the Witch

7. Gods & Dragons

About the Author

Kate Haley is a speculative fiction author who works predominantly in fantasy and horror.

While currently content to fill their days with writing and table-top RPGs, their grander plans involve world domination. Something akin to the tyranny of the greatest city atop the Disc would be an acceptable standard. They believe a super-villainous overlord would be an upgrade, given that our current villains lack style and imagination.

After all, super-villainy requires Presentation.

If you like their references, consider visiting their website www.katehaleyauthor.com for short fictions and merchandise, and join the mailing list for early access and exclusive cool stuff.

You can also get in touch through the website regarding their work, your position in future slave armies, or a general interest in all things nerdy and wonderful.

TOMB OF ENDLESS NIGHT

Printed in Great Britain
by Amazon